SHADOW OF SILENCE

JUDITH ERWIN

Emerald Cat Press

USA

Judith Erwin
Emerald Cat Press
Jacksonville, Florida

Publisher's Note: This is a work of fiction. Names, characters, places, and incidents are a product of the author's imagination. Locales and public names are sometimes used for atmospheric purposes. Any resemblance to actual people, living or dead, or to busi-nesses, companies, events, institutions, or locales is completely coincidental.

Book Layout © 2018 BookDesign

Shadow of Silence/ Judith Erwin

Second Edition - 2018
ISBN 978-0-9863367-9-9 - 2018
ISBN-978-1-61133-949-9 – 2014

Library of Congress Control Number: 2013923709

Editor:	John C. Boles
Cover Painting:	Nancy H. Duty

For Mother and Daddy

Acknowledgements

Without the support of my two families, the traditional and the literary, I could not have written *Shadow of Silence.*

Perry, Allison, Bill, Lynda, Judson, Sarah, Trevor, Brooks, Caroline, and Amelia—thank you for being the best part of my life. I love you all.

I have to give a special thank-you to Nancy Duty, who is my constant sounding-board and the talented artist who painted the perfect cover.

Finally, I give immeasurable thanks to the writing family who read, reread, and gave shape to what would become this novel: John Boles, editor extraordinaire; Julie Delegal, Jennifer Grannis, and Keith Gockenbach, outstanding writers and generous friends; and last, but not least, Retired Special Agent, Craig L. Dotlow of the FBI, who was generous with his time and knowledge.

There are many others who shared a part of the journey, including Betty Bergmark and Donna Freyberg; however, to attempt to list them all would risk leaving someone out—they know who they are.

The cruelest of lies are often told in silence.

R. L Stevenson

PART I

CHAPTER ONE

July 2001

Her clammy hands grasped the steering like an aerialist gripping a trapeze. Tiny beads of perspiration rose on her pasty-white forehead. Her pale blue eyes stared as though hypnotized, glazed over with tears on the brink of soaking her face. Without benefit of counsel or support, twenty-seven-year-old Annie Cameron was about to make a choice that defied her desires and violated her principles.

How can I be driving to an abortion clinic? Nine weeks ago I was driving to a fertility clinic.

Weeks of agonizing mental debate and prayer had produced no acceptable solution to her dilemma. *What if I'm wrong again?*

Although having the abortion was breaking her heart and condemning her soul to iniquity, revealing the truth would cause suffering to those she loved. Dan was coming home in ten days, so the time for deliberation had expired.

As Annie drove through her private hell, nature was smiling on the Georgia countryside. Streaks of sunlight burned through the morning haze, promising a pleasant summer day, which mocked her misery. It was almost eight o'clock, and she was more than an hour from her hometown east of Atlanta. However, with the passage of each mile, her courage faded. As hard as she tried to forget, the memory of her last trip with Dan to the Atlanta fertility clinic kept surfacing. *We were actually considering in vitro fertilization.*

The smell of the leather upholstery aggravated the nausea she had struggled with since her feet hit the floor that morning. Enya's "Only Time" played in the CD player but failed to soothe her anxiety.

"This can't be happening," she said aloud as an image flashed across her mind. She shut it down faster than a computer screen in a power failure.

"I will not go there."

Seeking distraction, she tried to concentrate on her surroundings but found it hopeless. Only shabby mobile homes, crumbling cabin-like houses, and property desecrated by decaying junk were within view.

I'm turning around. I can't go through with this.

In desperation, she took a hand from the wheel to reposition an air-conditioning vent. The cool breeze felt good as it dried her damp skin and blew the long, blond hair away from her face. As much as Annie wanted to go home—she couldn't.

No one knew she was pregnant. The secret trapped her inside an invisible tunnel, bound by fear and gagged by guilt. She wanted desperately to confide in someone—to tell Dan. Three days before, as he was leaving home to begin a temporary assignment in Washington, on an impulse, she had called after him.

As he put his travel bag into the black, government-issue SUV, he turned, eyebrows raised, and asked, "What did I forget?"

Trembling, she had the overwhelming desire to blurt out the whole story—to hand over the truth and trust him to fix it. To Annie, even after five years of marriage, Dan Cameron could slay dragons. The simple sound of his footsteps still caused her heart to race.

At the last second, she knew she couldn't tell him. This was no clogged drain or stubborn jar cap. With all his wisdom and strength, this was not something he could fix. As Dan walked back toward her, Annie knew that to confess would be to drag him into hell with her. She had made a choice, albeit with the best intentions, and now she had to live with it—alone. She hesitated for a moment and then said with a smile, "Nothing. I just need one more hug before you leave."

Grinning, he came up the porch steps. Reaching the doorway where she stood in her cotton robe, he wrapped his arms around her waist, sweeping her petite frame against his dark suit. "I'll be back before you know it, angel. I'll call every night; I promise. Don't worry if it's late. You know the drill when I'm on a TDY." Saying that, he had hugged her, kissed the top of her head, and left.

As Annie's van descended a small hill, a stream of sunlight penetrated the window, ricocheting off the surface of her gold wedding band. The flecks of light caught her eye. She stared at it for a second and wondered if the sparks formed an indecipherable message. Ever since suspecting she was pregnant, she had prayed for direction and looked for signs of an answer everywhere. Were the lights applauding her decision or trying to warn her of yet another wrong choice? She made a mental note to remove the ring.

Morning traffic was sparse in both directions, providing a clear view of the road ahead, but there was no sign of the church where she had been told to turn. A computer map lay folded on the passenger seat, next to her small Bible. *I have to remember to get rid of that map before I go home.*

As she rounded a curve in the road, a stronger wave of nausea caused her to hold her breath for a second. Swallowing hard and clutching the wheel even tighter, she managed to quell the relentless threat but felt her body grow weaker and her head fill with more fear. *What if I never get pregnant again?*

Passing a brick wall on her left, with a sign identifying a future housing development, Annie decided she was probably close to the clinic. The thought sent a ripple through to her fingers, extracting what little strength she had. Her entire body felt weak and helpless. It didn't help that she had barely eaten for days. However, despite the hunger pangs roaming her stomach, the thought of food was repugnant.

Between the anxiety and the onset of the nausea, she had lost eight pounds. Her clothes hung loosely on her body. Her fair complexion had become uncharacteristically pallid and drab for midsummer. Even the cashier at the Piggly Wiggly had noticed her weight loss when checking out groceries for Annie the day before.

"Goodness, child. What's the matter with you?" Tammy-Jo asked. "You're white as Georgia cotton and skinny as a string bean on Jenny Craig."

"I'm fine," Annie said. "I had a little stomach bug last week."

Looking at Annie with an all-knowing expression, the clerk raised an eyebrow and said, "You're not pregnant, are you?"

"Gosh no," Annie lied. "That would be fantastic, but unfortunately not so."

As she watched Tammy-Jo put the groceries in bags, she forced a smile to hide her annoyance, hoping there would be no more invasive questions.

So far, Dan had failed to notice her condition. Work assignments had consumed his time and attention for several weeks. Even when home, he was preoccupied. However, she couldn't hide the pregnancy much longer if outsiders were suspicious. For the first time in their marriage, she was glad the FBI had sent him out of town. As she had loaded the grocery bags into the van, Annie replayed Tammy-Jo's comments in her mind and knew that resolving the pregnancy was imperative. If she had the procedure early the following week, she should recover by the weekend when he was due home from DC.

If I don't do this, I will destroy the lives of nearly everyone I care about. Although the decision was made, coming closer and closer to the procedure was brutal. Squeezing her eyes closed for a second to clear her focus, she whispered, "Who is driving this car?" In that moment, Annie felt like a spectator, rather than a participant, in her life.

A tear slipped from the inside corner of her eye and drew a wet streak along the side of her nose as it slid to her mouth. *Will my conscience ever let me forget?*

Continuing to look for external guidance, Annie grasped at the idea that if she couldn't find the clinic, it could mean that she wasn't meant to go through with the abortion.

"Oh, Dan, why didn't I tell you at the beginning?" she whispered, tears flowing down her face. "Why did trying to protect others have such a heavy price?"

The image of Dan's smiling face—his warm, brown eyes as comforting as hot chocolate on a cold winter night—filled her mind. She could almost feel his embrace—smell his fragrance. *How could trying to do the right thing in a wrong situation make such a horrible mess?*

Suddenly, an 18-wheeler zoomed by on the narrow road, jolting her back to reality and causing the van to shake slightly—just enough to cause another tingle to pass through her hands. Bracing herself, she glanced down at the Bible on the passenger seat. Annie wanted to pray for the strength to complete the mission, but her moral conflict stood in the way. How could she seek divine support to break a commandment? *Life was so easy when right was right and wrong was wrong.*

"God, I know I can't ask you to help me through this. I want a baby—even this baby. Please forgive me." As she whispered her prayer, Annie eased her right hand across the seat and let it rest on the Bible, the one her grandmother had given her when she was twelve. On the white cover, her name, Anne Máire Brennan, was etched in gold. *Granny Máire, I miss you so much. If you were still here, you would have known what I should do.* In large part, Annie had chosen the clinic because of the Irish counselor she spoke with when making the appointment. The woman's accent and attitude had reminded her of her grandmother, a native of Ireland.

Never before in her twenty-seven years had Annie faced a serious problem alone. She always had Dan, her parents, her grandmother, and her faith. Now, when she needed it the most, even her faith had failed. *Is it possible that I have a problem for which even God has no answer?*

Forcing her attention back to the road, Annie strained to see farther in the distance, looking for the church that would signify where she was to turn. The nausea had progressed to the point that if she didn't find the clinic soon, she would have to stop. As she was about to pull over, she saw the church. Breathing a sigh of relief, she whispered, "You're nearly there. Hold on."

As she made the right turn, jitters resurfaced. Passing the church property, she felt a need to turn back and go in for one last attempt to find guidance. *Maybe since I'm so close, God would send me an answer if I ask just one more time.*

But, she didn't turn around. *Face reality, Annie. Abortion is your only option.*

CHAPTER TWO

It seemed far longer than four weeks to Annie since she made the trip into Atlanta to buy pregnancy tests. However, the horror of watching test after test produce a positive result was still raw. Returning home to Providence in a near trance, she had faced the uncertainty of what to do. Since missing her period and the onset of morning sickness, she had struggled to disguise her fear and hide her condition by avoiding her family and keeping as much distance from Dan as caution would permit.

Now, just over a month later, her means to the end was in sight. Approximately two blocks from the main road, Glenbrook Women's Clinic stood on the left. The red-brick, two-story building in the Georgian style looked as though it might have been a rather grand family home at some time in the past. As she turned onto the drive leading to the back of the building, Annie's heart raced.

I can do this. I have to.

Just as she reached the edge of the parking area, a squirrel darted across the drive from her right. Annie stomped on the brake pedal, causing a jolt. Her body tensed, then went a little weak from shock and relief. "That was close!" *Thank goodness I didn't hit him. Killing a squirrel would have been devastating.* Before she resumed forward motion, a second squirrel scooted across, chasing the first up a tree on her left and causing Annie to smile. She eased the van forward, watching for more wildlife.

Parking in the designated area behind the clinic, she turned off the ignition, but remained in the driver's seat, her forehead pressed against the steering wheel. *Pull yourself together, Annie. You've got to go in.*

You've gotten this far. Taking a deep breath, she raised her head from the wheel and leaned back against the headrest.

Remembering the phone conversation she had with the clinic counselor, Annie hoped to meet Molly O'Brien, but cautioned herself. *Just because she has an Irish accent doesn't mean that she's like Granny.*

"You've to know that whatever be your situation, 'tis you that must make the decision. Only you can know the right of it, luv," Molly had said, when Annie seemed hesitant to commit to an appointment.

Despite the warmth of the conversation, Annie had been careful not to reveal many details about her circumstances. She said only that she needed to terminate her pregnancy.

"You'll be needing to come in for counseling so we can explain all of your options, dearie," Molly said.

Annie didn't want to hear a lecture about options, and she didn't want to think any longer. "Are you saying that I have to make two trips to the clinic?"

"I'm afraid so, dearie."

Making a face, Annie said, "That's going to be hard. I don't live in Atlanta."

"Maybe you should try a clinic closer to you."

The phone was silent while Annie mulled over the suggestion. She wanted it over with and certainly didn't want to go to a clinic on the east side of Atlanta. That was too risky.

"That's okay, I'll figure it out," Annie said.

Annie was determined to both stay away from her in-laws' upscale neighborhood in the northeast section of Atlanta and the hospital where her father-in-law, Russ Cameron, practiced. *I have to go as far as I can from anyone I know, and there's something about this lady that I like.*

As Annie sat in her vehicle outside the clinic, she gazed out the window, struggling to make herself take the next step. *I'm here. I can do it.*

The squirrels that had crossed her path were coming down a tree. They scampered into shrubbery surrounding the building. *They have no worries, just run up and down trees all day.* With no one else in the parking lot, the area was quiet, except for the chattering of blue jays in a nearby tree.

A twig hit the top of the van, and she flinched. *I have to stop thinking. Reality is what it is.* Taking a deep breath, she tucked the Bible in her purse. *The sun is shining. Birds are singing. God is in his heaven— and nothing is right in my world.*

Opening the door of the vehicle, the early morning scent of honeysuckle and freshly mowed grass rushed forward, igniting memories of childhood—days spent sucking the droplets of nectar from honeysuckle blossoms with her best friend, Eva. Annie almost smiled at the thought of gentle times. *We were so innocent. How did life go so wrong?*

With purse over her shoulder, she blinked back tears, stood up, and adjusted her blouse in the waistband of her slacks. *There's no use tormenting myself. I'm pregnant, and I can't have it.* As she took the first step toward the clinic entrance, she prayed. *Holy Mary, Mother of God, pray for me.* As she got closer, her mind took an abrupt turn.

Why did I let Alex talk me into having that party?

CHAPTER THREE

The party was Alex's idea—not surprising to anyone who knew the Brennan sisters. Five years older than Annie, Alex Dalton filled every room she entered with her larger-than-life personality. Always quick with a witty retort, Alex was a risk taker who scoffed at protocol and devoured anyone who crossed her. Although she idolized her sibling, Annie was her polar opposite—responsible, punctual, and cautious. Annie kept a calendar and made lists. In contrast, Alex survived on her verve, luck, and irrepressible charm. She drank in life like kid with a soda pop on a summer day. Dark haired, with dancing brown eyes, she was wholly organic, while light-haired Annie, with faded-blue eyes, was ethereal.

When Alex came up with the party idea in early May, Annie was resistant. She had invited her sister for lunch to show off the new waterscape and the flowerbeds she had cultivated in the backyard.

Dan and Annie's home was a large, frame house in the Victorian style, which for many years anchored a cotton plantation. In the 1980s, the old cabins that had housed tenant farmers on the plantation were torn down and the farm subdivided, leaving the antebellum house standing at the center on a tract of land four times larger than those allotted the new homes. However, the Atlanta developer remained faithful to the architectural style of the old house in the construction of the smaller homes.

The previous owner of the house, a childless widow of the last man to farm the land, passed away four years before Annie and Dan married, and the building remained empty until the Camerons acquired it in 1998. As a rookie with the Bureau, Dan had been assigned to the Jacksonville field office during the first two years of their marriage. By the time he was assigned to the Atlanta office, the old dinosaur was in a sad state of disrepair with peeling paint, rotten wood, a leaking roof, and antiquated plumbing. The restoration was finally complete.

The final project had been the backyard, which had been Annie's focus for several months. She loved flowers and designed her beds to produce those that would give color to the yard and could be cut for the house. The waterscape, her pride and joy, was located at the left corner and was flanked by wrought-iron benches. On the right side, near the house, there was a pool, bordered with brick, and next to a covered patio where Dan's gas grill was mounted in a brick barbeque pit. A tall privacy fence, stained a reddish-amber, enclosed the yard and provided a complimentary backdrop to the green foliage.

"Wow!" Alex said as she stepped out the French doors of Annie's breakfast room to the back porch. "You have been a busy bee."

"Do you like it?"

"What's not to like? It's perfect, just like you."

"Was that meant to be serious or sarcastic?" Annie asked, frowning slightly.

"Calm down. It was meant to be a compliment," Alex said, as she walked to the middle of the yard.

"I'm sorry. It's just that you make 'perfect' sound like a character flaw, not that I'm close to being perfect," Annie said as she trailed behind.

"Come on, Annie. You know you've colored between the lines since before you could talk. It's just your nature. But that's a good thing. I'm just jealous, but once in a while, you should loosen up—try something new."

"What did you have in mind? Skydiving or motocross?"

"Don't knock it until you've tried it. But all kidding aside, the yard looks great. I'm impressed. It's like one of those elegant English gardens you see in the magazines," Alex said, as she leaned over to smell a rose bloom.

"That was my goal." Annie smiled with pride.

"Well, enjoy it while you can. When you have kids, they'll tear it up, but right now, it looks fantastic with the style of the house," Alex said, waving her right arm around in a grand gesture.

"If we have kids," Annie said, a slight edge to her tone.

"Cut it out. Of course you're going to have kids. You've just got to loosen up. Maybe if you and Dan made spontaneous love out here one night, instead of on the pristine sheets in your bedroom, you might have better luck with that. I'll bet you calendar sex like a dentist appointment."

"Was that your recipe?"

"Trust me, sugar pie, I didn't need a recipe. My three popped out like refrigerated biscuits when the can splits," Alex said, pulling the elastic off of her chestnut ponytail to redo it.

"I only wish that it were that easy," Annie said, in a melancholy tone. "The clinic doctor keeps saying that I'm fine and that even though Dan's sperm count is a little low, it's not low enough to keep me from conceiving. But I've just about given up."

With her last sentence, Annie's voice dropped, indicating her despair. Moving closer to her sister, Alex put her arm around her shoulder.

"Take your big sister's word for it. Relax…chill out. Haven't you heard about people adopting because they thought they couldn't have a baby, and then the wife got pregnant?"

"Well, we haven't reached the point of adoption yet, but we are considering in vitro."

Dropping her arm, Alex stepped back with a surprised look on her face. "You're kidding, aren't you?" she asked, looking Annie straight in the face.

"No. We really are. Dan says if I want to, he'll go along. It's just that it's so clinical and makes me feel kind of strange to think that my baby might begin in a petri dish." Talking about her failure to conceive caused Annie's mood to fade further. "Let's drop that subject and enjoy this beautiful day. Want to have our lunch out here?" she said, regaining spirit in her voice.

"Great idea. The weather's too perfect to be inside."

Back in the house, Alex helped by pouring glasses of iced tea and collecting napkins, placemats and utensils, while Annie arranged mounds of chicken salad, fruit, and pecan muffins on plates. Before carrying the food to the patio, Annie flipped on the sound system.

"I feel like a proper English lady having a spot of lunch in the garden, music and all," Alex said, in a pseudo-pretentious tone, as she put a napkin in her lap.

"I know it's not your taste in music, but it was already in the player, and it seems right for the occasion."

"You're right on both counts. It's not Tim McGraw, but it fits the mood."

As a piano rendition of Schumann's "Traumerei" played, a cardinal flew by, landing on the three-tiered fountain and was joined by his apparent mate.

"Aren't they gorgeous?" Alex said, pointing at the birds.

"I think they're building a nest in the magnolia tree."

"That is so neat. This is a really great atmosphere. Like I said before, you should set up a little romantic evening out here. Serve Dan a candlelight dinner with a nice bottle of champagne. Have some sexy music playing on that fancy system. After dinner, the two of you could dance on the patio, and you could whisper in his ear that you're not wearing anything under your skirt."

"Alex!" Annie said, shocked by her sister's audacity.

"Hush now. Pay attention and hear me out. Between the music, the candles, the wine, and the gurgling waterfall, I bet Dan would rip your clothes off and have his way with you right there on that thick grass," she said, nodding her head to confirm her statement. "That's the way you make babies."

Annie's face had turned beet red. "Or in the backseat of a car? You've been living with Cole too long. Your mind is getting as bad as his."

"Muff, you've got to keep the spice in your marriage. Admit it. That turned you on a little."

"Not going to happen, and can we change the subject?"

Alex tossed her long, dark hair back over her shoulder and stood up, lifting her empty plate and Annie's. "Tell you what, Miss Muff. I've got another idea. Why don't you and Dan have a party to debut your house and garden? Your anniversary and Memorial Day are coming. Pick a theme. I'll help."

Annie frowned. "Don't call me that dumb nickname. No one calls me that but you and Cole. Even Dad stopped a long time ago."

"Chill out. I think it's cute. You were adorable when you were Miss Muffet in the kindergarten play."

"That was about twenty-two years ago, and I don't do parties. You're the party person, not me."

"Bullshit. It would be great. What's the point in having a pretty house and yard if you don't show it off?"

"The house is not finished."

"Sure it is. It looks terrific, and you need to step off that straight line of yours occasionally."

Even though Annie refused to admit that having a party was a good idea, after Alex left, she kept thinking about it. *Much as I hate it. She's right. We don't have much of a social life.*

As she mulled it over, she thought about the social obligations they could repay, but remained definite that she would not label it an anniversary party. At dinner that night, Annie introduced the idea to Dan. Without hesitating, he expressed his approval.

"Why don't I barbeque?" he said. "Alex can help you with the rest, but try to keep it civilized. If we invite guys from the office, we have to remember that they don't speak the local language."

"Very funny, Mr. Seinfeld," she said, making a face at him. "I'm thinking a patriotic theme for Memorial Day. Who are you thinking about inviting from the office?"

"Mark Norman and maybe the new guy, Tony. You've always liked Mark and Sandy, and it'll give you a chance to show Tony and his wife some Southern hospitality. She's having trouble adjusting to Atlanta. It may be the capital of the South, but it falls short of New York and Paris."

"Wasn't she a ballerina with the Paris Opera or something?"

"Yeah, I think she was. I know she's French. You shouldn't have any trouble talking to her with your knowledge of music," Dan said, crumpling his napkin and putting it on his dessert plate. "But you might want to steer her clear of your local football heroes. She may not know how to handle a good-ole-boy pass."

"What are you talking about? Gabe Patton wouldn't hit on another woman...but you're probably right about Ray Brantley. Alex says she wouldn't trust him any further than the length of his zipper. I don't know why half the girls in Providence were so crazy over him. I guess it was the football thing." Gabe, the husband of Annie's childhood friend Eva was a college drop-out and car salesman. Ray, the husband of Alex's best friend Martha, couldn't pass the academic threshold required to take advantage of the football scholarships he was offered. However, he made a good living as a long-distance truck driver. Like Al Bundy, neither had accomplished anything surpassing their football successes in high school but rode high on them in Providence.

Annie paused for a minute to take a bite of her chocolate pie and to think over who they might invite. Swallowing the pie, she looked across the table with an apprehensive expression and said, "Maybe we should have two parties: one for your friends and one for the locals. It's probably not safe to mix your guys with the local cowboys. Can you see Mark trying to have a meaningful conversation with Ray?" She made a face. "Even Alex, with her take-no-prisoners mouth, is likely to offend everyone."

Dan smiled. He was fond of Alex and found her sharp-tongued wit amusing.

"Don't you smile, Dan Cameron. You know Alex puts her mouth in motion thirty minutes before she invites her brain to the conversation," Annie said as she lifted her tea cup to her mouth. "We're playing with fire."

Glancing up from his coffee, Dan said, with a chuckle, "Yeah…Martha will probably ask Tony's wife whether Swan Lake is done in English."

"That's a pretty cheap shot." But she smiled because she agreed that Martha's cultural experience was limited to country music, soap operas, and town gossip. If dance wasn't done in jeans and boots, Martha wouldn't know the difference between break dancing and ballet."

Wiping his mouth with his napkin, Dan said, "Maybe we could leave out the Brantleys?"

"Wrong. We can't snub our next-door neighbors."

"Just kidding," he said, raising his hands in mock surrender. He smiled, loving to tease her.

"Well, it should be an interesting party. Maybe we should hire a translator," Annie said, a devilish look on her face.

Dan stood and began gathering his dishes to take to the kitchen. "Maybe not an interpreter, but I'll make sure the guys have up-to-date passports and check their weapons at the door."

Annie thought about it for a minute before saying, "It should work if we invite enough from each group. That way the locals can talk beer and wrestling while your people talk clues and evidence."

Dan smiled. After three years of living in Providence, he was acclimated to the local culture. Although Ray Brantley's uneducated and opinionated conversations were boorish, Dan was patient and patronized his neighbor's limited viewpoints, provided they were limited by a ten-minute shelf-life during one-on-one encounters. In contrast, Dan respected his brother-in-law. What Cole lacked in formal education and social sophistication, he made up for in street savvy and business sense.

He owned the local hardware store, cotton gin, and a small farm. All of which he had parlayed with an inheritance from one of the town barons, who had taken Cole in when he was a near-homeless teen.

By the end of the discussion, they had added a few more names to the guest list, decided on the menu, and determined that the party would be on Sunday before Memorial Day to give everyone a day to recuperate.

The next morning, Annie called Alex to tell her that they were going to follow her suggestion.

"Awesome! What can I do to help?"

As it turned out, Alex was a big help with the preparations. She knew where to buy decorations, how to set up a bar, and how to plan a cookout menu. She loaned Annie serving dishes, folding tables, and volunteered Rosa, her housekeeper, to assist with the before and after chores.

"What are you wearing for the soirée?" Alex asked about ten days before the appointed day as they finalized the to-do list.

"I haven't thought about it, but probably a pair of jeans and a blouse."

"No, no, no. You've got to be dressed for the occasion. You're the hostess. You've got to have flair."

"I don't do flair, Alex. Besides, how do you do flair at a barbeque?"

"I'll show you. We're going shopping. We've got to go to Atlanta to pick up the rest of your decorations, so we can just swing by Lenox Square and find something sharp for both of us."

Annie knew there was no stopping Alex when she was on a mission. Three days later, the sisters made the trip to a trendy boutique in Atlanta.

"This is not me," Annie said, as Alex started through the entrance of the shop. "Where's the Gap?"

"Forget the Gap crap. It's a party. For once in your life, let go. You're not wearing Preppy 101 to this party," Alex said, her brows furrowed and nose wrinkled in display of disgust. "Your clothes set your mood, and you can't be in a party mode wearing uptight, suburban chic."

Annie rolled her eyes but followed Alex. Inside, she surveyed the array of sequined jeans and flashy tops—all styled to be provocative attention-getters; she wrinkled her brow in disapproval as Alex pilfered through the racks.

"Alex, this is a store for teenagers. I didn't even wear this stuff when I was in high school."

"Get over it. Let your wild-child out of the trunk for one day in your life."

After arguing over several of the pieces Alex thought were perfect and Annie considered trashy, they finally compromised on a pair of tight-fitting, belly-button-revealing jeans, paired with a red halter top, cropped at the bra-line. Annie had to admit that the outfit was flattering to her face and figure.

"That's the look!" Alex said, exuberantly, as Annie assessed her reflection in the three-way mirror. "Now, if I can just get you to work it."

"Are you sure I don't look like a hooker on the stroll?"

"A man likes his lady to have a little hooker in her, kiddo. It brings up the heat, and you're going to light Dan's fire in that outfit."

"Dan's fire is just fine," Annie said under her breath.

"What?"

"Nothing. Let's just get done so we can have lunch."

Annie had to admit that she felt a little sexy in the outfit, but she wasn't going to let on to Alex, so she retreated to the dressing room to change.

Alex turned her attention to her costume for the party and came up with a pair of white shorts, teamed with a multi-colored, strapless top, which she took to a cubicle before Annie came out.

Coming out of the dressing room, Alex modeled her choice for Annie in a jazzy, runway walk to the beat of Queen's "We Will Rock You" that blared from the shop speakers.

"No one will ever accuse you of being inhibited," Annie said, half embarrassed at the flamboyant antics of her sister—and half impressed. *Much as I hate to admit it, she looks fantastic for a thirty-something mother of three.*

"Can we go now?" Annie asked when Alex had changed back to her own clothes.

"Not yet. You need to accessorize your outfit," Alex said, as she picked up a gaudy bracelet.

"Forget it. I'm done. Not going any farther down this tunnel, so just put that back, and let's go get lunch," Annie said, and began walking out of the boutique.

Alex knew she had pushed the envelope to capacity and followed.

CHAPTER FOUR

By the morning of the party, with the help of Alex and Rosa, Annie had the house sparkling. Red, white, and blue garlands hung around the backyard, gathered up and clipped at intervals with small flags. Two folding tables with dark blue coverings, topped with crisscrossed runners of red and white, would hold the bowls and platters of food. On each table, a centerpiece of red and blue carnations interspersed with white gladiolas stood at attention. A portable bar, brought from Alex's house, stood on one end of the wraparound back porch, with a keg of beer on the other.

It had been a welcome distraction for Annie to put it all together. For the three weeks preceding the event, her depression over failure to get pregnant had been trumped by enthusiasm for the party. On the last trip to the fertility clinic, she and Dan had discussed in vitro fertilization with her physician but were putting off the final decision.

"As long we keep trying the old-fashioned method of conception, I'm on board," Dan had said.

Annie wasn't sure, but told herself that if July came, and she wasn't pregnant, then in vitro it would be.

Decorating for the party had been a fun project. Annie loved the house and was excited to show it off to some of the invited guests for the first time. The restoration and furnishing had taken a lot of time, money, and hard work, but the end result was all she had envisioned when they had toured the property after Dan received notice that he would be located in Atlanta.

The Connor House, as it was known in Providence, was built in 1870 by Edwin Connor, a Yankee physician turned successful cotton farmer. When Dan's family gave them the two-story home—with its porches, gables, and Victorian mouldings—it looked like it was one rotten board away from condemnation. Dan's mother, Margaret, had opposed the idea, with less than stellar motives. Dan was the center jewel in her crown. She expected her only child to establish his home nearby, in an upscale Atlanta neighborhood, which she justified as only practical since he would be working in the city.

"That's sheer folly," Margaret said to her husband on the morning he revealed his intention to purchase the property as a belated wedding gift for Annie and Dan.

"Have you forgotten that we told them when Dan got a permanent assignment, we would give them a house? They've made up their minds to live in Providence. You saw the look on their faces when they described the house to us, yesterday," Russ said.

"You mean Annie's face," Margaret replied in a tone that failed to conceal the little green-eyed demon possessing her maternal nature.

"They both love it, Margaret," Russ said.

They won't be able to afford to make the necessary repairs, and it's certainly not habitable from the way they described it," she argued, neatly arranging a stack of books on the Hepplewhite desk in their bedroom.

"It will give them a good project to work on together," he replied, as he put on one of his favorite cashmere cardigans. "Dan has a good job, and without a mortgage, they will have the ability to do all the renovating they like."

Rolling her eyes toward the ceiling, she dodged slightly as he passed by and attempted to kiss her goodbye. "I suppose you don't care if your grandchildren are raised like a herd of country bumpkins."

"If that's a question, my dear, I hardly think Annie is a country bumpkin; and she was raised in Providence," Russ said, leaving the bedroom to go to his office.

Not to be ignored, Margaret followed him down the stairs. "They don't need a house that large. Dan said it has five or six bedrooms. And what about the commute for him? He'll have to drive over two hours every single day."

"I don't think he minds. But in any case, it's not your problem."

"I'll bet it's her idea," Margaret said. "Dan grew up here. His friends are here."

Taking his medical bag from a table in the front hall, Russell turned around, facing his wife, and said, "You're wrong, my dear. Dan wants the quieter lifestyle, and he just may want to have a little distance between his two families." He then leaned toward her, kissing her lightly on the cheek and walked out the door.

The message in his last statement had completely eluded Margaret.

Failing to dissuade her husband, Margaret took her case to her son, later the same morning.

"I don't mind the drive, Mother. I like Providence, and I expect the job will have me traveling, so I want Annie near her family. We've made our decision."

"I'm just thinking of you, darling."

His mother's declaration made Dan smile because he knew that Margaret always thought about Margaret first, which was exactly why he did not want to live in Atlanta. As hard as she tried to mold her only child in her image, Dan had inherited the conservative genes of the Cameron clan—eschewing Harvard for the University of Georgia and a prestigious position in a silk-stocking law firm in favor of a career with the FBI.

If attending a plebian, state school and working in a government job weren't disappointing enough to Margaret, her golden boy had the audacity to choose a simple nobody from the provinces over the bevy of Atlanta debutantes who ranked him one of the city's most desirable bachelors. Any one of them would have married him instantly and given her mini-Margaret grandchildren. Although Dan rebelled against his mother's choices, like his father, he had a way of dodging her darts and politely doing as he pleased, with finesse.

Dan treated his decision to live with Annie in Providence just as he had the other decisions that went contrary to Margaret's agenda. He loved his mother but liked her better the less he was exposed to her unedited opinions and blatant intrusions into his personal space.

"Mother will trample Annie, if she has a chance," Dan had said to his Dad over lunch at the hospital a few weeks before. "Annie is accommodating, and you know how manipulative Margaret can be." Dan often addressed his mother by her given name, not out of disrespect, but rather like it was her title. His instincts told him that the success of his marriage lay in direct proportion to the distance between their homes.

Russ had agreed.

By late afternoon, Annie was a nervous wreck. She had Rosa in charge of the food, Alex the bar, and Dan the grilling, but she was barking orders like a drill sergeant.

"Damn, Muff. Chill...out," Alex said.

But Annie wanted perfection. She was terrified she had forgotten something that would ruin the party.

"If you don't calm down, I may have to invoke an IITO," Dan said.

"What?"

"An involuntary inpatient treatment order,'" he said, grinning at her frustration. "You're definitely in imminent danger to both yourself and me right now, because if you don't calm down, I'm going to shoot you."

"You're real funny, Dan Cameron. Did they give you comedy classes at Quantico?"

"Annie...Annie. It's going to be great," Alex said, putting her arm around her sister's shoulders. "We've got it under control. Go on upstairs and get ready.... And take your time. Dan and I can handle anyone who arrives before you're ready." Taking her by the shoulders, Alex turned Annie in the direction of the stairs and pushed.

Although she started to protest, she saw the expression on Dan's face and relented.

Upstairs, she ran a hot tub, hoping the water would calm her jittery nerves. It helped. By the time she dressed and went back downstairs, guests had arrived and were out on the lawn consuming drinks and appetizers.

Taking a deep breath, she opened the door leading from the breakfast room to the back porch and made her entrance, feeling a little self-conscious in her new outfit, but a little feisty at the same time. Looking over the yard, all appeared in order. Equally important, the weather had cooperated by providing both pleasant temperatures and a soft breeze as the sun dropped on the western horizon.

Alex had turned on the stereo system so that a mix of pop and country music was playing softly in the background. The local guests were scattered about the yard, chatting—most holding a beer. Gabe Patton was laughing at something Cole had said. The Providence guys, Gabe, Ray, and Cole, shared their football stories whenever together. Each played for the Providence Wild Cats at a different time. However, Gabe was the only one with enough talent and academic aptitude to make it into a major college.

Dan stood by the grill in his preppy uniform—khaki shorts and a blue golf shirt—which Alex obviously had no hand in choosing. Over his clothes, he wore an apron with an American flag design that read, "We grill only American beef," which was chosen by Alex. Ray Brantley was bending his ear, which Annie knew Dan hated. Only the two FBI couples and Dan's college roommate and his wife had not arrived.

As Annie descended the stairs to the yard to greet her guests, a wolf whistle pierced through the sounds of conversation and music. It had come from Ray Brantley. Annie blushed, feeling self-conscious—the cool air tickling her mid-section. Never having worn hip-hugger jeans before, much less a brief top, she felt naked.

For an instant, she had a desire to run back upstairs and change, but caught a glimpse of Alex, who stood by the bar, grinning like the Cheshire cat and nodding her approval. *Have a glass of wine and think Shania.* It had been Alex's advice when Annie tried to dodge buying the outfit. According to Alex, if she would just play the part, she would be fine. After all, the popular singer was sexy in a wholesome sort of way.

Shaking her head and slightly frowning, Annie attempted to squash Ray's gesture, but Gabe Patton wouldn't let it go.

Loud enough for all to hear, Gabe called out, "Don't fight it Annie, you're a damned sure knockout in that outfit."

Giving Gabe an indulgent smile, she turned to Ray and said, "Thank you, Ray, I'm flattered."

"I call 'em like I see 'em," he replied.

Glancing over at Dan, she could see that he was smiling. He didn't seem at all disturbed that his wife was garnering attention from other men. In fact, he had a proud look on his face.

The moment passed, and Annie crossed the yard to greet the other guests, giving Eva a hug and Martha an outreached hand. As she circulated, Rosa brought six additional guests to the yard—the two FBI couples and Doug and Caroline Burton. Dan and Doug had maintained their friendship from college despite the Burtons living in Brunswick. The men immediately went over to Dan, who had moved toward the porch upon seeing them arrive. The Bureau men shook hands, with Tony introducing his wife to Dan and Annie, who had walked back to greet them. Doug gave Dan a combination handshake and man-hug.

Annie immediately went over to welcome the newcomers, wanting them to feel comfortable among the locals, especially Christiane. Sandy and Caroline were both Georgia girls from Atlanta, so they could partially understand the Providence natives. Those two soon found mutual ground discussing their respective children while sipping white wine.

Christiane was another matter. Childless, like Annie, she had nothing in common with the other women, other than the fact that her husband worked with Dan and Mark. Between her heavy French accent, her ballerina presence, and her striking beauty, she was like a priceless piece of antique porcelain in the middle of the country fair craft table.

Although retired from ballet for several years, she had retained the long, lean body of a dancer.

Alex sensed the awkwardness imposed by the presence of Christiane and zoomed in to bridge the social gap. What she lacked in higher education, Alex made up for in her intuitive rapport with people. To Annie's relief, her sister moved in with ease, striking up conversation with a woman who fit in the group like a French poodle at a cat show.

Circulating through the group, Annie noticed that Martha and Eva had connected. *So far—so good. The local guys have their little "remember when" thing going, and Dan's buddies are talking shop.*

After paying her respects to each guest, Annie went back into the house to bring out the trays of meat for Dan to grill. As she delivered the first platter, he grabbed her by the waist and pulled her close.

"You sure look good, angel." He kissed the top of her head before releasing her.

It sent a chill down her body. *Maybe dressing a little sexy wasn't such a bad thing.*

With the vanishing of the sun, afternoon turned to evening. By seven, Dan's grilled meat had been eaten and praised, plus enough alcohol had flowed to put the party in high gear. After Alex loaded the music player with down-and-dirty rock and roll, mixed with a few sultry ballads, she and Cole started the crowd dancing.

"A party is not a party without dancing," she had told Annie when she convinced her to rent a portable dance floor.

While Annie wanted everyone to have fun, by nine o'clock, a few were having more than their fair share. The local men seemed to be competing for the Olympic medal in beer consumption, and even Eva Patton was over her legal limit in wine coolers. Although she was aware of the state of intoxication of several guests, Annie was having too much fun to protest.

"Where's your drink?" Martha asked as she passed by Annie, beer in hand.

"I'm fine. I had a glass of wine a little while ago," Annie responded.

"Have another," Martha said, slurring her words. "You and me can handle it. We ain't driving."

"Maybe later," Annie said, brushing her off. "I'm one and done." *There's no way I'm going to risk slurring words and losing my dignity like Martha and Eva.*

During the evening, Annie danced with nearly every man attending, even the reserved Mark Norman. Dan's friends were perfect gentlemen, but the hometown boys were pushing boundaries, either because they knew her so well, or because their liquored-up libidos were on the loose. Gabe Patton was sloppy drunk. He repeated himself throughout a dance with declarations of how gorgeous she was and that if he had noticed her first, he would have married her instead of Eva.

Annie knew it was the liquor talking, but even so, it made her uncomfortable. Eva was dancing with Dan and did not seem to notice her husband slobbering all over her best friend.

Dancing with Ray Brantley was uncomfortable as well. Always coarse in social situations, Ray fell back on off-color jokes to maintain his place in a conversation, which repelled Annie. Ray could give mashed potatoes a sexual connotation. The more he drank—the raunchier his language and stories. While dancing, she felt his right hand slowing inching toward an unacceptable zone. As he neared the target, she grasped his hand and firmly guided it to its proper place. To his credit, he seemed to get the message.

At one point during the evening, Cole claimed her for a dance. Percy Sledge's sensuous rendition of "When a Man Loves a Woman" played as he moved her seductively around the floor. He was a strong lead and without a doubt the best dancer at the party. Annie was intoxicated by the music and the movement. Cole guided her effortlessly through the sultry rhythm, punctuating the choreography with rapid turns, ending on the crescendo of the music with dip nearly to the floor. Holding her parallel to the floor, he paused before slowly and sensually lifting her back up in a raw demonstration of his strength.

Observing them from the side of the floor, Gabe shouted out to Alex, "You'd better watch out, Alex, your husband's getting it on with your little sister."

Gabe's remark silenced the party, leaving only the sound of the music fading away.

"No sweat," Alex replied, as most of the guests turned their attention to Annie and Cole. "Not that I'm stupid enough to trust him," she said, pointing her finger at Cole. "Brad Pitt couldn't seduce virtuous Annie. Her moral compass is straighter than a carpenter's plumb line." Lowering her voice, she continued, "Besides, she's not woman enough to take my man."

Laughter broke out among the group, especially the local men. Those not in range of the discourse moved closer to hear better. Far from amused, Annie was mortified.

"Don't be too sure of yourself, honey," Cole interjected. "She may be the quiet one, but Annie's got all the right stuff in the right places. We guys know still waters run—you know...."

Standing on the sideline with Martha, Eva chimed in on the banter. "Alex, have you forgotten the crush Annie had on Cole when we were kids?"

"Annie and every other female past the age of puberty in Providence," Martha said, under her breath. It was true. Cole had the pick of the girls in Providence. His cocky confidence and bad-boy mystique combined with his rugged good looks and sinewy physique to give him more than his fair share of sex appeal. He was every girl's secret fantasy and every parent's worst nightmare—and he knew it. The Brennans had expected him to lose interest in Alex and move on, but when she got pregnant three months before her eighteenth birthday, they were forced to sign for the marriage and welcome him into the family.

"Eva, I was twelve years old," Annie protested, her face turning pink as she attempted to pull away from Cole.

"Yeah, Eva," Cole said, tightening his hold on Annie. "That was before she discovered that in love and marriage—blue-blood trumps redneck every time." He paused and added with a wink, "But maybe not between the sheets."

"Cole!" Annie said, reproachfully, her face turning scarlet as she looked around for Dan to rescue her.

The local guests were enjoying the exchange at Annie's expense. Dan's friends were less amused and wore uncomfortable smiles. Annie wanted to leave the floor but feared it would give the scene credence.

Cole's sarcasm piqued Dan's defenses. He was dancing with Caroline Burton and stiffened at Cole's reference to blue-blood. Several guests turned to look at Dan, knowing about his privileged background versus Cole's diametrically opposite childhood.

Cole had grown up in a crumbling, four-room shack with five brothers, a perpetually drunk father, and an abused mother who cleaned houses six days a week to earn enough to put food on the table. In contrast, Dan came from the upscale Buckhead section of Atlanta. The only child of Russ and Margaret Cameron, Dan was heir to a considerable real estate fortune. While Dan learned to play tennis at the prestigious Piedmont Driving Club, Cole hustled lunch money in the schoolyard by shooting marbles.

True to her nature, Alex reentered the exchange. "Pay no attention to Cole. He's just jealous because Dan gets to legally strap on a gun every day." With that, she went over and pulled Dan away from Caroline, coaxing him to dance with her just as another song began.

Seizing the moment to break away from Cole, Annie went over to the food table to begin removing empty dishes. Ray followed. As she leaned across to pick up a platter, she felt him brush against her hips and heard him say in a near whisper, "You sure look sexy tonight."

Grabbing the dish, she straightened up, positioned the platter between them, and said, "I'll take that as a compliment. But I think it's coming from Jack Daniels, not you."

"I—I may have had a teeny little drink or two," he said, pinching his thumb and index finger together, "but that don't give me no hallucinations."

"I think it was more than a little," she said, forcing a smile. Annie had no respect for Ray.

"Come on, Annie, no shit, you're a real sexy gal. I 'member you from school, when you come to my games with Alex and Martha. You were just a little runt. No one paid you no mind, 'cause you were so, so, what do you call it…stuck-up? I knew back then you were gonna be somethin'. Only trouble is you grow'd up to be colder than a witch's tit in a brass bra in January."

Annie wasn't sure which she disliked more, his clumsy compliment or his vulgar language. "Ray, you're drunk. You wouldn't want Martha to hear you talking like that," she said, looking around for Martha, Dan, or someone to rescue her.

Ignoring the rebuff, Ray leaned over the platter and said in a near whisper, "Know what I would give to—"

"No, I don't think I want to know," she interrupted. "You need to get yourself a cup of black coffee." With that she walked away, leaving him leaning against the table. *This is getting out of hand.* Her radar sent a warning signal as she carried the dirty dishes into the house. *I don't want my next-door neighbor thinking he can come on to me.* It had been all she could do to stomach Ray since the day that Alex told her about his cheating on Martha.

"If I were Martha, I'd crown him with my iron skillet. She's home changing diapers and pregnant with the fourth kid, while he's fooling around with a hussy down in Sandersville," Alex had said. "Got her pregnant, too."

"How did Martha find out?" Annie had asked.

"The bitch called, screaming over the phone that Martha had to give the bastard a divorce. But the devil takes care of his own, and the little she-devil miscarried. Put the fear of God in Ray Brantley for a while, but I doubt that he's cured."

Appalled, Annie had asked why Martha didn't kick him out.

"Simple, Muff—a mortgage, car loan, crap-load of credit card debt, and all those kids. Ray makes good money driving that truck all over the state, but they spend more than he makes. And, where the hell was she gonna go with three kids and number four on the way?"

"Well, now she's got five. I would never stay with a man who cheated on me, would you?" Annie had asked.

"Annie...sweetie, you're so naive. Life isn't like your silverware drawer where you line the knives and forks up neat and tidy, and like good soldiers, they stay at attention until you come back. Life, Muff, is what happens when you're busy writing budgets and to-do lists. Martha stays because she's trapped. You do what you gotta do. Ray's an alley cat, but he puts food on the table."

When Annie reached the kitchen with the dirty dishes, she turned them over to Rosa, who had been watching a movie on TV. Before going back out, she resolved to stick close to Dan the rest of the evening. She wouldn't let Ray ruin the party for her. She was having too much fun and secretly enjoyed the little flirtations.

CHAPTER FIVE

As the hour grew late, Dan's two colleagues paid their respects and quietly left. They wanted to get back to Atlanta while still reasonably sober. Not having to drive, Dan went past his standard two-drink policy. Annie had limited herself to the one glass of wine, partly in deference to her quest to become pregnant. Alex had consumed her share of beer but switched to coffee an hour before the party wound down. Cole was drunk but still on his feet. However, it was Eva who had gone way past the finish line. She was one drink shy of comatose, and Gabe little better.

Taking Dan aside as the others were leaving, Annie said, "I think Alex is okay to drive. She's been drinking coffee for the last hour, but someone needs to drive the Pattons home. Neither one of them should be behind the wheel of a car."

"You're right," Dan said, "but I think I've had too much to drive."

"I'll do it, but I'm taking our car. They will just have to come back tomorrow and pick up theirs."

"I don't like the idea of you driving alone this late."

"I'll be fine. You stay here with Doug and Caroline. I won't be long, but tell them not to feel they have to wait up for me. I can see them in the morning before they leave to go back to Brunswick."

With Dan helping Eva to the van, she managed to climb into the back and immediately fell supine on the bench seat.

I hope she doesn't get sick and throw up. Maybe I should have driven their car, Annie thought as she looked at her friend sprawled in the back.

Gabe took the passenger seat alongside Annie for the drive to the other side of Providence. For the first five minutes or so, the van was silent. Annie was thinking about Dan back at home and wishing she didn't have to make the round-trip. He would probably be asleep by the time she got back. As they passed the Providence Bank, the feel of something warm touching her thigh snapped her to attention. Gabe's hand eased its way over her leg, apparently on the way to forbidden territory. Her impulse was to slap him, but she didn't want to alert Eva as to what was happening. Instead, she used her right hand to push his hand away, hoping he wouldn't persist. *This may be a long thirty minutes*, she thought.

It was a temporary fix. The hand found its way back within seconds. In an effort to dissuade the offensive move, she called out to Eva, who had not made a sound so far on the journey.

"Eva, are you okay back there?"

Gabe's hand flinched at hearing Annie's voice. However, there was no response from Eva. After several failed attempts to elicit any activity from the backseat, Anne decided her friend was out cold.

With increased assurance that Eva was not a factor, Gabe's hand continued to creep back over Annie's leg after each rebuff. Annie's actions became more emphatic with each attempt until finally, she said, "Stop it, Gabe! You're off base."

"But Annie—I'm just thinkin' how pretty you are."

He sounds pitiful, she thought, waiting a minute to respond.

"I appreciate the compliment," she said, with a slight chill in her tone, "but you need to keep your hands on your side of the car."

"I'm just lonesome, and you gotta be lonesome, too, with Dan gone all the time."

In a quick response, Annie said, "You need to understand that I certainly miss Dan when he's traveling, but I'm not interested in an understudy. Why are you so lonely? Eva's home all the time."

"Me and Eva, we ain't going so good these days.... We've been sleeping in separate rooms." His hand was still on the seat next to her like a cat waiting to pounce.

"That's really none of my business," Annie said. *Eva hasn't said anything to me about any problems.*

"We've been a talkin' about a divorce."

The words took her aback for a second. "Gabe, no. You can't be."

"Yeah, we are. She don't want to sleep with me no more. All she cares about is the kids, how many fuckin' cars I sell, and her mama."

"I don't believe that. You need to talk this out with her," Annie said. "Maybe you guys should see a marriage counselor."

"Naw. I ain't going to one of them know-it-all, freakin' shrinks and listen to him tell me what a turd of a husband I am when I bust my balls working to give her and the damned kids everything they fucking want."

"Great sentiment, Gabe," Annie said with another layer of ice on her tone. "You're willing to walk away from a woman you've been with since high school—and from your kids?"

"I ain't walkin'. She's pushing, pushing me right out the door. She don't love me no more; I don't want her. If she hadn't got pregnant when I was playing ball with the Tide, we wouldn't have got married so young, maybe never."

"She loves you, Gabe. She always has."

"Naw she don't. You just don't know, Annie. She went and let herself go. I need a woman like you. You took care of yourself real good. You're prettier than when you and Eva was at Georgia."

There's no use arguing with him. You can't reason with a mind-altered person, she thought. *Dear God, just let me get these people home.*

Finally, they reached the Patton house. It was apparent to Annie that she would have to help Gabe with Eva. He was none too steady on his feet, and Eva was completely out of it. She drove the van up the drive as close to the front door as possible.

It took both of them to get Eva in the house; the smell of alcohol choking Annie as she supported Eva on the right, while Gabe held her on the left. The house was dark, and Gabe fumbled to find the wall light switch, which caused Eva's dead weight to fall against Annie. As Annie struggled to keep her balance, the light finally came on.

They managed to get Eva safely to the living room sofa. Paying no attention to Gabe, Annie tried to make Eva comfortable, tucking a throw pillow under her head and putting her dangling leg on the couch. Satisfied that Eva was settled, Annie was about to leave when she felt a hand on her derriere. Startled, she yelped and slapped Gabe's arm aside. "What the heck do you think you're doing?"

His balance compromised by alcohol, he stumbled backward, flailing his arms in the air to keep from falling. Annie seized the opportunity to dart for the door.

"Take care of Eva," she shouted, hoping Eva would wake, but not stopping.

Once in the van, trembling, she locked the doors, and looked back to see if he had followed her, but he hadn't. *What just happened?*

As she drove home, the events of the last hour haunted her. Was Gabe making up the problems in the marriage as an excuse to hit on her? Did the liquor rob him of reason? Or, had their lives unraveled? In high school, Gabe had been the pride and joy of Providence—the football hero with an athletic scholarship to Alabama. Eva, like Annie, won an academic scholarship to UGA; but before finishing her freshman year, Eva was pregnant. She and Gabe both dropped out. *Getting pregnant crushed their dreams; not getting pregnant is crushing mine.*

The headlights of an oncoming truck momentarily blinded Annie, snapping her out of her thoughts. She flinched and grasped the steering wheel, intent on keeping the van steady in her lane until past the semi. Meeting a large truck on the narrow, two-lane road, even in daylight, made her nervous.

Calming down, her mind went back to the Pattons. *Eva and Gabe were like bread and butter. Once spread, butter doesn't come off. Could that ever happen to us? Never.*

Nearing home, Annie felt a strong sense of gratitude for the quality of her marriage. *Thank goodness Dan is there for me.* Thinking about him brought a warm surge through her body. *I hope he hasn't gone to sleep.*

The house was quiet when she opened the front door. It appeared as though everyone was asleep. Downstairs, the only light was coming from a living room lamp. There was no sign of Dan, or the Burtons. The silence was almost eerie, especially with Heidi, their German shepherd, missing. She had taken the dog to her parents' house for the weekend to keep her out of the way. *Darn, he must be asleep already*, she thought as she walked over to turn out the light. *I really wanted to at least hug him.* Reaching under the shade for the switch, she hesitated. *I'd better leave the light on for Tom and Carol.* The Burtons were staying in the first-floor guestroom.

To her surprise, when she tiptoed upstairs, the light was on in the master bedroom. Dan was propped up on the bed, reading. "I didn't hear you come in," he said.

Annie smiled, happy to find him awake. "I tried to be quiet so as not to disturb anyone."

He closed his book and laid it on the night table. He looked especially handsome in the warm glow of the incandescent light. His thick brown hair was slightly tousled, and his eyes were reading her body like the pages of his book. "Come here," he said in a tone that gave her the sensation of a teenager in heat.

She lowered her chin, cocking her head slightly and said, "Give me a minute to get out of these clothes."

"If you don't mind—I'll take care of that for you," he said as, palm up, he beckoned her toward him with two fingers.

CHAPTER SIX

As Annie walked across the parking area of the abortion clinic, the party was as clear in her mind as the night it took place. When Dan took her in his arms that night, he stripped her body of all that stood between them and her mind of all worldly thought. It had been so natural to give herself without reservation. *Will it ever be like that again?*

The door to the clinic opened easily, revealing a waiting area with the capacity to seat fifteen or sixteen people. Only three were seated in the mint-green chairs lining three sides of the room. *I'm here,* she thought, a wave of nausea cresting as she stepped into the room. Directly opposite the entry was the standard check-in window for a medical office. Left of the window was a door marked "Restroom." Pausing, she debated which to access first. The nausea was taking charge, regurgitation imminent. *I've got to get to the restroom. Checking in will have to wait.*

She walked quickly, oblivious to others in the room, praying the facility was not occupied. Reaching for the door handle, she held her breath. It was free. Once inside, Annie put her purse on the sink, leaned over the toilet, and retched, but could not vomit. Spontaneous tears filled her eyes and ran down her cheeks. She retched again and managed to expel a small amount of fluid, leaving a bitter taste in her mouth. At least that relieved the nausea. She looked around for a paper towel. *Please don't have one of those hot air hurricanes.* Luck was holding out. On the right, there was paper towel dispenser. She pulled several out and wet them with cold water. Putting one to her forehead, she dabbed her lips with the other, and then leaned down to the faucet to rinse her mouth. Relaxing, she sat down on the toilet seat, fully clothed, and attempted to pull herself together.

When her strength returned, Annie washed her hands; however, the aroma of the antiseptic soap nearly brought back the nausea.

Once her composure was intact, she walked into the waiting room and to the reception window. The chill of the air conditioning sent a shiver through her thin body, causing her to wish she had brought a sweater. Signing a pseudonym on the check-in sheet and receiving forms to complete, she took the clipboard to an empty chair and began completing the questionnaires. The pen made it through less than five words before arbitrarily ceasing to write. She dug deep in her purse, fumbling for a substitute.

Aware of the need to give accurate medical information and to protect her identity, she scrutinized each question carefully before answering. In the financial section, she marked "cash" for method of payment and moved the clipboard aside to check her purse for assurance the money was there.

After completing the registration process, she chose a recent copy of People from the table and returned to her seat. Unable to garner any interest in the magazine, Annie gazed around her surroundings, speculating about the other women waiting to be seen. *I wonder how they ended up here.*

One woman, seated a few chairs over, bore the hard look of a gal who had been around more than one block—too much make-up, too much jewelry, and avant-garde costuming. *She looks like she's at least forty. Is she here for an abortion?*

The woman's hair was dyed shiny-black—like patent leather shoes. It looked as though the color might rub off on your hands if you touched it. The hair contrasted sharply with her pallid skin and deep-red lipstick, creating a garishly absurd appearance.

Two young girls, sitting on the opposite side of the room, appeared to be eighteen or nineteen. They were dressed in similar, brightly colored tee shirts, teamed with short shorts–very short shorts, which rode low on their hips. Large designer handbags were on the floor, next to bejeweled thong sandals, exposing nude feet with gilded toenails. Both had cute figures and were probably popular with the opposite sex and spoiled by their parents. They reminded Annie of Alex—capricious and carefree. Neither girl displayed any sign of stress, as they smiled and chatted between themselves. *How can they be so cavalier in a place like this? Surely they're not both here for abortions? Of course not—one must be the friend, here for support.*

One other young woman sat in the corner, looking like a frightened deer. She wore a horizontal-striped, knit shirt of multi-colors—with long sleeves. At the end of her skintight, Lycra pants were leopard-print flats. Her bleached blond hair was straight and stringy, cut Dutch-boy style just below her ears. The expression on her face caused Annie to believe she was a first-timer, with no support and as afraid as Annie.

The first woman looked bored with the whole situation. Her gaudy jewelry clanged when she turned the pages of her magazine. Her hands, with Lily Munster nails, were both covered with rings.

Comparing her own preppy style with the splash and dash of the others in the room, Annie felt like a nun in a brothel. She was alien in both appearance and attitude. No one else in the room seemed to share the guilt plaguing her, except possibly the deer-girl in the corner. Or maybe that girl had no money to pay for the abortion—or to have the baby. Trying to take her mind off the situation, Annie flipped through the pages of the magazine, but it was useless.

The front entrance opened, and a man and woman walked in, catching Annie's attention. The man was considerably older. Father, lover, or husband? The woman looked to be twenty-five or younger—the man, closer to forty-five, maybe fifty. They were nicely dressed and neatly groomed. *Upper middle class,* Annie thought. *Bet he's not her father.* To his credit, the man appeared protective of the woman. *She's the bicycle pump for his ego. Somewhere in the suburbs there's a dumb, devoted wife, like Martha, doing his laundry, raising his kids, and trusting him.*

After signing in, the couple took seats close to the tawdry woman but focused their attention exclusively on one another. *They're lovers—no question.*

Shortly, a door on the opposite side of the room opened and a nurse, with clipboard in hand, called out the name Chelsea,

The prettier of the two frisky, young girls stepped forward, turning to give her friend a "thumbs up" sign.

Why doesn't she have the baby and give it up for adoption? Annie's gaze followed the young woman as she disappeared behind the door. *Maybe she's more upset about terminating her pregnancy than she appears to be.* Returning her attention to the remaining girl, who was digging through her purse for something, Annie felt guilty for feeling judgmental about the girl. *Throw no stones, Annie. You're a card-carrying member of this club.*

A short, heavyset woman appeared at the interior door, clipboard in hand. She was dressed in business apparel, and called out, "Amanda?"

For a moment, Annie failed to realize she was being summoned. When it struck her that she had used the name Amanda, she quickly got up, placing the unread magazine back on the table, and followed the woman through the door.

Molly O'Brien led Annie down a long hall to a small room with a brass plate on the door bearing the word "Counselor." Inside, she motioned for Annie to take a seat in one of two matching, winged-back chairs. She took the other. With the clipboard on her lap, Molly began presenting the required information to Annie.

Although she couldn't quite read the name on Molly's lapel pin, it took only a few words for Annie to recognize the voice. As expected, the information was more in-depth and tedious. Annie tried to appear as though she were listening but screened out about half of what Molly said. She just wanted to get to the bottom line. *When can I get this over?*

After explaining options available to assist in having a child rather than aborting, Molly described the procedure. Annie would undergo a standard examination, pregnancy test, and blood work. If all were positive, then an appointment for the procedure could be scheduled. Afterward, Annie would need a companion to drive her home. The last part Annie heard.

"What if I don't have anyone who can drive me?"

"There's an inn down the road, luv. If you take a room, the hotel van will drive you. 'Tis not a fancy place, but 'tis clean, safe, and private. I think you will find it to your liking."

Annie frowned. This was not in her plan. *Stay overnight? I don't like that idea.* But she didn't say anything.

Molly took a hotel brochure out of her desk drawer and handed it to Annie. "There's a little refrigerator in each room where you can tuck away some drinks and a bite for your dinner. You will likely sleep a bit on the first day, but you should have no trouble walking about the day after. You might think of bringing a book or magazine to read."

I guess I don't have any choice, Annie thought, watching Molly as she spoke.

"Whatever you do, don't drink or eat after midnight the night before." Seeing apprehension on Annie's face, she added, "It'll be over before you know."

Annie looked at the kindly woman with nearly all white hair. She wondered how many times Mrs. O'Brien had gone through this same speech.

"Your job must be hard. If you don't mind me asking, how did you come to work in this type of clinic?"

"No mind, luv. Back home, 'tis abortion that's illegal. Because of it, I lost me baby sister."

"Oh, I'm so sorry. I didn't mean to pry."

"'Tis but a long time now. When I was a nurse in Derry, me home in the North of Ireland, Siobhan got herself in the family way without telling the rest of us. We didn't know 'til after she was gone. A hemorrhage it was that took her life away. If the abortion would have been legal in Ireland, Siobhan wouldn't have needed to bleed to death on the kitchen table of a back-alley butcher."

"I am so sorry." Annie's expression was of genuine concern. "My grandmother was born in Dublin."

"Was she?" Studying Annie's face for a minute, Molly nodded and said, "Yes, you remind me the bit of Siobhan, you do—eyes the color of the summer sky and hair near the shade of a light beer. But to answer your question, it was losing that dear girl, with her gentle spirit—her life about to begin—that made me decide to come where abortion was legal. 'Twas a young and foolish thought that I might save Irish girls from what happened to Siobhan."

"But you didn't go back."

"No. That's a long story—you could just say that I'm no martyr to the cause like Mamie Cadden. But here, here, luv, we best be getting you along."

Annie had listened intently to Molly. As the counselor began making notes on the clipboard, Annie gazed around the office, coming to focus on a white Belleek mug sitting on the desk. It was of a basket weave design—a spray of shamrocks painted on the surface, along with the word "Herself" in gold. The rim was chipped. *Old John Bloomfield wouldn't be too happy that a piece of his china was out in the world with a flaw.* Annie remembered her grandmother telling about the founding of the factory by Bloomfield. His declaration that a piece with any imperfection was to be destroyed was still followed nearly 150 years later. Annie's great-grandfather had worked in the Belleek factory, and the family still had many pieces of the Irish porcelain. *My life is just like that cup. Three months ago, it was perfect; now it's forever marred.*

Completing her notes, Molly looked up and said, "There. You be all ready to see the doctor."

Turning her face to Molly, her eyes glassy, Annie said in a near whisper, "I think so."

"Child, you don't have to do this. There are people who can help you."

Pulling herself together, Annie replied, "No. I do have to."

"Maybe you should talk with your priest or your pastor."

Closing her eyes to fight the tears, Annie shook her head.

"No. I'm sure. Can we please set up the appointment?"

Molly paused, looking at Annie with compassion. "I can schedule you, pending doctor's approval." She stood up and walked to the opposite side of the desk to look at her computer screen. "We have openings on Monday morning and Wednesday afternoon."

Annie thought for a minute. *I can be ready by Monday. That will give me all week to recover before Dan comes home next Friday.* "Monday would be good."

CHAPTER SEVEN

The exam and blood work indicated Annie was slightly anemic, definitely pregnant, and in sufficiently good health to have the abortion. I guess I'm cleared for take-off, she thought as she dressed and prepared to leave the clinic. The doctor had estimated that she was approximately six to seven weeks pregnant. Seven weeks and two days, to be precise, she mentally clarified as he spoke.

Passing through the waiting area on her way out, she glanced around at the women waiting to be seen. *They look like extras in a Woody Allen film while I'm living in a Shakespearean tragedy.*

Having put the plan in motion, a sense of relief veiled Annie's depression. She was finding her way through the nightmare, at least physically, if not spiritually. Walking to the parking lot, she congratulated herself on having taken charge of the problem.

Once back in her van, an inspiration struck as she buckled her seatbelt. "I'm going to cut my hair," she said aloud, the sound of her voice startling her.

With solemn resolution, she turned the ignition key. Lowering her tone to a whisper, she continued, "Cut it—short." Nodding her head affirmatively, a smile crept across her face as she said, "That's exactly what I'm going to do."

Exhilarated by the thought, she was certain that a drastic move was exactly what she needed. *I can overcome this. One step down, one to go. There's a new Annie coming.*

As she pulled out of the clinic parking lot, she focused on where she could have her hair cut. Since high school, she trimmed split ends herself. About every three months, she went to the only stylist in Providence to have it professionally cut. *I'm not going to open myself up to an inquisition from Carlene today. She has a wider circulation than The Register. But I can't just go anywhere. I want a new style, not a disaster. Margaret and Eleanor would certainly know good stylists, but that's not an option.*

Eleanor Howell was the mother of one of Annie's sorority sisters. She owned an exclusive designer boutique in Atlanta and sold jewelry that Annie designed and made. Jewelry design, which had begun as a hobby, had now grown into a small business that provided Annie pin money—thanks to Eleanor's support.

Determined to take the drastic step before her adrenalin evaporated, Annie racked her brain for how she could implement the plan. "I'll just have to take a chance with Lenox Square. I should be able to find a salon that accepts walk-ins," she said aloud. "If by some chance Margaret is out shopping, she would go to Phipps Plaza and never anywhere in Lenox but Neiman's. If the worst happened, I can always say I was shopping for a picture to go over the living room fireplace."

The plan gave her a sense of confidence; however, first she needed to make a reservation for Monday night at the inn Molly had suggested.

She had no trouble locating the hotel but was surprised to find that it was larger than expected and occupied a substantial tract of land, complete with a golf course. She could see a sign pointing to tennis courts and thought how great that would have been if she and Dan were staying there together. *We've haven't played tennis in a long time. His time has been so consumed with work since the director at the Bureau resigned.*

Tennis was Dan's sport. He had played on a championship team at the University of Georgia. Annie could not think about tennis without remembering the day they met. She was a freshman with no formal instruction; Dan was a senior, serving as a teaching assistant to the coach. The first day of class, he was on the court when she arrived. Annie was instantly attracted to the handsome young man, three years her senior, in white tennis attire. Not only was he incredibly handsome with his thick, dark-brown hair and perfectly proportioned physique, he also moved with phenomenal agility. With little experience dating, Annie never expected a popular, upper-classman to be interested in the shy girl from the country. But she was wrong. His words that day at the end of class were still fresh in her mind.

"You have a lot of potential, Miss Brennan. I would like to work with you."

Annie could hardly speak.

Dan immediately made her tennis training his mission and within a few private lessons had asked her out for a movie. The rest was history. Although she became a decent player, she was never a match for him, but he let her win enough to keep her interested.

Parking on the circular drive in front of the hotel entrance, Annie went into the lobby. The interior was neat and clean, but as Molly said—not luxurious. The furnishings were serviceable, rather than decorative; however, the desk clerk exuded Southern hospitality in a thick Georgia accent, making it easy to accomplish her purpose. Annie paid in advance, again using the name Amanda Cox. It was getting easier each time she used it. She paid with money, from her jewelry business, that Dan insisted she keep in her own account. She folded her receipt and put it in her purse, carefully reminding herself to keep it hidden.

The reservation made, she drove back toward the Atlanta mall. Nearing her destination, she became slightly agitated. Although determined to have the haircut, an uneasy feeling lingered.

Am I flirting with discovery at Lenox? In choosing Glenbrook Clinic, Annie had been confident that the location was sufficiently remote and foreign to the Cameron family to avoid an accidental encounter. Margaret Cameron was not likely to soil the tires of her BMW outside the upscale neighborhoods of Atlanta. However, Lenox was risky. Margaret did shop at Neiman Marcus. A shudder came over her as the thought of what Margaret would say if she knew where Annie had been that morning. The guilt was quickly followed by a glimmer of satisfaction at having the courage to take a step that would shock her mother-in-law. *I shouldn't think that way about Margaret. She's not so bad, just a little pretentious…. No, make that a lot pretentious.*

In contrast to his mother, Dan was a down-to-earth, unassuming man, far more like his father than his mother. Oddly enough, while Russ Cameron's family was the source of their comfortable financial position, it was Margaret who acted as though she were born to royalty.

Once in the mall, Annie easily found a salon open to walk-ins. The stylist assigned to Annie turned out to be talented—despite having a woodpecker hairstyle, a nose stud, and multiple tattoos.

"I want a total change," Annie said as she sat in the swivel chair. But looking at the woman's image in the mirror, she added, "Nothing crazy, just something short and sassy."

After running her hands through Annie's hair, the trendy stylist flipped through several books and then pointed to a flirty bob.

"You've got the volume for this style, and I believe your hair has enough natural wave to make it work."

"I like it," Annie said, surprised that it had been so easy. Apparently the girl knew her trade, despite her own atrocious hairstyle. *Here goes. I'm relying on Grandpa's old story about the man who chose the barber with a terrible haircut over the one with a great cut on the theory that they cut one another's hair.*

When done, the haircut exceeded Annie's expectations. Walking out of the salon, she felt a new vigor in her step. Her hair was still smooth, but cutting the weight off had released the natural wave. Chin-length, it curved forward on one side with an "S" wave on the other in a short Veronica Lake style.

Taking her makeover plan a step further, she left the salon in search of a new outfit.

While carefully avoiding Neiman Marcus, Annie found an equestrian-styled outfit in a small boutique near the salon. Although she fell in love with the neatly tailored, plaid jacket with a velvet collar, the price was overwhelming. *I'm game for radical action today, but not that radical,* she told herself, putting the garment back on the rack. Further along in the mall, she discovered a navy pant-set in a nautical design on sale in another specialty store.

Forgetting her quest to change her style, she purchased the conservative pant-set, left the mall, and headed back to Providence. Traffic was heavy, but she refused to let it stress her. For the first time in weeks, she thought she might enjoy having something light for dinner.

Nearing home, a morose mood began to edge in. As the depression escalated, she flipped on the radio and searched for an upbeat station. When she found Pat Benatar singing "Invincible," she sang along—her mood taking a dramatic change.

If not for Heidi greeting her at the door when she arrived home, Annie's mood would have faltered, but the sight of the dog brought on a smile. *Thank goodness, she's here. I couldn't stand to come home to an empty house.* Dropping her purse and package on a chair, Annie sat down on the living room floor with both hands scratching the sides of the shepherd's head.

"How do you like my new look?" Annie asked.

Responding to the attention, Heidi rolled onto her back, presenting her chest and stomach to be scratched.

"I bet you need to go outside," Annie said. "Where's Deli?" Looking around the room, she saw Delilah, their black Persian, coming around the wall dividing the living room and dining room, tail waving behind her like a fringed flag. Annie reached out to the cat with one hand, while continuing to rub the chest of the dog. Ignoring Heidi, Deli rubbed her face against Annie's hand and purred. Having the warmth and affection of the animals gave Annie comfort.

For most of the evening, Annie held her spirits intact and even ate a light dinner of eggs and grits. When Dan called, as he did every night, she had dozed off with the television set still on. It was a short conversation because he could tell she was groggy.

"I don't want you to have trouble going back to sleep," he said, "so I'm just going to tell you that I miss you and that it still looks good that I'll be home next Friday night."

Much as she loved hearing his voice, she did not protest. Talking to him was hard because keeping the secret was insufferable. When he signed off with his usual, "Sleep tight, angel, you know how much I love you," her eyes filled with tears.

I've never felt less like an angel in my life.

CHAPTER EIGHT

Friday morning, Annie slept until after eight—the latest she had slept in weeks. As she woke, her mind overflowed with the arrangements and chores necessary to prepare for the abortion. The first priority was withdrawing enough cash from her account to cover the clinic expense. *I'm not going to the bank until Mary-Sue Crandall goes to lunch.* The local bank teller would likely ask what the large withdrawal was for, and Annie wanted no questions.

Opening her eyes, she saw Heidi lying on the floor a few feet away. Seeing Annie's eyes open, the dog got up and came to the bedside, resting her chin near Annie's face.

"Good morning," Annie said, reaching out to pet her. The shepherd put a paw on Annie. "No, girl. You don't need to get on the bed," Annie put her arms around the dog's neck and her face against her head. "I have to take you to a kennel for a couple of days, but I promise you won't be there long."

Sitting up brought on the onerous nausea. Nudging the dog aside, she moved quickly to the bathroom and gagged over the toilet. *Thank goodness Dan isn't here.* After brushing her teeth, she went downstairs, let Heidi out, and made a cup of strong tea laced with extra lemon. Siting at the kitchen desk, she made a list of what she needed to do. Unsure as to what limitations would be imposed by the abortion, Annie wanted every base covered. The list included stocking the pantry, preparing casseroles for the freezer, watering the yard, and thoroughly cleaning the house. Whether or not it was necessary to do all the things on the list, concentrating on the chores kept her mind away from depressing thoughts.

Finishing the tea, she felt better and decided to address the matter of Heidi's care. Thumbing through an Atlanta phone directory, she found an ad that impressed her in an area she thought would be easy to locate. After making the call, she struggled to shake a gnawing guilt. *I have to leave her in a kennel. I can't ask Mom to keep her. There would be too many questions.*

Annie knew her mother. Claire wasn't intentionally intrusive but thought it her maternal duty to know everything going on in the lives of her two daughters. Normally, Annie took it in stride. It was Alex who rebelled.

"I wouldn't be surprised if she asked me whether I have orgasms," Alex had once said, when complaining about a conversation with Claire.

"You are terrible," Annie said, smiling. "She doesn't mean any harm, and she certainly wouldn't use the "O" word."

Alex wrinkled her nose.

"Don't you remember the time that Tommy Jenkins told me to say 'fuzzy duck' but to switch the first letters?" Annie asked. "When I did, he laughed his head off at me? I asked Mom why he laughed and what it meant, and she told me to look up "adultery" in the dictionary."

Alex smiled. "Yeah, and you came to me."

"Alex, I know she can be a pain, but she just loves us so much and is interested in everything we do. She has no clue that she's prying."

Although she wouldn't ask her mother to dog-sit, Annie knew that she would have to create a reason for not answering her phone on Monday, which reminded her of Dan's nightly calls. If she didn't answer the house phone, he would think the worst. *We vowed we would never lie to one another, but what else can I do?*

Annie wasn't afraid that Dan would probe. It wasn't his nature. It was betraying his trust that sent rivets of guilt through her.

Shortly before noon, she made the dreaded trip to the bank. To her chagrin, Mary-Sue was not at lunch. *Just my luck! This is probably the only day this week that she's not out to lunch at noon.*

The teller enthusiastically greeted Annie as she approached the counter.

"Well...hel...lo, Annie Cameron," Mary-Sue said in a Southern drawl thicker than guava jelly. "How fetching you are looking today."

What a hypocrite. I look like the devil. Annie smiled, handed her a check, and said, "I'm surprised that you're not at lunch."

"I know," Susie purred. "I oughta be, but Mr. Foster had to go to an important meeting, so I just had to take my lunch break early. But, I wouldn't have got to see ya, if he was here." Looking down at the check, Mary-Sue said, "My goodness, darlin', you must have a real big shoppin' trip planned."

I knew it—I knew she would ask. "Not really, but you know Atlanta sales this time of year, and some of the small stores don't take AmEx," Annie lied and looked at the teller for traces of doubt. She bought it. *Now let me get out of here.*

The remainder of Friday passed without incident. Her conversation with Dan that night was considerably longer than the night before, but she could not find the courage to mention Monday night.

Saturday went well, like the calm after a storm. She awoke relaxed, and with very little nausea. Shortly after she got out of the shower, the phone rang.

"Good morning, sweetheart," said Claire. "What are you up to today?"

"Hi, Mom. I'm just working around the house, cleaning out closets." It was almost true. She was cleaning.

"Oh my, that's a chore—at least it is for me. But, honey, I called because Dad and I are grilling ribs tonight for Alex, Cole, and the girls. Since Dan's still away, why don't you come over and spend the evening. You could stay over and go to church with us in the morning."

Annie bristled at the idea. "Sounds like fun, but I have a mess over here, and I want to get it done."

"Oh, that's too bad. I know the girls would love to see you."

"And I would love to see them too." *Here goes my cover story.* "By the way, I had a phone call from an old sorority sister from Kentucky. She's in Atlanta the first of the week and wants me to spend the day with her on Monday."

"Who?"

"Sylvia Blanton. You probably don't remember her. We weren't that close."

"You're right. I don't remember her. Is she married?"

And so the inquisition begins. "Yes, Mom. She's married."

As expected, Claire asked a dozen questions with Annie filling in false answers until able to terminate the conversation. *Practice makes the liar perfect,* Annie thought as she hung up the phone.

Sunday morning arrived. Annie opened her eyes and immediately thought: *Tomorrow. Tomorrow is Monday.* A ripple of anxiety charged through her belly, leaving a wave of nausea in its wake. *I should go to church. But going to church would mean family, conversation, and potential questions.* She could not bring herself to go—an omission she later blamed for everything that went wrong.

The frustration began when, taking a cup of tea to the patio, she bumped her elbow on the doorjamb and dropped the cup. It was one of a set she and Dan had purchased on their honeymoon. Annie loved the china for both its beauty and the memories it held. On Sunday mornings, she and Dan enjoyed a continental breakfast of fresh breads and Darjeeling tea before church. She always used the special cups as a reminder of the Sunday morning in London when they had tea and croissants at a Covent Garden café, while a string quartet played classical music. Dan bought a cassette tape of the group from a hawker on condition that the musicians autograph the copy. No one played cassette tapes any longer, but she still treasured the souvenir and played it often on their Sunday mornings.

Now only three cups remained. She wanted to cry but chided herself and moved on to clean up the spilled tea and broken china. "It's only a piece of china, and I still have three," she sniffled as she swept up the pieces and mopped the wood floor.

The broken cup set the tone for the day. Annie seemed to drop or spill everything she touched. When taking a dish of lasagna out of the oven, she burned her hand on the rack and almost dropped the casserole. Maintaining her composure, she grabbed an ice cube and then cut open a piece of aloe from her kitchen plant and rubbed sap on the burn. The first-aid treatment a success, she turned to washing the dishes only to cut her finger on a paring knife in the soapy water. *What next?*

After bandaging her finger, she finished cleaning the kitchen and started outside to dispose of the kitchen garbage only to step on one of Heidi's toys. The misstep caused her to twist her ankle and lose balance. Although she wasn't injured, the last event was the breaking point. She sat on the ground and cried for several minutes. Sensing her mistress was upset, Heidi trotted over to lick her face. "If this day doesn't end soon, I may seriously injure myself," she sobbed to the dog.

When the phone rang around five, Annie faced the dreaded, final chore—lying to Dan.

"Hello, angel. How was your day?"

"Pretty routine." *He sounds so cheerful. How do I lie to him?*

"How was church?"

"I didn't make it today."

"You aren't sick are you?" Dan said with concern.

"No." *I'm not lying. I'm not sick.* "Not at all. Just lazy. I need you home to motivate me."

"You've got it. I'll be home next Sunday, and I'll see that we both get there," he said with a smile in his voice.

Here goes. I've got to get it out. "When you call tomorrow night, you might better call my mobile," Annie said, trying to keep her words steady.

"Sure, hon, but what's up?"

"I'm going to Atlanta for some errands and to visit with one of my old sorority sisters." Annie squeezed her eyes shut, grimacing as she spoke.

"Anyone I know?" The innocence in his tone etched a scarlet "L" on her heart.

"You probably don't remember her—Sylvia Blanton. We weren't really close friends, but she's in town for a couple of days and wanted some of local sisters to get together. We all might sleep over at the hotel with her and reminisce."

"You're right, I don't remember her, but it sounds like a fun hen-fest. I'm glad you're getting to socialize."

"We may go shopping."

"Then, buy yourself something pretty."

When she hung up, she buried her face in her hands and cried. "How many lies am I going to have to tell? If he ever finds out, he'll hate me. God, I promise, if I get through this, I will never, never tell another lie."

CHAPTER NINE

Sunday night, Annie's sleep was fitful. She woke several times with a gnawing in her gut. While exhaustion allowed her to fall back asleep each time, at four-thirty, she gave up. Turning on the television, she surfed the channels, frantically chasing a distraction from the day ahead. Her mouth was dry, and the shadowy vexation of morning sickness threatened to emerge with any sudden move.

Station after station offered infomercials, lawyers professing justice for no cost, or ads promising to cure erectile dysfunction. Disgusted, she turned off the set and got out of bed. *Why couldn't I have slept until the alarm went off? I have too much time to get ready but not enough to ease my dread.*

Outside, it was still dark. When Annie turned on the table lamp, Heidi stirred from her place by the bed. Blinking, the dog looked up at her mistress. Deli slept on Dan's side of the bed, unfazed by light or motion. "Come on, girl. Let's go downstairs."

Heidi got up, stretched, and followed Annie out of the room. As they reached the entry hall, Annie sat back on the bottom step and began rubbing the shepherd's back. "What would I do without you?" she said, nuzzling her face against the dog's neck. "I promise you'll only spend tonight at the kennel. I'll get you as early as I can tomorrow." Oblivious as to what she was being told, the dog soaked up the attention.

Starting to get up, Annie gave the dog one last hug and said, "What I would give for a cup of tea right now. Why is it that you're never as thirsty as when you can't have a drink? But, I'm not nauseated."

Once in the living room, Annie took a deck of cards from a table drawer. For the next hour, she played solitaire on the sofa, whipping the cards down each time she dealt. When the grandfather clock chimed six, she breathed a sigh of relieve and put the cards back in the box. "Thank goodness, I can finally get ready," she said to the now sleeping dog.

After taking a shower and dressing in a warm-up suit, Annie attended to Deli's needs for the two days and wrote the name of the kennel on the kitchen dry-erase board. *If something should happen to me, Dan would have to know where she is. I know he would check if I just leave the name.*

Satisfied that she had put everything in place, Annie took Heidi's leash from a hook in the utility room and prepared to leave. Seeing her leash, Heidi perked up. The dog's enthusiasm added another layer on guilt for Annie.

Traffic was light on the road until they neared Atlanta, where commuters began to bog the flow, but not enough to botch her schedule. Leaving Heidi at the kennel was emotional for Annie, despite telling herself that it was only until tomorrow. *I can do this. One day and it's over.* Her heart was pounding and her hands shaking as she got back in the van for the last leg of the trip.

Jaw clenched and knuckles white on the wheel, she drove to the hotel where she checked in and then deposited her overnight case and several cans of soda in her room before returning to the lobby to catch the shuttle to the clinic. By the time she boarded the hotel van, she was calm—almost numb.

CHAPTER TEN

In the clinic dressing room, Annie robotically removed her clothing and wristwatch, the only piece of jewelry she wore that morning. *So far, so good*, she thought and took a deep breath. *I'm here; it's about to happen... I'm okay.* She tied on the hospital gown, then neatly folded her clothing and placed it in one of the lockers, together with her watch and large purse that held a book to read and her Bible. Before closing the locker, she reached into her purse to touch the Bible, and then crossed herself. "Forgive me," she mouthed, silently.

It wasn't long before a nurse returned and led her to an examining room, where her vital signs were taken, and she was injected with a muscle relaxer. Annie stared straight ahead, avoiding eye contact.

"My name is Jenny, and I'll be your nurse until you're discharged this afternoon," the young woman said in a chipper tone. "I'm just going to start an IV right now. It might pinch a bit."

Annie nodded, still not looking at the nurse.

Once the IV was in place, Jenny brought a wheelchair to transport Annie to the operating room. The walls moved by in a blur as she rolled down the corridor. Annie felt detached, as if she were watching an episode of ER. At the end of the hall was a set of wide doors, like those in a hospital. Jenny pushed a large silver disc on the wall, and the doors opened. Once through, Annie surveyed the sterile area with its intimidating array of equipment. The room was icy cold. A shiver went through her body, causing the hairs on her arm to rise.

"Just lie down on the table, Ms. Cox." Seeing that Annie was shivering, the nurse said, "I'll get you a warm blanket. The doctor will be here shortly."

This is not me. I'm not here. This is Amanda Cox. Amanda is having an abortion, not me. Tomorrow it'll be over.... Tomorrow.... With the help of the nurse, she stood up and boosted herself backward onto the table. As she lay back on the small pillow, a doctor walked in, wearing a grin that instantly repelled Annie. He was not the doctor who had examined her on Thursday. This one was older with white hair. There was nothing sinister about the man; but to Annie, he might as well have been Dr. Jekyll for the diabolical feeling he cast.

"And how are we doing?" he asked, trying to be friendly as he took her chart from the wheelchair pocket and began to scan it.

Annie said nothing. She just looked at him, a frozen expression on her face.

"Are you okay?"

She didn't respond. Suddenly, her body began to tremble. She couldn't breathe. Panic gripped her, and she heard herself scream. "No…! No…! No!" Each no echoed louder than the one before.

"Ms. Cox, it's alright. You'll be fine," the doctor said, putting his hand on her shoulder.

"No…. No, don't touch me. I won't do it. I can't," she said, her emotions escalating.

"Of course you can. You'll be fine. You'll go to sleep, and when you wake—it'll all be done."

"Don't say that!" Glaring at him, vicious sparks flying from her eyes, she lowered her voice to a guttural level. "Hear me…. I won't do it. I'm not going to take my baby's life. I won't do it. Keep the money, just let me up." She pushed his hand away and sat upright.

The nurse stepped up to the table and tried to calm Annie by taking her hand, but Annie jerked it away.

"Don't touch me." Like those of a cornered tiger, her eyes challenged them to move.

The nurse backed away, and the doctor stood with a helpless expression—his insipid grin gone.

"This is my baby you're going to kill," Annie said, her tone turning from hysterical to hostile. She yanked the IV out of her arm and attempted to stand, sobbing profusely. The relaxer was not working.

The doctor turned to the nurse and said, "Call for Molly." He then turned back to Annie. Laying her chart on the table, he took her gently by the shoulders.

"Ms. Cox, please. Sit down—here in the wheelchair. No one is going to do anything you don't want. Trust me."

Annie just looked at him, frozen.

"Here, sit down. We'll find another place where you can think about this for a few minutes."

"There's nothing to think about. My brain is burned to a crisp with thinking. It was thinking that brought me here. It didn't work. This is wrong," she said, her tone escalating, then abruptly ceasing as she stared at the physician.

For the next few moments, the room was silent.

Breaking the silence, Annie said, "I'm going home," her voice lowered to a resolute tone as she fought to regain composure. Buried in her state of confusion, she knew that a complete breakdown would strip her of control, which she could not let happen. A breakdown would have been a relief, but a fatal error. *They could have me committed, find out who I am—call Dan.*

In seconds, Molly appeared. Walking into the surgical room, a frown came over her face.

"Amanda, luv, what's wrong?"

Relieved to have someone else take over the situation, the doctor released Annie and stepped back. Turning to Molly, he said, "Ms. Cox has decided not to go through with the procedure. I've told her that it's completely her choice, but she's still upset. Maybe you can help her."

"Of course I can," Molly responded. Turning to Annie, she asked, "Would you like something to drink, luv? Jenny here can bring something for you."

Annie nodded, and Jenny left the room. Molly continued in a soothing tone, "Come now, luv. Let's go to my office."

"I'm going home."

"Of course you are. But first, we've got to help you calm down a bit."

The doctor watched stoically as Molly took charge. When he saw that Annie was calming, he turned to leave. "Call me, if you need me."

Molly nodded and thanked him as he left.

Still distraught, but starting to relax, Annie said, "I'm sorry. I just can't do it." Her chin dropped, as she sat back on the surgical table. The disconnected IV tube lay nearby creating a wet spot on the surface.

"'Tis no need for apologies, dearie. 'Tis me what should be doing the apologizing. I should've seen you were too fragile to handle this by yourself."

For a moment, there was no response. Annie was delicately balanced between calm and chaos. The trembling had ceased, but tears continued to form, re-wetting those drying on her cheeks.

"I guess I freaked them out," Annie said weakly.

"Give them no thought. 'Tis you that we're worried about. Is there a friend or family member that we can get for you?" She squeezed Annie's hand. "Who can I call, luv?"

Annie just shook her head from side to side in silence.

Molly did not press further. Instead, she pulled slightly on Annie's hand in an upward motion and said, "Come now, dearie. Let's get you out of this chamber to a place where we can be comfortable."

Annie started to get up, but grabbed at the gaping hospital gown. "My clothes. Can I have my clothes?" she said as she sat back on the surgical table.

"Surely, I'll have Jenny fetch them," Molly said, nodding her head reassuringly. "Just take a seat in the wheelchair, and I'll take you to my room."

"I can walk."

"I know you can, but 'tis more comfortable in the chair, and you wouldn't have to worry about that flapping designer gown you be wearing."

Annie smiled a little and followed directions. Just as Molly took the handles of the wheelchair, the nurse came through the door with a can of cola and a bottle of water.

"Jenny dear, can you fetch Amanda's things from the locker and be bringing them to the counseling room?" Molly asked, removing Annie's locker key from the wheelchair pocket.

The nurse nodded, handing the drinks to Annie.

Traveling down the hallway, neither woman spoke. Annie was relieved that no one else was in the hall. She felt self-conscious about creating the scene—the last thing she ever wanted to do.

When they arrived at the room, Annie recognized it as where she had her interview the week before. Molly motioned to one of the wing-back chairs and said, "Make yourself comfortable, and I'll go check on your things."

Annie sat in the chair, leaned back, and closed her eyes.

Returning shortly with a small basket containing the personal items, Molly handed it to Annie and left her to dress in private.

Discarding the hospital gown felt good—like shedding an unsavory cloak that had shrouded her since first entering the clinic. Once dressed, she was infinitely calmer and sipped the soft drink as she waited. Molly returned within minutes and took a seat in the companion chair.

"I don't want to pry into your affairs, luv, but would like to help," Molly said. "Just say what you would have me do."

"There's nothing you can do. There's nothing anyone can do. I have to work this out by myself."

"The father knows—doesn't he?"

Annie adamantly shook her head. "No. Never. He will never know."

"He's married to another lass?" Molly asked.

Annie paused before responding and took a deep breath. Ignoring the question, she said, "He doesn't exist."

"Luv, 'tis his problem as well. You need his help."

"No! Absolutely not. I'd die first."

"'Tis not fair for you to take it all on your wee shoulders," Molly said, shaking her head.

"You don't understand." Annie's voice was filled with anger, her eyes with fire as she looked straight at Molly—eye to eye.

"I was raped."

CHAPTER ELEVEN

Annie stared at Molly with the intensity of a cat stalking prey. But the image she saw was Cole's unshaven face, his piercing green eyes, as she escaped his grasp and fled to the bathroom two months before. She heard her voice crying hysterically, "What have you done?"

Despite how hard she had tried to forget that day, the image remained so vivid that she could smell the odor of sweat-infused Polo—smell his sun-scorched skin. The sound of his Matthew McConaughey drawl echoed in her ears.

In minutes, her life was irreversibly changed. Cole, on the other hand, casually hitched up his jeans and buckled his belt with an air of self-satisfaction—absent any sign of guilt or regret.

"You raped me," Annie whimpered, as she fled to the bathroom where she grabbed a large towel in an effort to protect her modesty.

Pants in place, Cole sauntered to the bathroom door. "Don't think so, Muff. You've been a'wantin' that since you were a kid. Don't think I didn't feel the fire comin' off your crotch Sunday night." He stood, blocking her exit with one hand high on the doorjamb—his unbuttoned shirt hanging open, exposing his tanned washboard abs.

As much as Annie wanted to avoid looking at him, something compelled her to lift her chin and stare him in the face. His eyes cast that cut-to-the-corner, cocky look that in another time and place some women would have found seductive.

"Your pretty little ass was craving it," he said with a smug smile, one eyebrow slightly cocked.

Gathering strength from the insult of his tauntingly capricious attitude, she lashed back, "You're disgusting. That's a lie, and you know it." Venom streamed through every syllable. "You raped me. You're going to prison."

"Really? And who do you think you're goin' to tell—Barney Fife down at the Sheriff's office? Or maybe you're going to tell ole Dan so he can put the FBI on me. They gonna pin my picture up at the Post Office? Naw…. Last I heard, adultery ain't a federal offense."

He mocked her, like he had done when she was an adolescent in awe of her sister's relationship with him. When visiting Alex, he would tease Annie by snatching a book she was reading and then holding it barely out of reach while she scrambled in vain. Although she acted angry, she had basked in the attention.

"It wasn't adultery, it was rape. And don't think I won't tell—especially Alex," Annie said, with fire in her eyes.

"Don't think so, darlin'." His eyes twinkled arrogantly. "Alex, for one, just ain't gonna believe you. She knows how hot you were for me back in the day. She'll forgive me, 'specially when I plead temporary insanity at the sight of your bare ass in front of me." He reached up and scratched his head. "Naw, she'll believe me when I tell her that you're just suffering from—what do they call it—buyer's remorse?"

He broke into a grin that Annie wanted to slap off his face. "No sugar," Cole said. "Alex'll forgive me…. But I ain't so sure she'll forgive you."

Against her will, Annie's anger went full circle back to tears. "And to think you're the father of those precious girls." She shook her head, looking him right in the eye. "The only remorse I have is in trusting you—letting you in my home."

"Come on, little sister. Why'd you want to cause a whole big hoo-ha over one little bitty ole romp in the hay? It's all in the family."

His smirky, patronizing attitude was almost more insulting to Annie than the act he committed. "You want to embarrass poor ole Dan—let the whole town know that one of the no-good Dalton boys has been in his sweet little wife's panties?"

She looked down at her hands, clutching the bath towel around her waist, her bikini top still in place. Taking a deep breath, she said calmly, "You arrogant bastard, you don't have a clue what you've done." Then, in a voice she didn't know she had, sparks flying from her eyes, she shrieked, "Get out of my house. I never want to lay eyes on your despicable face again."

"Amanda." Molly spoke sharply, trying to snap Annie out of her near trance. Then lowering her voice, she said gently, "Do you want to talk about it, sweetie?"

Blinking, as though to clear her eyes, Annie whispered, "No.... I can't."

"Are you okay?"

"I'm fine," Annie lied, shaking her head slightly and avoiding eye contact. "But don't call me Amanda. My name is really Anne—Annie." Turning her face to Molly, her eyes, floating in a body of tears, she silently implored Molly to probe no more.

"Then Annie it shall be," Molly said, nodding in agreement. She paused a moment, then said, "You'll be needing to see a counselor, luv. What you've been through is much too big to have a go at by yourself."

Annie shook her head emphatically. "No. I can't do that. I'll just have to figure it all out."

"What will you do?"

"What can I do?" Her voice was pitiful. "I'll have my baby." Annie looked down at the floor. "I'll pretend.... I won't think about it ever again, and no one will know that it's not"—she caught herself before speaking Dan's name—"that it's not my husband's child."

"You're married?"

"Yes—five years."

Molly smiled. "Do you have other wee ones at home?"

"No." Again a rush of tears flowed down Annie's cheeks. Neither woman spoke for a moment.

Gathering her composure, Annie said, "We've both wanted a baby, but it just didn't happen, no matter what we did. I don't know why it had to happen right now."

Molly's face relaxed and her eyes grew larger as she asked, "Could it be that this is your hus—"

"No," Annie said, abruptly. Thinking a second, she added, "Maybe. There's a tiny chance, but I really don't think so."

"A DNA test can be done from the amniotic fluid before the babe is born, child."

"No. Absolutely not." Annie's expression was adamant as she shook her head.

"Why not, luv? If your husband's the daddy, would solve your problem."

"Mrs. O'Brien, we've tried for four years to have a baby. There's no way he got me pregnant the week this happened," Annie said, wiping tears away with the sleeve of her gown. If I don't have a test, there's always a tiny hope that I'm not lying to him—and to everyone else."

"If he's a good man, he would understand."

"Don't you think I've thought about that?" Annie looked straight at Molly, her blue eyes wide in a desperate plea for understanding. "He would try, but how could he really love another man's child, especially under the circumstances? And what about his family? What would we tell them? I couldn't brand my child."

Molly thought for a moment before responding. "I think I understand. Tell you what," she said as she leaned forward, took Annie's hands, and squeezed gently. "Promise me that you'll be staying in touch with me. I've a stout Irish shoulder you can lean on." Releasing Annie's hands, she went over to her desk and took a card from the holder. Turning it over, she wrote her home phone number on the back and handed the card to Annie.

"Call me whenever you need to talk, but at least once a week so that I know you be doing okay. Promise me, luv?"

When the call came that the hotel van had arrived, Annie stood to leave. As she passed by, the older woman rose and reached out. Hugging the shaky young woman, Molly said, "You are going to be fine, Annie Whoever. You've a soldier's spirit."

A wisp of a smile appeared on Annie's face. "I will call you. I will."

Back at the hotel, Annie washed her face and put on a little makeup. She changed out of her warm-up suit as though the experience of the morning had somehow contaminated the clothing. She wanted a fresh start for the day and time to sort out what she had done and what she would do next. The room was prepaid for the night, so there was no hurry to leave. Hair brushed and fresh clothing on, she walked down to the hotel restaurant. She was actually hungry but decided to order from the "lite" selections on the menu to avoid stressing her stomach. The nausea had miraculously subsided.

I'm not going to think until after lunch. I'm just going to work on calming down. There's plenty of time to decide what to do next.

When she finished eating, she went back to the room. After gathering her belongings, Annie sat down on the bed and took the Bible from her purse. "I couldn't do it, God. Thank you for stopping me, but please, please give me the strength and wisdom to get through the rest." Crossing herself, she returned the book and started for home.

Once in the van, the questions lined up. *I made one decision I thought was right, but it wasn't. How do I know what to do now?*

Although back where she started, Annie had ruled out one major option. She could not abort the baby. The rest had to be dealt with one thing at a time. *I'm still in the same mess, but somehow, I feel relieved.*

Relief was brief. As she drove through Atlanta, the thought of how she would tell Dan sent her back into panic mode.

Driving toward Heidi's kennel, she stopped at a traffic light and noticed a service station with a carwash. The van didn't need gas, but for some reason, when the light turned green, she crossed the intersection and turned into the station. After filling the tank with less than five gallons, she selected the deluxe wash option on the pump. The kennel wouldn't close for another three hours, and she was avoiding the trip home where reality was inescapable.

Inside the carwash tunnel, Annie found security in being narrowly encased within the concrete walls. Shortly after the spray of water began plummeting the van, streaming down the windshield in torrents, tears began to run down her cheeks. As the tears escalated, she pounded the steering wheel with her palms. "Why? Why did this happen? What have I done to deserve this?" She didn't resist the hysteria, giving herself permission to totally breakdown—if only for the length of a carwash.

When the wash cycle was complete, Annie didn't move. The floorboard of the van was littered with crumpled tissues, but she was not finished draining her emotional reservoir. *I've got to get all this out once and for all. I'm going to cry until there is no tear left—then I'm never going to cry about it again.*

With no cars waiting behind the van, she circled the small building, dug into the console for change, and purchased another wash via a device at the entry. It took three cycles before she was ready to proceed to the kennel. After the final wash, Annie was spent and wished for water to splash on her face. A once-over of the service station squelched the notion of going to the restroom. She opted instead to purchase a bottle of water and a fresh package of tissues. Back in the van, she drank half of the water, and then used wet tissues to blot her face. *Putting on makeup was certainly a waste of time,* she thought as she cranked the van.

At the kennel, Heidi was exuberant at the sight of Annie. Tail wagging, and straining on her leash, she nearly pulled the attendant down trying to reach her mistress, which gave Annie a moment of joy.

"I'm so glad that you don't have to stay here overnight," Annie whispered, as Heidi rose up on her back legs to greet her beloved Annie.

Dogs are so forgiving. She's so happy to see me that she doesn't blame me for bringing her here.

In the van, Heidi resumed her place in the passenger seat, sitting majestically erect and looking out the window as though surveying her kingdom. Annie knew she should make the shepherd get in the back, but she didn't have the heart to disturb the smiling dog and secretly liked having her near. "We're going to have a baby, old girl. I need you to help me get through this."

CHAPTER TWELVE

When Annie arrived home, dark clouds covered the sky. She took Heidi to the backyard and then retrieved her things from the car. Before unpacking her overnight case, she took the various papers and receipts connected to the abortion out of her purse. Disposing of the abortion evidence was critical to Annie. Five years of marriage to an FBI agent, plus being a fan of fictional crime stories, made her paranoid about erasing every trace of her day.

As she held the documents in her hand, contemplating a method of obliteration, the kennel receipt reminded her of the note left about Heidi's location. She immediately went to the kitchen and cleaned the dry-erase board, and then took the papers to Dan's shredder and ran them through. When the machine stopped grinding, she lifted the lid and surveyed the remains. The sliver-thin strips lay at the bottom like grey straw. Annie should have been satisfied that no one would suspect the original identity of the ribbons, but she wasn't. Scooping up the small pile, she carried them to the fireplace, tossed them in, and ignited the shredded paper with one of the long-stemmed matches kept in a brass box on the mantle. In seconds, the paper turned to ash.

Hearing a clap of thunder and satisfied that her mission was accomplished, she went to bring Heidi in from the yard. As she walked to the backdoor, she thought about what the clinic would do with the money she paid. Molly had indicated that she was entitled to at least a partial refund, but Annie never gave her real address, or even her full name. It didn't matter. Her need for anonymity far surpassed the few hundred dollars in question.

After calling Heidi back into the house, she picked up the kitchen phone, planning to deliver a cover story about cancellation of the Atlanta excursion to her mother, but her fingers wouldn't punch in the number. She wasn't ready for conversation with anyone, least of all her inquisitive mother. *The more questions that she asks, the more lies I will have to invent.* Lying to her mother was almost as bad as lying to Dan. Not only was Annie being forced to adjust her moral compass, she was also having to betray the trust of the most important people in her life.

For the next hour, she sat in the living room, listening to the thunderstorm outside, reviewing the scene at the clinic, and contemplating her next move. The pets hovered around—Delilah in her lap and Heidi on the floor with her chin resting on Annie's foot. Like a hot water bottle, the warmth of the cat soothed the tension in her stomach. As the storm faded, the house grew still. Without a TV playing, the silence was suffocating, but Annie made no move to turn on sound or light.

She tried to map her course of action, but the details scrambled for priority like paparazzi pursuing a celebrity. The only thing she could check off the list was the abortion issue. Thoughts of when to make the pregnancy known and what measures to take to cover the secret overwhelmed her. The one thing clear in her mind was that any information she revealed had to be carefully thought out in advance. A slip could be fatal. She shuttered to think how many lives would feel the impact if the truth were discovered—Dan, his parents, Alex, the Dalton girls, and most of all—the baby. The criminal act of one despicable man could shatter the lives of so many innocents. The key to their happiness was in Annie's custody.

While announcing she was pregnant and letting the rest take care of itself seemed like the simple solution, Annie knew it was not. She had to avoid Cole doing the math and realizing it was his baby. She could not imagine that he would want it known but knew that the only person who can be trusted with a secret is a dead one. Further, she could not bear the idea of him looking at the child with any paternal attitude. That would create an insufferable bond between them.

"I have to tell Dan—soon," she said, breaking the silence.

Although the idea paralyzed her, she knew that delay would create suspicion. But Dan would expect her to be euphoric. She was not ready to pull that off. *This is the most important thing that has happened to us in our entire life together. If I can't act like I'm crazy with excitement, he'll wonder what the heck is going on.*

As she struggled to formulate a plan, a tear eased down her cheek. It should have been one of the most thrilling times of her life. Grappling for a plan, she came up with an idea that would serve a dual purpose. She would fudge the baby's due date. It could buy her time to adjust to the situation and prepare for the disclosure, plus allay any dangerous notion Cole might develop.

"What's one more lie? I've already told more than there are pills in Dad's pharmacy."

Shortly before nine, it was totally dark in the room. Her mind staged a mutiny, refusing to sort her thoughts. Her stomach growled, and a hunger pain cut through, causing Annie to grab her abdomen, which in turn disturbed Deli. As the cat left her lap, Annie stretched in place to increase circulation in her stiff body thereby displacing Heidi. "I can't think anymore, guys, and I need to eat," Annie said, her arms outstretched over her head. "I'll bet you're starved, Heidi. It's way past your dinner time."

Turning on a lamp, she got up and went to the kitchen, with both animals following. After feeding Heidi and checking Delilah's bowl, she made a plate of scrambled eggs, instant grits, and toast. Although her stomach was begging for satisfaction, she had no appetite, but made herself eat everything. *I have to take better care of myself for the sake of this baby.*

After clearing away the few things in the kitchen, she went upstairs, took a shower, and put on a comfortable gown and robe. Fatigue and letdown closed in, causing her to feel drowsy. Not wanting to alarm

Dan by failing to hear the mobile ring, she took it with her and went downstairs to watch television.

Settling on a *Law and Order* rerun, she tried to concentrate on the drama, but found her mind creeping back to the issues she faced. By eleven, Dan still hadn't called, and Annie was struggling to stay awake. She turned off the set, unaware of what the episode had been about, and went back upstairs.

In her bedroom, she found Deli already down for the night on Dan's side of the bed. The cat was curled up like a round fur pillow—eyes closed. Her black coat contrasted nicely with the stale-red of the Jacobean-print bedspread. Smiling, Annie said, "Had a hard day on bird-watch at the window? Didn't get your usual sixteen hours of sleep?" Sitting down, she dropped the phone on the bed and reached over to pet Deli, who instantly began to purr. Heidi had followed Annie and nuzzled against her thigh, seeking attention.

"Jealous are you?" Annie said, using her free hand to scratch behind the dog's ears. "What am I going to do, guys?" She curled her bottom lip under her front teeth for a minute or two before continuing her conversation with the pets.

"I'm right back where I was before my foray into Atlanta. There's still going to be a baby, and the world is going to know it soon. How am I going to break the news?"

Laying down, cuddled around the cat, she closed her eyes, ignoring Heidi. The dog moved onto the bed as though by right, lying as close to Annie as she could. The warmth of the big dog against her back, coupled with the purring of the cat, brought a sense of security to Annie. "I'll figure this out, guys. I have to."

Fatigue overcame her and she fell asleep. She slept about forty-five minutes before waking when Heidi jumped off the bed. *Oh my gosh, what time is it? Has Dan tried to call?* Rising to look at the clock, while reaching for the phone, she blinked her eyes, trying to clear her head. It was nearly midnight. *Did I sleep through his call?*

Flicking the phone to "calls received," she was relieved to some extent that no call had come in, but apprehensive as to why he had not called. *I don't want to talk, but I want to hear his voice.* As she stared at her phone, she weighed the pros and cons of letting him continue to believe she was in Atlanta with Sylvia. *I don't need to lie more than necessary. I'll just tell him that the plans changed, and I came home—which is absolutely true. I don't have to say what plans changed.* Annie knew Dan well enough to trust that he would not press for details.

Without turning the covers back on her bed, she reclined against the pillows and began making mental plans. She would need to choose a doctor for her prenatal care and delivery. She immediately ruled out Doctor Martin. As the only physician in Providence, he not only delivered both Annie and Alex, but he was also a family friend. If she told Dan she was pregnant, he would expect her to rely on his father for a referral. That would be too close to home. Even with the confidentiality of doctor and patient communications, it was not a good idea to have a friend or colleague of her father-in-law as her doctor. What if she talked under anesthetic? Or what if he suspected she was lying about her last period?

Concentrating on who she knew in Atlanta, she remembered Molly O'Brien and her offer of help and decided to call the counselor the following day.

It was not much, but a plan was beginning to form. She decided that she would tell Dan after having a prenatal check-up. She could use the appointment as an excuse for not telling him sooner. She could say that if it turned out that the drugstore tests were wrong, she did not want him disappointed. Only one loophole remained. How could she explain her independent choice of doctors—why she did not consult his father for a referral? *Every lie leads to another, but I can't work them all out now. First step is decided...which is enough for tonight.*

As she formulated her plan, Annie was becoming more and more reconciled with the fact that she was having a baby. When the thought of how the baby was conceived crossed her mind, it wasn't given an opportunity to fester.

By the time Dan called at half past twelve, she was agitated, fearing something might have happened to him. When the phone rang, she jumped, but was relieved. He apologized for calling late, fearful that he woke Annie and her friends. He explained that a meeting had gone far into overtime. Annie told him that she was back in Providence and briefly touched on her sorority sister's change in plan. As expected, Dan accepted the explanation without question. The conversation was brief.

"You sound exhausted," Annie said. "We can catch up tomorrow night when you're not so tired."

He agreed without protest and ended the short conversation with his usual terms of endearment. However, before hanging up, Annie was able to confirm that he expected to be home by the weekend.

The nap, plus the stimulation of the phone call, caused Annie to lie awake on the bed, returning to plans of how to reveal the pregnancy. *I'll need to tell the doctor that I had a cycle in June. That way, he will give me a later due date.*

Rubbing her stomach, she said, "I guess you're going to be a pretty big premature baby." She brought a hand up to rub her forehead and continued the soliloquy. "Now, I've got to work on the courage to tell your daddy—the one you are going to believe is your father." The fact she was having a baby began to take full hold, and she smiled. I'm really going to be a mom. *There's a baby growing inside me—a little girl...or a little boy.* Her expression instantly changed.

A boy could look like him. What if I have to see him on my child's face every day? Could that affect how I feel about my own baby? Would others notice a resemblance and be suspicious?

Taking her Bible from the night-table drawer, she held it to her heart and prayed, "Dear God, it's got to be a girl...please." Tears rolled down her face.

CHAPTER THIRTEEN

When she finally dozed off, her hand resting on the Bible, Annie slept well. Whether from faith or fatigue, her anxiety was temporarily neutralized. Tuesday morning, she woke with a spirit of determination. Although there was a queasy moment when she first stood up, the nausea was all but gone—replaced with an appetite. After tending to the needs of the animals, she toasted a cheese and tomato sandwich, which she ate with a cup of hot tea. The food tasted good for the first time in weeks.

Mid-morning, she called her mother and told a convincing story of going to Atlanta when the sorority outing failed, shopping for materials for her jewelry projects, and visiting the library for creative research. Though the lies slipped smoothly from her mouth, guilt sent her into a frame of mind similar to what she experienced at the clinic. Her mouth spoke the words, but her mind heard them coming from a stranger.

"It was late when I got home, and I was just too tired to talk," she said.

Claire asked a few questions but seemed to accept the fabrication.

"Being gone yesterday has me behind with my schedule, so I'd better not talk long. I just wanted to touch base with you before I got started," Annie said, her list of lies growing.

With the house clean from her preparations over the weekend, the only thing remotely behind in Annie's life was her jewelry work. Although she wasn't inspired to design, she decided it would provide a good subterfuge until she was more in balance. "If you talk to Alex, Mom, tell her that I'm going into hibernation to get some designs done for the boutique, so I might not answer my phone."

To sooth her aching conscience about lying and to kill time until evening when she could telephone Molly O'Brien, Annie scanned her collection of art books and the Internet, searching for ideas for the fall collection. At the start, it was hard to focus, but as some of the images sparked her creative side, the time passed faster.

After microwaving a frozen dinner that evening, she took out Molly's card, copied the number in her address book with a pencil under the "M" heading, and burned the card in the kitchen sink, before dialing. Unsure as to whether to identify Molly, she left the name line blank. She could always enter it later. As the phone rang, butterflies stirred in her stomach. *I hope she meant it when she told me to call.*

When Molly answered, Annie felt a twinge of regret and had to resist an impulse to hang up.

"Mrs. O'Brien, this is Annie…Annie from the clinic yesterday. I'm so sorry to bother you, but you told me I could call."

There was no reply, but Annie could hear voices in the background. *Oh my gosh, she was just being polite to the crazy woman. I shouldn't have called her.*

"I'm the woman who backed out at the last minute," Annie continued.

The background noise subsided. "Of course, I remember, luv. The telly was too loud, and I just didn't hear you so well," Molly said. "How are you, child?"

"I'm much better. I actually ate three meals today without throwing up."

"Wonderful, luv. Have you told the hubby he's to be a daddy?"

"No. Not yet. That's why I called. I want to see an OB/GYN before I tell him. But I don't know who to see."

"There's no one in the town where it is that you live?"

"There's only one doctor here, and he delivered me. I live in a very small town, Mrs. O'Brien. He and my father play golf together."

"Call me Molly, luv." Hesitating for a moment, Molly said, "I see your point. Of course you can't."

"Can you help me get an appointment this week with someone really good, but not on the east side of the city? I can go anytime this week."

"Three days might be a problem, but I'll give it a go first thing tomorrow morning. You call me back in the evening."

"Mrs. O'Brien—Molly, it is really important that I see someone before Friday afternoon." Annie's voice quivered as she spoke.

"I understand, luv, but I'll be needing your full name—the real one."

Of course she would have to register with the new doctor under her true identity. How could a doctor deliver a baby, if he didn't know who she was?

After a brief pause, Annie said, "It's Anne…Anne Cameron."

Sensing the hesitation in Annie's voice, Molly said, "Your identity is safe with me, luv. I'll do me best to have you an appointment before the week is done."

True to her word, Molly made a Thursday afternoon appointment with an Atlanta obstetrician whom Molly worked for before going to Glenbrook. Whether by accident or design, the doctor was a woman. Annie never thought to specify a gender preference when she asked for the referral. Doctors were all men to her—Doc Martin, Russ Cameron, her fertility doctor, and the sinister one at the clinic.

Having an appointment was a relief. As she thought about it, Annie was pleased that the obstetrician was female. Her situation was taking root. She could use a feigned preference for a female doctor as an added excuse for circumventing a referral from Russ. *The more distance I can keep between the Camerons and my baby, the more comfortable I will be.*

Annie arrived at her appointment in the Stone Mountain area of Atlanta a half hour early. When Dr. Windsor walked into the examining room, Annie was surprised at how pretty the physician was and disconcerted by how young she appeared. Annie's face must have signaled her discomfort because the doctor immediately said, "You were expecting an older man, weren't you?"

Embarrassed, Annie replied, "I'm sorry…no, I knew you were a woman—"

"Let me put you at ease. I'm older than I look," the doctor said, and pointed to a diploma on the wall that indicated she completed medical school in 1976. "People from India are fortunate that time is a little more merciful," she said as she pulled on a pair of surgical gloves.

"You were born in India?" Annie asked.

"No, no. My father was from Bombay and received his medical training in London where he met my mother."

Once the initial surprise wore away, Annie was impressed with her new doctor. Kareena Windsor was a consummate professional, performing a comprehensive examination and taking the time to answer all of Annie's questions. As hoped, the doctor accepted her date for her last menstrual period and announced that Annie could expect the baby around St. Patrick's Day. If after examining Annie, Dr. Windsor had any suspicions about the date, she reserved comment.

Leaving the office with a prescription for prenatal vitamins, a packet of information to study, and a list of ways to combat her morning sickness, Annie began to contemplate how and when to make her announcement to Dan. She had to make certain that she was able to manifest the enthusiasm he would expect—but that would be tricky. *I'm beginning to accept this, but how much excitement can I project? I can't look in his eyes without guilt being written all over my face. Should I tell him the minute he walks in? Maybe the excitement of seeing him will pass for joy about the baby.*

She debated the options all the way back to Providence. The thought of his enthusiasm over becoming a father tortured her. She feared having a breakdown like the one she had at the clinic. Although she was stronger, her nervous system was not completely repaired. Annie knew that Dan would want to share the news with his family immediately, adding another layer to her guilt. Margaret and Russ would be excited about their first grandchild—she could hear Margaret gushing over her grandbaby—only it wasn't hers—not one single drop of Cameron blood would flow through the baby's veins.

Dan's plane was due to arrive at Hartsfield a little after seven on Friday night. It would take him another hour or more to retrieve his car and make the drive to Providence. She had told him not to eat, that she would make a special dinner since he had been gone for nearly two weeks. He promised that the prospect of a home-cooked meal, after so many days of restaurant food, was well worth the wait.

I'd better stop at the store before I go home. I should have stopped in Atlanta, but it's too late now. I'll just have to do with what I can find at the Piggly Wiggly. Dan will be happy with meat loaf, mashed pota-toes, and cabbage.

On Friday after lunch, Annie took a shower and started to dress. Be-fore putting on a pair of shorts and a T-shirt, she looked at herself in the full-length mirror on the back of the bathroom door. Her abdomen was still flat, but her breasts were definitely changing. *There's really a baby in there,* she thought as she passed an open hand down the length of her torso. *I'm really pregnant. I'm going to be a mom.* A slight chill passed down her arms, causing the hair to rise a little. *My baby.* It felt good for the first time. With a renewed feeling, she finished dressing and went back downstairs.

Before heading to the kitchen, Annie went out to the mailbox at the front of the property. In addition to a magazine and some mass-market-ing fliers, there was a package from Eleanor Howell. She took it to the small room off the breakfast nook that she used for a studio. She knew the package contained a portfolio of fashions the boutique would be carrying for fall, together with fabric swatches. Her job would be to design complimentary jewelry. Eleanor wanted samples by August each year. Looking at the box, Annie was aware she needed to produce an exciting collection so she could replenish the money taken from her account for the abortion, but the assignment would also give her a diversion.

Once in the kitchen, she chopped onions and green pepper, mixing them with ground beef and catsup. Dan liked the meatloaf with a lot of catsup. When the two loaves were formed, she poured a can of vegetable juice over the top and put the casserole dish in the refrigerator. It was only four o'clock, but she decided to peel her potatoes and put them in cold water so that in the evening, she would have little to do to complete the meal. Butterflies began buzzing around her stomach like the Blue Angels. "Calm down, Annie. You've got to stay in control. You can't let on that anything has changed until you're ready to deal with telling him."

The following hours were agony as she tried to fill the time and stay calm. Thoughts fluctuated from worry about how she would act when he walked through the door, to thoughts about the gender of her child. "Please, dear God, let it be a girl," she whispered as she combed her hair, fluffing up the new style with one hand as she combed with the other. "If it's a boy, the Camerons will expect dark hair, brown eyes, and his name to be Daniel Russell Cameron, IV, not a green-eyed, blonde. It's got to be a girl."

CHAPTER FOURTEEN

At half past six, Annie put the meatloaf in the oven. Afterward, she took a shower and put on makeup, comfortable knit pants, and a loosely fitting pullover. Dan would be home soon. It seemed liked months since he'd left. Although she desperately wanted him back, there were moments of panic over his potential questions about the fertility efforts. There was no way that she trusted herself to tell him about the baby. Making the decision to have the child did not provide the strength to control her guilt over the deception, or to show the requisite enthusiasm. She needed more time. Annie prayed Dan wouldn't notice any change in her appearance or demeanor. Once dressed, she returned to the kitchen to complete meal preparations. Slightly past seven, the phone rang.

"Hey there, angel. I'm down and on my way."

Annie's whole body smiled. It was the voice she loved—sexy and sweet—something Dan pulled off well.

"Dinner will be waiting for you."

"Sounds good, but I'm hungry for a little more than dinner. Wear something sexy."

Annie looked down at her clothing. *Don't think this is what he has in mind.* "You've got it. Drive safe."

Now what? Change? How sexy? She wrinkled her brow. She hadn't felt sexy in quite a while and was surprised to feel a stirring in the right place as she pictured his arrival. *I'm definitely not telling him tonight.*

It took Annie most of the hour between Dan's call and his arrival to choose what to wear. Fortunately, the food was prepared and table set before she went back upstairs to begin her search. After taking out and putting back a number of pieces, she finally decided on a pair of black

Lycra pants, a black camisole, and a tomato-red silk shirt that complimented her blond hair. Usually, she would have buttoned the shirt and worn lingerie. Observing her image in the full-length mirror, she felt a little self-conscious. As she was about to turn, a light struck the mirror. Coming through the window, it was the headlights of Dan's car on the drive. There was no time to change—he was home.

Practically skipping down the staircase, she barely hit the next-to-last step when the door opened. There he was. She stopped on the bottom step as he placed his suitcase to the side of the entry with one hand and looked up.

"All…right," he said, in a low voice, slowly looking her up and down. "That's what a man[1] likes to see when he comes home." As she moved toward him, he brought a rose from behind his back and extended it out to her.

Annie jumped into his open arms, hugging him as tight as she ever had.

After squeezing her close for a minute or two, he took her by the shoulders and held her away, looking at her hair and shaking his head—one eyebrow raised.

"Something's different," he said in a flirtatious tone, his head tipped slightly at an angle.

"I cut my hair…I mean I had it cut."

"I'll say you did."

"Do you like it?" she asked, sheepishly.

He paused, studying the hairstyle. "It's attractive."

"You don't like it."

"I didn't say that I don't—"

"Dan Cameron, you hate it," she said, playfully pounding a fist on his chest.

"Tell you what. I'll take you upstairs and show you how I feel about it."

At six-thirty the next morning, Annie was awakened by a physical urgency common to pregnancy. Exhausted from two weeks of sleeping on hotel mattresses, combined with a grueling work schedule, Dan was deep asleep.

Not wanting to wake him with a sudden move, nor trigger her morning sickness, Annie eased slowly out of bed and went to the bathroom, taking a package of saltine crackers from the nightstand drawer with her. Dr. Windsor had recommended nibbling frequently, particularly in the morning, to ward off the nausea. It seemed to help.

Returning to the bedroom, Annie considered sliding back into the bed but chose instead to curl up in a plump chair by the window and watch Dan as he slept.

He's so handsome, she thought as she watched him. *Ever since I fell in love with him, I've dreamed of having a little boy who would look just like him.* Soft tears glazed her eyes. *I am so lucky that he still treats me like a princess. He is so trusting. How did I let this happen to us?* Trying to find a comfortable position, she wriggled around, pulling an afghan around her shoulders as a barrier against the stream of cool air coming from the overhead vent. Dan liked the room cool, and Annie wore only a sheer negligee, which she had slipped on when leaving the bed. Nestling down under the snug cover, only her face was exposed.

Dan lay on his stomach, the sheet carelessly draped across his hips and one leg. The other leg was stretched precariously close to the edge of the bed. Although relaxed, the muscles in his upper back and arms had the definition of many rigorous hours in the gym. His dark hair was tousled; his face, as peaceful as that of a sleeping kitten. He was still the most handsome man she knew.

As Annie watched Dan sleep, her thoughts strayed to a comparison of the way he made love to her with the way Cole had taken her. *Dan treats me like porcelain. He cares about my feelings. Cole treated me like a paper towel in a public restroom—something to be jerked around for personal purposes, then tossed aside.*

Curled up in the chair, thinking, her gaze drifted to the red rose on the night table. It stood at attention in a Waterford budvase—a proud sentinel standing watch over its charge. Dan always brought a rose when returning from a trip—one red rose—a symbol of his devotion. Annie always lit a candle in the bedroom window. It was their ritual.

Alex thought both customs endearing.

"I envy you having a guy like Dan," she had said to Annie while they were Christmas shopping the year before. "Cole has the sentimentality of a horny bull."

"What does that mean?" Annie had asked.

"Just that. He calls sentiment 'bullshit.' To his way of thinking, he takes care of me and the girls—gives me everything I need and most of what I want. To him, anything else is class 'A' crap. 'If you can't tell I love you, sugar, by the fact I'm here nearly every night, give you nearly every dime I make, and do you damn well in the sack, then no fucking flower is gonna make a difference,'" Alex said, mocking Cole. "Nope. Cole Dalton is hard-ass to the core."

She doesn't know the half of it, Annie thought, staring at what was left of the candle she lit the night before. She closed her eyes and tipped her head over, resting it on the wing of the chair.

Why does every thought I have end up with Cole Dalton? Is he going to haunt me the rest of my life? She took a deep breath, opened her eyes, and looked up at the ceiling. *Of course he's going to haunt me. He's the father of my child.*

Dan stirred and then rolled over. Annie sat quietly, waiting to see if he would wake. His hand went up to his forehead and pushed his hair back, then reached out to her side of the bed as if searching. When his hand found nothing, he opened his eyes and looked around.

"Good morning," she said quietly. "Sleep well?"

A smile crossed his face. "Absolutely. But then, I had a pretty good sleep aid."

"You did?"

"Come over here and we'll talk about it," he said, as he raised the sheet to allow her to join him under the cover.

Annie tossed the afghan aside and crawled in under the sheet. As she snuggled down, he untied her peignoir, opened the front, and pulled her close—flesh against flesh.

"There. That's better," he said, as he pressed his body against hers. "Let's get a little more sleep, angel." With his free hand, he caressed the back of her head and ran his fingers through her short hair. Kissing her, he pulled her head to him so that it nestled in the cave under his chin. They both slept.

CHAPTER FIFTEEN

When Annie awoke again, Dan was still asleep. It was almost eight o'clock, and the sun was streaming through the bedroom window, casting a beam of light across the bed like a laser. She eased out of the bed a second time, thankful for the absence of nausea, and made another trip to the bathroom. This time, she took a shower and dressed for the day. Seeing that he was still asleep when she opened the bathroom door, she tiptoed out of the room and downstairs to start breakfast—at least the coffee.

Should I tell him this morning? No. It should be in the evening— maybe over a candlelit dinner.

Once in the kitchen, Annie decided to prepare a batter for pecan waffles. Heidi lay at her feet, watching. With the aroma of coffee coming from the gurgling pot, the whistle of the tea kettle, and Dan in the house, life was good.

As she put the batter in the refrigerator, the phone rang and startled her. Annie grabbed for the receiver to avoid a second ring, almost tripping over the dog. It was Margaret.

"Good morning, sweetheart. Did Dan get home last night?"

Annie assured her that he was home and still sleeping.

"Dad and I are hoping the two of you will come over to Atlanta for Sunday dinner," Margaret said in her sugary, condescending voice.

It was not a weekend Annie wanted to spend with her in-laws, and she believed Dan felt the same. As gently as possible, she explained to Margaret how they could not come because Dan was exhausted.

"Any other time we would love to," Annie said. "But, you know how unusual it is for Dan to be in bed past six-thirty. Could we have a rain check?"

Margaret's tone changed, taking on a slight edge. Annie knew she had pushed the envelope but held firm. Dan would not want to spend his Sunday afternoon listening to Margaret's diatribe on how service at the club was becoming impossibly inferior, or how her bridge partner bid wrong and cost them the prize that week. While Annie did not want to field questions about their quest for a baby, she would only cross Margaret to protect Dan and their time together. Where he was concerned, her courage was limitless.

"But it's been ages since Dad and I have seen the two of you," Margaret said.

"I know. It's been too long, but Dan is just depleted. You know he never sleeps this late. Maybe we could come over next week."

"Are you sure he won't go out of town next week?"

Margaret was not going to give up easily, and Annie began to fear that she might suggest a Sunday get-together in Providence. *Think fast. If they come over here, we have no control over when they leave.*

"Dan's going to be working in Atlanta all week. I bet he would love to have lunch with you." *He's going to kill me, but it's the lesser of the two evils. He can always plead an appointment and make it a brief lunch.*

Reluctantly, Margaret gave in. The phone was barely back in its cradle when Claire called, inviting Annie and Dan over for steaks on the grill that night.

"Alex and Cole are coming," Claire said. "Alex said that she and Cole haven't seen the two of you in over a month."

You're darned right. If I have my way, it'll be a lot longer. Annie's mood had instantly changed at the mention of her brother-in-law.

"I know," Annie said, trying to sound disappointed. "But, I don't think tonight is a good night for us to come. He's really tired."

"Oh, honey, it wouldn't be any trouble for Dan. Your dad's doing the cooking. All you have to do is drive over," Claire said.

Damn. Why does she have to be so persistent? It's usually Margaret who can't take no for an answer.

"Mom, I don't think Dan wants to go anywhere this weekend, not even to your house. He wants to just relax in his own home."

With that said, Claire gave up, and Annie ended the conversation with a promise to touch base later.

By the time Dan came down the stairs in his boxer shorts, Annie had consumed a cup of hot tea and several saltine crackers. So far, grazing was staving off the morning sickness. Dan grabbed a cup of black coffee and went back up to take his shower while Annie finished making the waffles and bacon.

When he returned, they took their breakfast plates to the backyard and ate poolside, sharing the morning paper. When Dan finished his food and paid compliments on her cooking, he said, "You've been such a good sport about my neglecting you for the past few weeks that I want to make it up to you. Let's go down to Savannah tomorrow, have a nice dinner, and stay over in that bed and breakfast place you like so much."

Annie's expression betrayed her delight as she said, "What about your work?"

"There's nothing pressing right now. We wrapped up the project on Friday so I can take Monday off."

There's my cue. We'll have a romantic dinner tomorrow night, and I'll give him my news over dessert.... Dear God, I wish it were his baby.

"Sounds perfect." Annie got up and walked around the table to give him a hug.

On Sunday morning, they got an early start on what turned out to be a pleasant drive with perfect weather. After checking into the historic inn Annie loved, they went for a walk along the restored waterfront, and she bought a bone china vase, with a floral motif, in one of the antique shops. Dan found an old Thomas Jefferson biography in an antiquarian bookstore. Returning to the inn after their excursion, they relaxed in the room with Dan reading his new book and Annie reading her latest Jan Karon novel. She fell asleep after a few pages. About five-thirty, they showered, dressed, and went to Elizabeth on 37th Street, a highly rated restaurant, for dinner.

Once at the restaurant, Annie struggled to disguise how distracted she was over the thought of telling Dan that she was pregnant. In her mind, she rehearsed the script over and over, but could not find the words she wanted to use. While she loved the ambiance of the neoclassical styled mansion in which the restaurant was housed, and the food was superb, she could not relax enough to enjoy either.

The few days of adjustment to her circumstances, plus better control of her morning sickness, had brought back the color to her face and put a little flesh back on her bones. Physically, she felt the best that she had in weeks. For substantial periods during the day, she forgot her condition and would have thoroughly enjoyed the holiday if not for the task yet to be accomplished.

As she watched Dan spear a piece of his pepper-crusted filet, her thoughts turned to the source of the flaw plaguing her happiness. *What if I tell him the whole story? Put it all out there. What would he say? Would he believe that it was rape?* She took a sip of her carrot soup, avoiding the chicken entre. *Surely, he would believe me—he's never known me to lie—but how could he handle knowing the baby isn't his— that Cole was intimate with me?* She shuddered. *Maybe I could leave Cole out of it—pretend that it was a stranger.* The thought of creating a mysterious assailant was barely through her mind when she knew how foolish it was. No one would believe that she waited nearly two months to report such an attack, plus Dan would definitely launch a full investigation, thereby making her guilty of falsely reporting a crime.

As Annie's pondered all the scenarios, she knew that she could not tell Dan the truth without creating unfathomable chaos. At worst, he would have Cole arrested and leave her sister without a husband, and her nieces without a father. At the very least, family get-togethers would become unbearably awkward.

"You okay?" Dan asked.

"Oh, yes, absolutely. It's just a tiny bit chilly in here with the air conditioning."

"You want my jacket?"

"No, No. I'm not that cold."

Dan smiled and went back to concentrating on his food.

It would be such a relief if he knew. I could have the DNA test, she thought. With a DNA test, there would be closure. But could they deal with the results if her suspicions were accurate? Could Dan deal with sharing in the horrible deception—with raising another man's child—having that child call him Daddy? Would he look at her baby and be reminded every day of what had happened between her and Cole? She cut a piece of roasted chicken, determined to eat. It was excellent, but she could barely swallow.

As tempted as she was to spill out the story, she had to consider what would happen if Dan insisted on reporting Cole. *How would Alex react? Would she be destroyed— blame me?* But, Dan and Alex weren't Annie's only concerns. There were the Dalton girls—children who had no role in choosing their father. Finally, there was Frank, Annie and Alex's father. He had not dealt well with Cole impregnating his daughter at seventeen. What would he do if he found out the same man raped his other daughter? *Dad's not a violent man, but he could lose it and go after Cole.* Annie was sure that exposing Cole would have catastrophic effects on the family.

"How's your chicken?" Dan asked, interrupting Annie's deliberation.

"Umm—it's really good. I wish I knew how they made it so juicy and tender—and what spices they use to season it," she said, looking up from her plate. *If only he knew what I was thinking.*

Dan smiled. "How about dessert?"

"No, I'm good."

"Come on. How about that cream cake on the menu? You know you can't resist it."

He knows me so well. She looked at him with a smug smile and said, "Only if you split it with me. I can't eat a full serving."

The right moment to bring up the pregnancy never materialized at dinner, so Annie decided to put it off a little longer. *I still have time, tonight. I'll tell him when we're back in our room. Right before we go to bed.*

They finished dinner a little after eight thirty. Annie thought they were going back to the inn, but Dan had another surprise. He reached into the breast pocket of his jacket and pulled out an envelope.

"What's this?" Annie asked.

"Open it and see." He smiled as she pulled the flap out of the envelope.

"Oh my gosh. It's a cruise."

"A romantic, moonlight cruise on a riverboat, to be exact."

Her face lit up. "Just like our honeymoon in Paris?"

"Well, I don't think the Savannah River is quite the Seine, but it's the same moon."

"You didn't just make arrangements for this little trip, did you?" She looked at him with one eyebrow cocked and a knowing expression on her face.

"Not exactly."

"Come on, give. When did you do this?" She reached across the table and put her hand on his arm.

"About a week ago."

"How come?"

"You haven't had anything exciting since the party back in May, and we haven't been able to make any vacation plans this summer because of the bureau. You deserve a holiday. And by the way, we're not going home until Wednesday." He smiled smugly. He was obviously proud of his little deception and her reaction.

Annie was thrilled, but she suddenly remembered responsibilities at home. "What about the animals? We can't just leave them. I only asked

Mom and Dad to come over tonight and in the morning. And I didn't bring enough clothes for two more nights."

He smiled—again pleased with himself. "It's all taken care of. They're looking after the guys until we get back. And, last I heard, there are plenty of shops here in Savannah that carry your size."

His thoughtfulness overwhelmed her. She shook her head. Smiling, she said, "I love you—you do know that?"

"I suspected, but it's good to hear."

CHAPTER SIXTEEN

This is so good, Annie thought as she snuggled against Dan on the top deck of the paddle-wheeler purring along the Savannah River. The heat of the day had dissipated with the setting of the sun, and a cool breeze skimmed the water. Although not a full moon, it was still large enough to cast a nice reflection on the river, which combined with the shore lights to produce a romantic glow. *I can tell him when we get back to the room. This is too perfect a moment to interrupt.*

About fifteen minutes into the cruise, a small dance band began playing on the deck below. Squeezing her shoulder, Dan asked, "Want to dance?"

"As long as it's a slow piece."

They climbed down the stairs and joined a few couples already on the floor. The band played a nice arrangement of the romantic "Moon River." What Dan lacked in dance ability, he made up for with his strong lead. She felt so secure, so safe, with his arms around her. He doesn't need raw testosterone spilling out of tight jeans, or Cole's cocky swagger, to be sexy.

Back at the inn, Dan took her in his arms as soon as the door to their room closed.

"You haven't mentioned a baby in a while," he whispered. "Maybe tonight would be a good time to work on that."

It was the moment—finally—he had given her the perfect moment. As he slid his hands down the sides of her body, she slowly looked up and at him and said, "We don't need to work at that any longer."

Dan froze, then stepped back, his hands still on her hips. "Does that mean what I hope it means?" he asked, his eyes smiling.

"I think so. That is, if expanding the family to three is what you have in mind."

"Are you serious?"

She nodded, with a coy smirk on her face.

He pulled her tight against him. "We're going to have a baby!"

"To be precise, I'm going to have a baby," she said, stepping back and looking in his eyes. "You're going to watch. That is if the FBI will give you time off."

"Oh, my God." He was ecstatic with a toothy smile that would rival Tony Robbins. Looking up and down her body, he paused a second as his eyes reached her stomach and nodded. Pulling her back against him, he said, "You're really pregnant?"

"I'm really pregnant."

"When? How long have you known? You didn't tell me. Why didn't you tell me? Who knows? Do your parents know?" His questions came forth in rapid fire, not allowing her to answer.

"Slow down. Give me a chance to answer."

He had not moved and stood looking at her like he was a miner and she was a newly discovered vein of gold.

"Well, you have your little surprises, and I have mine," she said with a devilish look on her face. Taking on a serious look, she added, "Besides, I didn't want to jinx it. I was afraid that it was a mistake, or something might go wrong because I wanted it so much. As for who knows? Only me, the baby, the doctor, and you."

As she spoke, pangs of guilt stabbed her conscience. She could not even be truthful about who knew. Not that they mattered, but Molly and the clinic staff knew; and she had not been afraid of something going wrong. In the beginning, she hoped it would, which would have solved the dilemma. *I won't let the sordid truth ruin this moment for us. Tonight—this is Dan's baby. This is our time.*

"Have you seen a doctor?"

Anticipating the question, she was prepared and without hesitation said, "I have. I went to a really wonderful doctor in Atlanta. Her name is Windsor."

"Was she recommended by the fertility clinic?"

Annie paused, about to launch yet another fabrication. She could tell one lie and let him think the clinic recommended Dr. Windsor, or she could introduce Molly into their life. Thinking about how close she felt to Molly, despite the brevity of their relationship, she decided to go all the way.

"No. She was actually recommended by a lady I met at Eleanor's shop a few weeks ago."

Dan looked puzzled. "A stranger?"

"I know it sounds crazy, but Eleanor has known Molly for a long time. She worked for Dr. Windsor, and she's from Ireland, like Granny Máire."

"You don't want to go to one of Dad's colleagues?"

Looking him straight in the eye, she said, "I really like this doctor. I felt I could talk to her instantly. And I checked out her credentials. She graduated from medical school at Duke." Because that information was true, it flowed easily.

"Knowing how much this means to you, I know you've done your research, so who am I to question your decision?" he said, smiling at her.

"I have, and I trust Molly. She reminds me so much of Granny, and she understands how anxious I am. Eleanor told her how long we have been trying to have a baby. Molly insisted that I call her with questions anytime. She lives alone, and—she's a cat lover."

"Well, what better references could she have?" he said, with a twinkle in his eye.

"Will you back me up with your mom? You know she's going to have her own ideas about who I should use."

"With pleasure, and I'm sure Dad will, too."

Despite the fabrications she constructed, Annie capped her negative thoughts for the remainder of the evening—allowing nature to take its course by way of Dan's enthusiasm. If she had not been pregnant, chances are that after Sunday night in Savannah, she would have been.

Early, the next morning, they enjoyed coffee on the veranda of the inn and began a serious conversation about giving their families the news.

"I would rather wait until we get back to Providence to make the announcement, if you don't mind," Annie said. "This is too precious a time for us to allow the families to intrude. Your mom would probably want to come down here to check it all out."

"Touché." Dan smiled, not in the least offended.

"Can we just savor it privately for a while?"

"It's fine with me, if you don't mind the fallout when they discover how long it's been kept a secret."

"I'll just tell them it was your idea," Annie said with a twinkle in her eyes.

"Like hell you will," he said, reaching out to grab her in a playful gesture.

Wanting to divert the discussion, Annie suggested they concentrate on planning the remainder of their vacation. They agreed that they would like to play tennis but knew the clubs would be closed on Monday. So they decided to get as much sightseeing in as time and energy would permit.

After consuming an elaborate brunch in the dining room of the inn, they toured the historic district, learning about the city's past and walking through some historic homes. Afterward, they took a "movie" tour of the area that visited locations where films such as Midnight in the Garden of Good and Evil and Cape Fear were shot. By time the second tour ended, Annie was exhausted and Dan was starved. Stopping for lunch at the first appealing café, Annie ate light, but Dan devoured an enormous hamburger, fries, and a slice of pie. After eating, they shopped for enough items to cover the extra two days of the trip and returned to their room. Annie immediately curled up on the bed, while Dan checked in with his office to make certain there were no pending emergencies.

After more than a month of private hell, she was finally able to relax, falling asleep before Dan was off the phone. As soon as he finished his call, Dan settled into a lounge chair by the window with his Jefferson biography.

When she woke, Annie slowly opened her eyes, easing seamlessly into consciousness. Without stirring, she observed the room within her view from the four-poster bed. Dan's chair was in her direct line of vision. He was deeply engrossed in the book and failed to notice she was awake. *If only we could stay here forever. This baby would be his.* At that instant, Annie believed that by leaving Providence, she could erase Cole Dalton. *I would not have to face Alex very often, would not have to feel guilty that I can't warn her—can't tell her that she's married to an adulterous criminal.*

Thinking how Dan had choreographed the surprise vacation and how thrilled he was about the baby, she couldn't help but revel in the joy of the moment. *I love him so much. If only we could live here in one of those beautiful, old houses.* She closed her eyes and began painting a fantasy image across the landscape of her brain.

In her imaginary scene, Annie pictured buying one of the historic Savannah homes. She could see her family attending services at the ancient Episcopal Church. The furnishings she had collected over their marriage would fit appropriately in the Victorian style of the grand homes they had toured. *I can see the three of us on Sunday mornings. I would bake cookies for school parties and church bake sales. Dan would visit our daughter's school on career day and tell stories about catching bad guys with the FBI.*

In her mind, she could see him standing at the front of a classroom in his traditional black suit, wearing his warm and accessible persona. She saw a little girl with blond hair sitting on the front row, smiling, but

Annie couldn't discern her face. She would be so proud of her daddy. *Yes, it's a girl—definitely a girl. At Christmas, we might visit Providence and Atlanta, but we would have our private celebration, just the three of us, in our home in Savannah. Maybe we could have another child someday—a boy with dark hair, like his dad.*

Of course that was fantasy. The vacation could not last.

On Tuesday morning, they were able to start the day with an early round of tennis. Utilizing the reciprocal agreement his parents' country club had with a Savannah counterpart, they were able to purchase tennis attire in the pro shop and play on the local court. While Dan insisted Annie won a couple of their matches fair and square, she knew he "threw them." His championship days in college might have been eight years before, but he had not lost any artistry on the court. She was no match for him but would have enjoyed the morning if she lost every set. The fresh air and exercise felt great, energizing Annie's body and spirit after the confinement of the past weeks.

Throughout the morning, she caught Dan looking at her with a smug expression on his face. He was as thrilled with her pregnancy as she wanted to be. Several times, he began a conversation with: "This time next year, we won't be able to do this because we'll have a little one with us."

If only this were the real thing—our baby. It's as if we're renting the happiness, and the landlord is going to evict us one day without warning. She caught tears forming more than once, but somehow managed to conquer the emotion. Whenever a strong feeling of sadness or depression arose, she forced her thoughts in another direction. Amazingly, it worked. *Have I got a lifetime of this in front of me? Will I ever grow to accept the lie as truth?*

Clear skies and unseasonably cool temperatures graced Savannah throughout the Cameron visit. It was as though nature had purposely designed a perfect setting for the mini-holiday. After tennis, they showered in the locker rooms, dressed, and enjoyed a cold drink in the club before starting more sightseeing.

After strolling through boutiques and galleries near the waterfront, they had lunch, and then went on a "ghost tour" where they learned that Savannah was the ghost capital of the country. By the time the tour was over, it was after three o'clock, and Annie was done.

"Do you mind if we go back to the inn? I'm pretty beat," she said to Dan as they left the bus.

"Not a bad idea," he said, with a smile. "I could use a little down time before dinner."

Their last night in Savannah was perfect. They had an early dinner and went back on the riverboat. Snuggled under Dan's protective arm, Annie relaxed and soaked in the moment. *There's nothing like a moonlight ride on water to light the romantic fires.* The boat swayed gently, while the moon caused the vessel to cast a shadow on the water. *"Plus qu'hier moins que demain,"* she whispered—"I do love you 'more than yesterday, less then tomorrow.'"

***

Wednesday, together with reality, came in a flash, and they were driving back to Providence, talking about how and when to announce the big news.

"Maybe we should just have all the parents over for dinner and tell them at the same time," Annie said, as a soft rain began falling on the windshield.

"You don't want to just give each family a quick phone call?"

"Quick phone call? There's no such thing as a quick phone call to either one of our mothers. Maybe you want to try that."

"I pass." He grinned. "You're better at it than I am." They both knew how Dan hated getting caught on the phone with his mother. He generally tried to call when his father was home, to avoid what he called the "I gotcha now telephone trap." He joked that it was easier for a suspect to escape handcuffs than it was for him to get Margaret off the phone.

"Yeah, right," Annie said, making a face.

"If you don't want to tell them on the phone, then make a plan and let me know when to show up," he said and tipped his head slightly toward her with a smile.

"Let you know? Isn't it more like, you'll let me know when you're available?"

"Yeah, you're right," he said, turning on the windshield wipers as the rainfall increased. "I get your point. I've been gone too much lately. But, honey, once we have the new director on board, it should level out. My agenda will settle down, and I'll be home more."

"Is a new director going to eliminate crime so that your caseload is lighter?"

"Don't you be such a smart ass," he said, reaching over and grabbing her thigh in a devilish squeeze.

Playfully attempting to push his hand away, she said, "Stand down, mister, and keep both hands on the wheel, please. You're transporting precious cargo."

Dan smiled and relaxed his grip, caressing her leg in a gesture of affection, and then returning his hand to the wheel.

"Gosh, I'm glad the rain held off while we were there," Annie said, as she reached over to the dash and turned on the radio. Static blared from the speakers. Scanning the dial, the only audible signal she found was coming from a "fire and brimstone" station. Giving up, she turned it off. "What do you know about the man that President Bush has appointed to be the new director?" she asked.

"Not a lot. His name is Mueller, and he was the U.S. Attorney for San Francisco."

"Not an agent?"

"No, but I understand he has a lot of experience in white-collar crime."

"Well, he sounds like your kind of guy," she said, yawning.

Since joining the Bureau, Dan primarily worked fraud cases, including Ponzi schemes. Recently, he had been assigned to a money-laundering case that had tentacles in several states. His undergrad work in accounting, law degree and MBA from the University of Georgia provided the background to fit well into investigation of financial based crimes. Although his family, especially Margaret, expected him to become a corporate attorney in an upscale firm, Dan became attracted to criminal justice through a fraternity brother. After taking a criminology course, he applied and was accepted into the FBI internship program. Margaret thought the idea of a summer internship was clever but went ballistic when he decided in his final semester of law school to accept a job with the Bureau.

"What are you thinking?" Margaret had said, the night Dan announced his decision to follow a career in law enforcement. "You know that Tom Blankenship is expecting you to join his firm."

"It's not up for debate, Mother. I've made my decision and it is final."

"I suppose this idea is acceptable to your girlfriend," Margaret said, with a note of sarcasm in her voice.

"Fiancée, Mother. And yes, Annie is a little nervous about it, but she loves me and wants me to be happy—and that is not in a stuffy, corporate job."

Margaret left the dinner table in tears that night. Although she never openly expressed it, she blamed Annie for Dan turning his back on what Margaret considered his rightful place on the socioeconomic map.

The drone of the van traveling on the open road, plus the cool breeze from the air conditioning vent, was making it difficult for Annie to stay awake.

"Am I boring you?" Dan asked.

"Of course not. I'm just sleepy. When will you know about time off for the family affair?"

"Plan it for Sunday. That's the safest time right now. When you call the folks, just let them know I could have to postpone if something comes up."

"Oh, you're sly. You're going to be sure that it's me making the calls."

"You do it so well," he said, turning and winking at her.

"Dan Cameron, you lie. You want to dodge making the call."

He laughed. "Guilty as charged, but give me a break, I'm a busy man."

"Okay, you win." She knew all along that she would be the one making the calls.

"Tell me. Is this going to be the whole clan, including Alex's crew?" he asked.

"No," Annie snapped, instantly regretting the harshness of her rapid reaction.

"Well that was responsive," he said, raising an eyebrow in a mock startled expression. "Any special reason you're leaving her out? You guys have a tiff I don't know about?"

"No—not at all," she said, shaking her head while searching her brain for an excuse. *Why did I snap like that? I've got to have more control. Think, Annie. Make up something.* "It's just that it would mean preparing food for eleven people. I'm not sure I feel up to that."

"Go ahead and invite them all, hon. I'll grill the meat. You won't have to do a thing."

"There's a little more to a dinner than meat."

"Annie," Dan said. His tone was firm. "You know that your mom and Alex will insist on bringing food, and you can count on Margaret for anything she can buy at the bakery. You won't have to do a thing—just be the pampered mom-in-waiting."

She was cornered, but not yet ready to concede. "I think it would be better to just have our parents—but I'll think about it." *I'm not going to debate it now. He'll wonder why I don't want Alex, and I don't need that.* "It'll be fine. Remember how well the Memorial Day party went."

That was the last reference Annie wanted to hear, but she decided the best course was to not comment and hope the subject would go away. Closing her eyes, she said, "I am really sleepy. Do you mind if I take a short nap?"

Reaching over with his right hand, he patted her on the knee and said, "Of course not. You need your rest."

The next day, Dan left very early for the office. Annie was barely awake when he kissed her goodbye. She wanted to blame morning sickness or fatigue for her lethargy but knew that it was avoidance of the unpleasant. Would the Daltons be included? After a few minutes of wrestling with the pros and cons, she tossed off the covers, got out of bed, and announced to a startled Heidi that she was taking charge.

"I'm not going to keep dodging him forever," she said, adamantly, as she walked to the bathroom in her bare feet. "What can he do with the entire family around? Nothing!"

Heidi watched intently as though she fully understood.

CHAPTER SEVENTEEN

It turned out that Sunday worked for Dan, and the women offered to bring exactly what he had predicted. Alex was on board for a green bean casserole and Claire for coleslaw and potato salad. Margaret was only too happy to bring the bread, after establishing that she and "Dad" would cancel their plans to have dinner at the club with friends. In truth, she would have canceled an invitation to dinner at the White House in order to have time with her son, but she wore the martyr role with pride.

Curiously, no one asked why they were having a party without an occasion. Annie's call caught Alex on her way out the door for a hair appointment in Atlanta, but she didn't hesitate to accept the invitation on behalf of her family.

"We'd love to come, sweetie. Got to run now, but put me down for the green beans."

Both mothers were so caught up in wanting to know all about the Savannah trip that neither inquired as to the significance of the party. However, before the conversation with Margaret ended, she asked if the appointment of a new FBI director was going to affect Dan's work. Russ had heard about the change of command on the news. Annie assured her that Dan didn't expect any significant changes.

Once the cookout plan was in motion, Annie was relaxed until Sunday morning when she woke with the realization that Cole would walk through her front door that day. Tension seared through her body. *I can't look at him. What if he does the math and suspects it's his child? Why did I agree to invite them?*

She forced herself out of bed, pulled on a robe, and started downstairs. Dan was in the kitchen and had made coffee, which she smelled as soon as she left their bedroom. When she reached the kitchen, grits were boiling on the stove and a thick slice of country ham was frying in a skillet.

"Good morning, Sleeping Beauty. How are you today?"

Annie smiled as he reached out to pull her close.

"I hope you know that you look pretty silly with my apron on," Annie said.

Dan smiled. "What do you mean, woman? This is standard-issue undercover attire. We're all wearing ruffles these days."

His humor, plus the comfort of having him home, eased her tension until the guests began arriving.

Claire and Frank Brennan arrived first. Claire always liked to be early so she could help Annie with final preparations. In addition to bringing the coleslaw and potato salad, she brought two homemade cakes: one strawberry, Dan's favorite, and one chocolate, always a hit with the grandchildren.

"You didn't have to do that, Mom," Annie said, when Claire brought in her Tupperware cake containers. "I have cookies." As she took the cover off the first, she took a sniff and said, "But Dan is going to be thrilled when he sees this one."

"It was no trouble, sweetheart. Dad worked all day yesterday, and it gave me something to occupy my time."

As the two women arranged the food and utensils, Annie dreaded the arrival of the Daltons. Her mind was filled with strategies for avoiding contact with Cole. *Maybe, with a little luck, he will go straight to the backyard to find Dad and Dan.* Her obsession with Cole nearly caused her to forget the entire purpose of the gathering.

It was easy to tell when the Dalton clan arrived. The household tranquility took an abrupt change of course. Alex and the girls came inside, chattering as they carried bowls of beans and fruit salad, along with tote bags containing bathing suits. Cole was nowhere in sight.

Maybe he didn't come. Annie's heart began beating faster. *Maybe he is sick or had an emergency with one of his jobs. Could I be that lucky?*

"My gosh! We've got so much food. Mom brought more than I expected, and now you have too," Annie said to Alex.

"No big deal. You know I didn't cook any of it. Rosa is my savior. All I did was cut up the fruit; she made the dressing."

Annie couldn't bring herself to ask where Cole was, despite how much she wanted to know. Was he not coming? Was he out back? She tried to inconspicuously peek out the kitchen window, but without being obvious, she couldn't see anyone other than her father. *Surely, Alex would offer an excuse if he hasn't come. Is he coming later in a separate vehicle?* It was Claire who finally put Annie out of her misery.

"Where's Cole?" Claire asked.

"He went around the house to the backyard. He thought Dan would be outside, so he just took the shortcut."

Damn—damn, damn, damn, Annie thought. *But of course he knows the way to the back; he certainly took it eight weeks ago.* Annie felt her face tingle and quickly turned her back to avoid facing her mother and sister. *Why couldn't he have done the right thing and stayed away? He could have made up some plausible excuse for not coming.*

"Run along outside with your father," Alex said to the girls after all the food was placed on the kitchen counter.

Pointing to the chocolate cake on the kitchen table, Sunny said, "Can we have just a little, tiny piece please, Mommy?" Sunny was the youngest of the Dalton girls and the only blue-eyed blonde.

"Not on your best Barbie doll, darling. You know you don't have dessert until after your dinner," Alex said. "No spoiling your appetite before having the yummy steak Uncle Dan is grilling."

At six, Sunny was seven years younger than her sister Rhys and five years younger than Brandi. Her sisters and parents indulged her, which was easy to understand because she was a good-natured child.

Accepting her mother's verdict without further protest, she went to the downstairs bedroom to change into her swimsuit. Brandi followed.

"If I hadn't been the one on the table moaning the day that one was born, I would swear she wasn't mine," Alex said.

"Well, she looks just like Cole," Claire said.

"She may have his hair, but she's nothing like him—or me either for that matter. The other two are like us with their love of the outdoors and their reckless personalities, especially Rhys. But that one, she's more like Annie: quiet, accommodating, cautious. She even has Annie's eyes. I sometimes catch myself calling her Annie."

"I can see what you mean," said Claire. "She is a lot like Annie. Rhys is more like you."

"And you don't think that keeps me awake at night," Alex said. "Where is she right now? Not outside with her dad and sisters, and not in here with us. She's in the living room, talking on the phone—probably to some little wet-behind-the-ears troublemaker."

"I take it she has discovered the opposite sex," said Claire.

"Discovered them? She thinks she invented them, and the worst part is that they have discovered her. Cole said he intends on keeping his shotgun handy."

"Shades of your youth coming back to haunt you?" Annie teased.

"And don't you remind me," Alex said, just as Brandi and Sunny came out of the bedroom, ready for the pool.

"Where's Rhys? Isn't she going to swim with us?" Sunny asked, as Brandi tied a towel around her waist and headed toward the French doors in the breakfast room.

"She's too busy on the phone with Carl," her sister said, making a face as she tightened the knot.

"She's not talking to that squirrely little Atwater kid, is she?" Alex asked, making a face.

Brandi nodded affirmatively.

Turning to Annie and Claire, Alex said, "Last week it was Johnny Delano. I think our troubles are just beginning."

"As pretty as Rhys is becoming, with those green eyes and thick, brown hair, I don't think she's going to be content riding horses with her daddy much longer," Claire said, raising one eyebrow.

Alex rolled her eyes and shook her head. "Thanks, Mom. I needed that reminder."

As her sister and mother chatted, Annie's nerves were beginning to get the best of her. Her hands were trembling, and she could hardly concentrate on either the banal conversation or the chores at hand. *Get a grip. Don't let them see that you've got a problem.*

"Be right back," she said in the cheeriest voice she could muster and headed for the bathroom.

After closing the door, she turned on the lavatory faucet and dabbed cold water on the back of her neck and lightly on her cheeks and forehead. Facing the mirror, she said, silently, "You can do this. Just focus."

To back up her resolve, Annie practiced the script she had prepared as she patted her face dry, attempting to save her makeup. "Hello, Cole. Good to see you. How have you been?" she whispered to her reflection, forcing a smile. Hanging up the towel, she contorted her face in a stretching motion in an attempt to relax the muscles and then flushed the clean toilet to justify her absence. Continuing the soliloquy, she nodded to the mirror and said, "I'm great, just staying busy with my jewelry and the yard."

Her rehearsal finished, Annie closed her eyes for a second, took a deep breath, crossed herself, and opened the door.

Just as she came out of the bathroom, her in-laws arrived—Margaret with a large box of rolls from Atlanta's finest bakery and Russ with several bottles of vintage wine.

"Hope there's something here you like," Russ said. "Where are the menfolk?"

"They're out back, telling Dan how the country folk cook on the grill and consuming liquid refreshments," said Alex.

Annie went over and hugged both Margaret and Russ. "Just put everything on the kitchen table," she said. "We'll get it all sorted out.

With four women in the kitchen, not that Margaret was much help, everything was covered. Alex made Rhys get off the phone and take the platters of raw steak and chicken to Dan. Claire took the side dishes out, and Alex took out pitchers of iced tea. To her relief, Annie avoided any trips to the backyard until they were ready to eat.

When Annie finally went out into the yard, Cole was enmeshed in a game of croquet with Brandi and Sunny. He waved casually to her. She responded in kind. *Amazing! He acts like nothing ever happened. God, please keep him that far away.*

The food was excellent. Dan did a superb job with the meat, but Annie ate very little. Hard as she tried to fight it, she wondered throughout the meal how close Cole might be. However, she refused to look, forcing herself to engage in conversation with whoever was close. She flinched each time she heard his voice.

Three card tables were set up for eating with the Dalton girls at one, the men at another, and the four women at the third, thereby sparing Annie direct confrontation with Cole. After the group finished the main meal and slices of cake were distributed, Dan stood up and tapped his glass with a knife.

"Everyone, listen up." He turned to Annie's table and said, "Come here, sweetheart."

Annie smiled and blushed slightly, knowing what he was about to do. She stood up and walked over to him. He put his arm around her waist, drawing her close.

"We invited you over to share good news." The yard became as silent as church. "My beautiful wife is giving me the greatest gift a man can—"

"You're pregnant!" shouted Alex.

Annie nodded, and Alex ran to her and hugged her tight.

"Oh my word," said Margaret, putting her hand to her mouth. "I'm going to be a grandmother."

Claire beamed. "When are you due, honey?" she asked.

It was all happening so fast. Dan's words were burning in Annie's ears as everyone in turn came over and hugged her. *I'm giving him the greatest gift a man can receive, and it's not his child. What a colossal sham!* Her eyes were glassy, but no one paid any attention. No one in the family would be surprised to see tears, knowing how long she had waited for this moment. *Where is Cole? Is he counting on his fingers?*

She desperately wanted to see Cole's expression, but dared not look. To protect herself, she kept her head down. The Dalton girls were all excited, especially Sunny, once she realized what was happening. All three came to Annie with big smiles. *If only they knew that I'm expecting their little brother or little sister—not their cousin.*

So much conversation was going on simultaneously that a lot of it was lost in a blur. Questions came at Annie in rapid fire from all directions: When did she find out? Had she had a sonogram? Who is her doctor? Why did she wait so long to tell? She wasn't sure who asked what.

"I just can't believe it's finally happening," said Margaret. "It's a boy—I know it—Daniel Russell Cameron, IV."

I knew she would think that. She's already named my baby.

"I can't wait to start buying those precious little baby clothes they have now," Margaret continued.

"Hold on, Margaret," Russ said, "it might be a girl. Even if she has a boy, it's Annie's and Dan's prerogative to choose his name."

"But, family tradition—"

"Mother, try to remember whose baby this is," Dan said.

Hearing him interrupt, Annie felt a warm glow.

"This is Annie's baby—and a little bit mine," he added with a smug grin. "She's the one who has to go through what it takes to have the baby; she has the right to choose the name."

Listening to Dan claim paternity, the words "maybe not" screamed in Annie's head. Fortunately, they didn't come out of her mouth. However, the secret succeeded in destroying the magic again.

As the group began to separate into independent conversations, Annie heard Cole's unmistakable voice.

"Way to go, man. I knew you could do it. Just took a little practice." He was talking to Dan, and it made Annie feel like throwing up.

He's so vulgar, she thought.

"Excuse me, guys. I need to take a little break," Annie said, and went into the house. Dan started after her, but Claire put a hand on his arm, stopping him.

"She's probably had too much for one day," Claire said. "When you're pregnant, hormones play nasty tricks on your temperament. She'll be fine. We'll just cleanup the dishes and get going so she can rest."

Never one to volunteer for the domestic work, Margaret announced they would have to go because Russ had an early morning schedule.

"I hate to leave you all with the mess to clean up, but you know how it is with a doctor's life," Margaret said.

And so the party drew to a close with Alex and Claire cleaning up—Brandi and Rhys providing reluctant assistance. By the time they finished bringing everything in from the yard, Annie was sitting on the living room sofa with her feet on the coffee table. She started to get up and go to the kitchen, but both Alex and Claire were adamant that she was not needed and should rest.

"Go upstairs and lie down. We've got this covered," Alex said. "Between Mom and me, plus the girls, we'll have it knocked out in no time."

Seizing the opportunity to escape a possible confrontation with Cole, Annie did not protest further. After the exchange of routine hugs, she mounted the stairs. But upon reaching the second floor, instead of going left to the master bedroom, she went right to a dark room on the back corner of the house.

Without turning on a light, she crossed the empty space to a window overlooking the backyard and peeked through the louvered blind. Cole was drinking a beer and laughing with Dan and her dad. Sunny was curled up on the outdoor loveseat beside him. Her head rested in his lap. Annie stood by the side of the window, watching as though hypnotized for several minutes, being careful not to allow her silhouette to become obvious. It was like rubbing a sore muscle. It hurt, but she was compelled. *How can he be so comfortable with Dan, knowing what he did? He's a sociopath.*

Although focused on his interaction with the men, Cole subconsciously stroked Sunny's hair with a tenderness completely inconsistent with the man Annie encountered on May 29. "Who are you, Cole Dalton?" she whispered. "Don't think you have me fooled. I've seen the other side—and it's dark." While her hatred was not diminished, watching the child cling to her dad affirmed Annie's decision not to "out" him. *Even though he doesn't deserve protection, I couldn't take him away from those innocent girls. What good would it do? Sending him to prison won't make this baby Dan's, and it won't sanitize me.*

Slowly closing the louvers, she leaned against the wall and closed her eyes for a minute or two before going to the master bedroom. Once in her room, she lay down on the bed, fully clothed, not bothering to turn down the covers. Although she closed her eyes, she did not sleep, at least not right away. But pregnancy being pregnancy, drowsiness finally overtook her, and she dozed.

It was nearly an hour before the family left, and Dan came upstairs. Although he tried to slip in, she woke when he entered the room.

"Are they all gone?" she asked, rubbing her eyes.

"Everyone—animals and house secured and safe."

"They were genuinely surprised, don't you think?"

"Absolutely, especially Alex," he said, taking off his watch and putting it in the tray on top of the tall chest.

Annie watched as he went through his routine, stripping off his belt and shoes and putting them in the closet.

I love the shape of his hands. They are so strong—so masculine.

"I should get up and undress for bed." She rose to her elbows.

"I would help you with that, but I smell like barbequed beer."

"I like barbeque," she said, tipping her ear toward her shoulder with a smirk on her face, and watching him as he unzipped his jeans.

It wasn't sex Annie craved; it was the warmth and comfort of his embrace. Like Jell-O in boiling water, she wanted to dissolve in his arms.

Walking over to the bed, he pulled her to her feet and close to his chest. "Tell you what. Let's save on the utility bill and share a shower."

CHAPTER EIGHTEEN

Later that night, as Annie lay in Dan's arms, basking in the joy of the moment and the relief of making it through the announcement party, he brought up his mother's comments.

"Angel, this is your baby. Don't let my mother bully you. We're not royalty, and you can choose any name you like."

The words struck her heart like a cold stethoscope touching warm skin. Although he would never admit it, Annie knew Dan would like their son to bear his name—but the thought of naming Cole's son Daniel Cameron was onerous. Searching for a response, she didn't say anything, desperately wanting to preserve the intimate mood. After a minute of silence, she said, "I want your son to have your name," telling herself that it was not a lie. She did want his son to be Daniel Russell Cameron, IV.

Dan squeezed her tighter—no doubt pleased.

I guess I just outsmarted myself.

"And if the baby's a girl?" he asked.

"Faith," she said, without hesitation.

"Máire Faith Cameron. That has a nice resonance," he replied.

The thought of the baby having her grandmother's name added another layer to the subject. Annie was not sure she wanted Cole's child to have her family name either.

"We'll talk about it later," she said. "I'll be going to sleep now."

Silent for a minute or two, he whispered, "Máire Faith—that plays well." He kissed the top of her head and said, "Goodnight, angel."

***

The following day, Dan left early, and would be away for at least two nights. Annie despised saying goodbye and being alone again—she missed him already. The house was so quiet that Annie could hear the click-click of Heidi's paws on the bare floors. Before leaving, Dan had draped two suits to be cleaned across the arm of the living room couch.

Walking through the house, still in her robe and slippers, she stopped at the sofa and picked up one of the jackets. Holding it to her face, she breathed in the aroma of dry-cleaning solution, combined with wool and Armani's Acqua Di Gio. Holding the garment close, she curled up in the corner of the sofa with one leg under her and her head on the armrest. Annie wanted to absorb as much of Dan as she could draw from the fabric. Closing her eyes, she could almost feel that he was there in the jacket. Out of nowhere, a weight plopped onto her lap, interrupting her reverie.

"Delilah. Make yourself at home." Annie smiled at the black cat and began stroking her. At the first touch, Deli's motor turned on, and her front paws began kneading Annie's leg.

"No claws, please," Annie said as she put her hand under the offending paws.

"It's done, Deli. They all know. I guess it's going to be the centerpiece of every conversation for quite a while."

Impervious to Annie's comments, Deli continued her quest to create a nest in the only lap available—digging harder and harder as though on a mission.

"I've got to believe that today is the first day of the rest of my life," Annie said as she tried to guide the paws away from her skin. "Deli, I need someone to talk to—preferably someone who can respond."

The cat extended her chin upward, eyeing her mistress with the typical feline message of "Aren't I beautiful?"

"Yes, you're a great cat, but you're not helping me much. Since you're not going to participate in this conversation, I might as well clean up the breakfast dishes. If I know my mother, we may have company this morning."

As she washed the dishes, she continued thinking about her need for someone she could talk honestly with about the baby. *I need to get some of this anxiety out.* Dealing with the family's enthusiasm was oppressive—faking her own was tedious. She could not talk about the baby with family members and did not want to talk about it with any of her friends. Drying her hands on a paper towel and tossing it into a bin under the sink, she went to her kitchen desk and retrieved her address book. She reached for the phone and dialed the number under "M".

"Molly—it's me. Annie."

"My goodness, dearie. You've had me wondering. Did you see Dr. Windsor?"

"I did see her, and I like her a lot. Thank you."

"I'm glad to hear of it. But tell me, how are you getting on?"

It's so good to hear her voice. I can talk to her. "Well, everyone knows I'm pregnant, and that's a good thing. But, it's just so hard, Molly. Sometimes, I think I can't stand it—all the lies, hiding things. You're the only one I can talk to."

"Oh, wee one, you're not meant for the deceivin' life, are you now?"

"No…no, I'm not."

"Is there anything that I can do for you?"

"Could I take you to lunch or dinner sometime soon? I just need to talk." Annie twisted the phone cord round and round her index finger as she spoke.

"Sure's can be—that can be arranged. When would you like to meet?"

"The sooner, the better. I can come to Atlanta—maybe meet somewhere near the clinic?"

"Why don't we meet at the hotel restaurant down the road—the one where you were to stay."

"That's fine. Just tell me when. I'm free anytime."

"What about this Wednesday at noon? I work only the half-day on Wednesdays and Saturdays."

"That will work great for me. I'll be in the lobby at noon. And Molly, thank you."

***

True to her word, Annie was in the hotel lobby at noon on Wednesday. Molly arrived shortly thereafter and immediately embraced her.

"You be looking fit as a fiddle, lass," she said, smiling, "far better than when last I saw you."

Annie was dressed in a pair of pale aqua slacks, white sandals, and a loosely fitting white top. A pastel print scarf in a paisley pattern of pink, aqua, and beige was tied under her collar. Although much of the stress that Molly had seen when Annie was in the clinic was gone, she remained a fragile young woman, in contrast to Molly's sturdy, peasant-stock features.

"I'm feeling so much better—and eating, too. I've gained two pounds."

"Wonderful!" Molly smiled.

The hotel was quiet. They were the only ones in the lobby. Even the reception desk was devoid of a clerk. Molly pointed to a small restaurant at the end of the lobby, and they walked over. Only one booth was occupied.

After being seated by the hostess, Annie reached across the table to take Molly's hand. "You are so kind to meet me. I know you must have things you need to do."

"'Tis only me and me cat to tend to, so don't you be worrying. Tell me what's been happening for you."

Annie smiled at Molly's reference to her cat and then began telling her about the Savannah vacation and breaking the news to Dan. Molly was enthralled with Annie's description of Dan and his reaction.

"I would say 'tis a winner you have in that one, missy. You had a good share of the craic on your holiday. From the sounds of it, your Dan's to be a grand dad for your babe."

Annie looked at Molly with a puzzled expression. "I'm not sure what you mean?"

"That your Dan is to be a good father?"

"No, the craic part."

Molly chuckled. "I'm sorry, luv. You'd not know. For the Irish, the good fun is called 'the craic.' It's just a bit of the Old Country and probably doesn't sound so good here—that is with the cocaine probably coming to mind."

Annie raised her eyebrows and smiled and then resumed the conversation. "You're right about Dan. He is a winner, and he will be a fantastic father. I know that, which makes it all the harder to keep this secret. I feel like a felon."

"You've done nothing wrong, lass. Stop torturing yourself. You don't know that the babe's not his. You're the victim, and there's no law that says a victim has to report the rape."

Annie smiled. She really liked the older woman. There was so much honesty and sincerity with Molly. *She's the best thing that came out of my foray into the clinic. If not for her, who could I talk to?*

"Molly, the first thing my mother-in-law said was that I should name the baby after Dan. You can't imagine how ashamed I felt."

"But you've not had the test, have you?"

Annie shook her head. "There are so many reasons why I can't. I can't tell Dr. Windsor that my husband may not be the father of my child." Dropping her forehead into her right hand, she said, "I can't." Raising her face, she looked Molly straight in the eye. "Even if I could, I can't bear to read a report that officially confirms that it's not Dan's baby. That would make me even more despicable. I would have to tell him the truth, and it would break his heart—probably destroy our marriage."

Molly shook her head. "You're not despicable, and being he's the man you have described to me, luv, I think he could handle it all just fine."

"No. Trust me. It's too complicated. If I had been raped by a stranger, I think I could have told him. He is strong enough, sensitive, and mature enough to divorce himself from the idea of the conception. But the father of this child is someone he knows and will be around a lot—a constant slap in his face. It's hard enough for me; I can't make him go through that too." Her face was wide-eyed with the passion of her conviction. "And even worse, Molly, if he knew, he might refuse to stay quiet about it."

Before Molly could respond, the waitress came and took their orders. Annie chose a turkey sandwich on whole wheat with iced tea, Molly, a tuna salad with a cup of hot tea.

"You're not having the corned beef?" Annie asked, smiling.

"Not for me, luv. I hate the stuff. I have me a good meatloaf with the cabbage and potato cakes on St. Paddy's day every year." They both chuckled.

When the waitress walked away, Molly reached across to take Annie's hand again. "The baby could be Dan's. You don't know that 'tis 'Adam Henry's' child."

"Adam Henry?" Annie looked puzzled.

Molly smiled. "'Tis me Irish again, luv—Adam Henry 'tis our polite way of saying 'the asshole.' Might be I should bring an Irish dictionary for you."

Annie smiled, almost laughing. "I like that, and you've got it right— he is definitely an 'Adam Henry.'"

As Annie finished speaking, the waitress returned with their beverages. Molly released Annie's hand and reached for sugar packets before saying, "As for the name thing, what's the harm in the little fella being called after a good man? Your Dan's the daddy. 'Tisn't the blood that makes the father." She paused for a minute, and then looked Annie straight in the eye. "I think that you should find a way to do the test, luv. You find out the little one is your hubby's, and you find peace."

Annie's eyes glazed over as she thought for a minute. "I did research on prenatal testing. It's expensive, and there are risks. Molly, I've thought about this for weeks. When Dan was in law school, he used to talk about the balancing test—about weighing the positive against the negative. The only positive a DNA test could produce would be to relieve my mind, where a negative result would be disastrous. I couldn't let Dan believe the baby was his if I had absolute proof it isn't. When he found out, he would be devastated, and he might confront the father. It would not only destroy Dan, but also innocent members of another family and our marriage. My peace of mind isn't worth that risk or the risk of miscarriage because of the test."

"I didn't mean to push you, luv. 'Tis your life. I just want to help."

"You've been so kind. I don't expect you to solve my problems. It's just good to be able to talk to someone. Most of the time, I'm doing okay. Sometimes I cringe when I think of the future, but I'm trying to live one day at a time."

"Do you think that you would never want to know? I mean, shouldn't the child know at some time about his background, maybe for medical reasons?"

"I've thought about that. I have. Maybe when he's ready for college, I might find a way to have the test done."

Molly pressed no more about the testing. She never inquired as to who the father might be. It was as if she knew that was Annie's most guarded secret.

While they waited for their food, Annie related her struggle to display the expected degree of excitement about the pregnancy.

"The family is so happy for me. They've been through all my disappointments—my depression. Of course they expect me to be jubilant, but I can't. It's nearly impossible to act thrilled when there's a piñata full of bricks hanging over my head."

"You've got to concentrate on the little one. Forget the rest. Think about holding that warm little bundle in your arms and about how much love he's going to add to your life."

Before Annie could respond, the food arrived, and the conversation drifted in a different direction.

Watching Annie eat, Molly complimented her jewelry. "What a lovely bracelet that you be wearing."

"Thank you. It's one I designed," Annie said with a smile of pride, while holding her arm out for Molly to examine the aquamarine, silver, and pink quartz piece. "I make jewelry for a shop here in Atlanta. I would love to make one for you."

"Oh, I couldn't let you do that."

"Of course you can. I'm going to make one for you, so what color would you like?"

"If you put it that way…then make it something with green. If I don't eat the corned beef, I'd better well wear the green."

Riding back to Providence, Annie reflected on the conversation. *Could she be right? Should I try a DNA test? No. I can't.*

CHAPTER NINETEEN

As Annie expected, Margaret and Claire immediately assumed respective roles of chief advisors to the mommy-to-be, each with a signature technique. Margaret chose to direct the pregnancy with the self-anointed authority of an expert-extraordinaire, while Claire opted to hover like an ever-vigilant bee, buzzing over a pollen-rich blossom. Annie found both to be annoying, but reconciled herself to the phone calls, which by late August had become daily.

As Annie hung up the phone on the fourth Saturday in August, Dan came into the kitchen, hot and sweaty from working in the yard.

"Something smells good," he said, inhaling the aroma of roasting chicken and chocolate cake baking as he took a bottle of water from the refrigerator.

"I was making tonight's dinner ahead of time when your mother called."

"Whatever you're cooking smells good," he said, pressing the cold bottle to his forehead before opening it. "What did Margaret want this time?"

"Nothing really. She and Mom seem to feel that they have to call every day or else there may be a catastrophe of some kind."

"And did you expect them to be any different?" he asked, with a twinkle in his eyes, as he passed by her.

Annie thought about it for a minute before responding. "No," she admitted. "It's just that I didn't expect both of them to call every day."

"Honey, just speak up. Tell them you appreciate their concern, but you've got it under control," he said.

"I don't think your mother trusts me. You know she wants me to see an obstetrician they know from the club."

"Hmm...country club membership...great credential," he said sarcastically. "Don't pay any attention to her, hon. Haven't you learned by now that with Margaret it's all form and no substance? She equates skill with pedigree." His face was flushed and his shirt plastered to his buff torso.

Even in his grimy state, Annie admired his toned body, trim with firm, unobtrusive muscles earned by years on the tennis court and maintained with regular workouts. Looking down at her stomach, she thought of how her body was changing and would soon be swollen out of shape. It gave her a brief feeling of maternal pride.

Putting his empty container in the garbage pail under the sink, Dan said, "By the way, tell Bobby-Ray to take a little more time with the edging. He's missing quite a few places in the backyard, and he needs to take more care with the weed-eater around the fence."

Dan enjoyed yard work but rarely had the time to devote to it. They paid Martha and Ray's thirteen-year-old son to mow and edge, which Ray, Sr. monitored.

"If he doesn't do it right, just let me know," Ray had told Annie. "He'll answer to me."

Ray Brantley, with what Annie considered to be his opinionated, autocratic philosophy, was challenging to her patience. Intellectually, she knew that Ray compensated for his lack of education and cultural savvy by playing the tough guy with a know-it-all attitude, which usually exposed his ignorance. However, she had no respect for the narcissistic control he exercised over Martha and their children. *As despicable as Cole is, at least he's not a bully like Ray.*

"I will, if I can do it when Ray's not around. I don't want to get the boy in trouble with his dad. That man can be such a pig sometimes that I want to slap him," she said. "He thinks that being rough on his kids and controlling with his wife makes him important. It makes me sick. Especially when I know that he's only married when in Providence, cheating on Martha every chance he gets on the road."

"My…. We're in a bit of bad mood today, aren't we?" Dan said with a teasing note in his voice.

Annie paused for a minute before answering. "You're right. I'm being pretty judgmental of everyone, aren't I? I don't mean to be, but sometimes your mom makes me feel like she thinks I'm a dumb, country girl because I'm not going to the right doctor—kind of like my opinion of Ray."

"Ignore her. If Dad had any problem with your doctor, he would have let me know."

"Ignore Margaret? Easy for you to say."

Leaning against the kitchen counter, he took a drink of the water, and then said, "I'll tell you what. I'll tell her to butt out."

Annie frowned and shook her head. "Don't you dare say anything. I don't want to make her mad. You know how touchy she is."

Dan grinned, took his bottle of water, and headed for the door. "If you won't tell her, and don't want me to say anything, then I guess you're going to have to suck it up, sweetheart." With that, he went back to the yard.

Suck it up, Annie thought as she took the cake out of the oven. *Yeah, I have to. She's part of the package, and I've got to appreciate that if it weren't for her, there would be no Dan.*

***

The following Tuesday morning, Alex dropped in on Annie without warning. She had barely crossed the threshold when the Cameron phone rang. Before Annie could reach the living room table to answer, Alex grabbed it.

"Hello…. No, Margaret, this is Alex," she purred. "Annie's absolutely fine but not taking calls today."

"What are you doing?" Annie mouthed silently—grimacing.

"Oh…Margaret…you are so kind to check on Annie, but she's tied up right now." Alex's tone was as cool as a mint julep and as sticky sweet as maple syrup.

Annie was horrified and began making faces to try and squelch her sister's impertinence—but it was useless.

"I know how she appreciates your checking on her, but I bet it would be just fine if you only called every other day—or maybe a couple of times a week…. Oh, yes, I know you're concerned, and it's certainly thoughtful of you to check so often. It's not that she doesn't love talking to you…but you know how it is. She's got so much to do and so little energy. Surely you remember how you felt when you were pregnant with Dan."

Annie was flabbergasted.

As Alex terminated the call, she turned to Annie and said, "God, it's hard to believe that woman gave birth to a guy as sane as Dan. Are you sure he's her child?"

The wisecrack struck a dissonant chord in Annie for a moment, but stunned by her sister's audacity with Margaret, she said, "What did you just do?"

"Taking care of my little sister," she said, patting Annie on the shoulder as she walked toward the vestibule on her way to the kitchen. "I sure hope you have a pot of coffee made?"

"Alex…I don't believe you talked to Margaret like that."

Alex stopped as she reached the archway leading to the entry hall and looked back at Annie. "Just did what you've wanted to do, but wouldn't—because you're Miss Muffet and too damn nice." Tipping her head to one side, she continued, "I, on the other hand, am the spider, and I bite."

"She's going to be furious."

"Maybe, but it'll be on me, not you. If she says anything, just tell her you were in the shower and had no clue she called. Now, get dressed. I'm taking you on a girls-day-out. By the way, what time does our mother usually call?"

"You wouldn't."

"Ohhhh…you bet I would."

"Alex, you'll hurt her feelings."

"She'll get over it. Now go get ready while I have a cup of coffee and wait for the next meddling mother's call. You and I are going to Lenox for a grand day on the mall—credit cards, beware."

As Alex left the room, Annie stood for a moment, and said rather loudly, "It would be easier to fight Mother Nature than to dissuade Alex Dalton when she's on a mission."

"I heard that," Alex quipped, but kept walking.

Resolved to her fate for the day, Annie started for the stairs. *Who am I kidding? I could use a break, and a day out could be fun.*

As Annie climbed the stairs, she told herself that she had been in hibernation long enough. Although focusing on the completing the fall collection of jewelry for Eleanor's shop had provided the basis for a truce with her stress, the order was complete. Dan was currently tied up with a demanding case, and she was left to contemplate her condition. The past week, she had slipped back toward depression, which had shown on Saturday when she criticized Margaret and Ray to Dan. As she dressed for the excursion, she wondered if he could have put Alex up to getting her out of the house. As he left on Monday, Dan had urged her to start a project.

"You seem to be worried about something," he said, when she failed to respond to a menial question as they parted at the front door.

"No, I'm not," she had snapped.

"I think you are spending too much time alone in this house," he said. "With your jewelry order filled, why don't you begin decorating the baby's room?"

That had not been a suggestion Annie wanted to hear. She was in no way ready to begin working on the baby's room.

"I'd rather wait a while before starting on that. I don't want to jinx anything," she lied. She had thought about choosing baby furniture but pushed it aside, telling herself that there was plenty of time to do that later.

"Besides, what color scheme would I use? I can't very well choose pink or blue since we don't know if it's a boy or girl."

"What about green or yellow?" Dan asked.

"Not really exciting. I need to think about it for a little longer."

I hope Alex doesn't start on shopping for the baby. The thought of baby things still gives me knots in my stomach, and the last thing I need is another avalanche of anxiety.

The more she thought about it as she dressed, the more uneasy she became. Alex would expect them to shop for maternity clothes, baby clothes, and maybe baby furniture. Cole's name would be dropped far more than Annie wanted to hear. Even the brush with him at the party had not diminished her aversion to being exposed to anything related to Cole Dalton. Hiding her discomfort at the mention of his name would be a challenge.

Telling herself to get over it, she put on her lipstick, and then stepped back to look at her reflection overall. Deciding that she looked passable, Annie paused a while longer, contemplating the day ahead. From downstairs, she heard Alex calling for her to hurry up.

I've got to get out of my own way. I can't change the facts as they are, so I might as well take the good from everything I possibly can. I need new clothes. I can't button this skirt, and there's not a pair of jeans or slacks in my closet that I can wear now.

Tossing her hair, which was just beginning to grow out, she turned and took her purse from the handle of the closet door, then went downstairs to begin her day-long adventure with Alex. *Bring on the baby clothes. I'll even refer to the baby as "Danny." What the heck. My life is a play. I may as well aim for a Tony award.*

The Atlanta shopping trip was a success. For the most part, Annie was relaxed and enjoyed being out with her sister. Cole was mentioned far less than she had feared, and Alex was at the top of her game with witty wisecracks and tidbits of gossip. Only once did the conversation move in an objectionable direction. It occurred when Alex brought up Dan's extended absences.

"From what I hear from Mom, Dan is working so much that he's hardly home. You don't need to spend so much time alone in that house," Alex said as they meandered through the mall, looking in store windows. "Why don't you come stay with us for a few days?"

Annie grew tense and struggled to mask her discomfort. To eat dinner at the Dalton table would be torture, but nothing compared to the horror of sleeping under the same roof with Cole. *A lock strong enough to make me feel safe in that house hasn't been made.* "I couldn't do that," she said. "I can't leave Heidi."

"Hell's bells. Bring her with you. What's another dog at my house? She would have a blast running through the horse pasture."

Damn it, Alex. There's no way I will ever eat, sleep, and be merry in the house of King Cole. "I'm fine at home. Don't worry about me. Besides, Dan expects to be able to spend more time at home soon, and I just sleep better in my own bed."

Never willing to give up, Alex persisted. "You're pregnant, sweetie. It's an emotional time for women. You don't need to stay alone."

"Alex, I'm used to it. It goes with the territory." Annie tried to keep her tone upbeat, not wanting to give away how uneasy she was with the conversation.

Alex frowned, causing Annie to expect additional pressure. Fortunately, a maternity boutique in the mall distracted her, and the tension was alleviated.

The rest of the day went well. Annie purchased several maternity outfits she liked on sale. Although Alex pushed her through baby departments in the major stores, she continued to resist the idea of purchasing any baby items.

While poring over infant's wear in Neiman's, oohing and aahing over each miniature outfit, Alex spotted a display of bears across a broad aisle separating baby wear from toddler clothing.

"Muff...look over there. Those bears—they're calling us."

Annie looked at the display and could not help but smile. "Yeah, they are cute."

Walking to the display, Alex picked up a bear. "Cute? They are ir-resistible. Here…feel it," she said, thrusting the plush toy at Annie. "Tell me you can ignore this little guy."

The bear was about two feet tall and as soft as it was visually ap-pealing. It came in two versions: white with a pink ribbon bow, and tan with a blue bowtie. Annie squeezed it and nodded in agreement. "It's adorable."

"Which one do you want?" Alex asked, holding up one of each. "Auntie Alex is buying the little one his or her first toy."

"You can't. You don't know whether to buy the girl bear or the boy bear."

"I can solve that. I'll buy one of each, even if I know that you're having a boy since I had all the girls. You know that Cole is going to be green, don't you?"

Did she have to say it that?

"If you do have a baby girl, she'll probably like having brother-sister bears. If you have a boy, you can either save the white one for when you have a girl or give it to one of mine. They all love stuffed animals."

Thus, two bears went home with Annie—the first sign of a baby in the house.

When they got back to Providence, Alex helped carry in the pack-ages.

"Where do you want me to put the bears?" she called out to Annie, who had gone to the kitchen to make lemonade.

"I have no idea. I guess you can just put the bag in the empty bed-room upstairs, the one next to ours."

"I'm not going to stick these precious little guys away by themselves in an empty room. They need to see and be seen."

"You're crazy. They're stuffed toys," Annie said, as she brought two glasses of lemonade into the living room.

Ignoring her, Alex said, "I'm going to put them on your sofa. You need a baby presence in the house." She placed a bear at either end of the sofa, folded the shopping bag, and stood back to admire her arrangement before taking a glass from Annie.

And so the bears remained until after Alex left. As soon as she was gone, Annie went upstairs to get comfortable. She hung up the new clothes, holding each outfit in front of her and observing the reflection in the full-length mirror. *I'm really having a baby.*

Going back downstairs for a bowl of soup and to tend to Heidi, she passed the bears holding court on her couch. "What am I going to do with you?" The bears seemed to look back at her with pleading expressions like puppies at the pound. "You're just stuffed toys. I admit you do look like you're talking to me with those eyes—but you can't stay here."

Picking up the two bears, she walked into the guest room, a room she still liked to dodge—the room where the nightmare began. "Here," she said to the inanimate objects. "You can sit here until there is a nursery for you to live in." She positioned the two bears at the head of the bed, behind the throw pillows, and left, closing the door behind her.

CHAPTER TWENTY

Two weeks later, the bears were still in the guestroom, and no progress had been made toward getting a nursery ready for the baby.

As Annie was doing her laundry on the second Tuesday morning in September, she thought about the fact that she was fifteen weeks pregnant. Dan was in New York on a temporary assignment. A few days before, she had felt a little flutter in her stomach that thrilled and frightened her. She felt it again as she smoothed the wrinkles out of a warm towel. *Is that a little foot, kicking? This is a little person inside me. If only I could stop feeling like it's all counterfeit, then I could work on a nursery.* She knew that time was moving fast. The holidays were not far away, and she had taken no steps to prepare for the little one. If Dan had not been away so much, it would have been harder for her to procrastinate. *I have got to make myself start soon, but I'm just not ready.*

Every time anyone inquired about her nursery décor, she brushed the question aside with a response that she was waiting until Dan was home and had time to be part of the project. With Dan, she used the excuse that not knowing the gender of the baby, she couldn't decide on a color scheme. A sonogram was scheduled for her next appointment. If she wanted to know the sex of the baby, Dr. Windsor had said she could probably find out that day. But Annie didn't want to know. She couldn't face the possibility that she might be expecting a boy—a mini-Cole.

"I would really prefer to wait," she had said to Dr. Windsor. "I'm old fashioned. It would be like opening a gift before Christmas."

As Annie removed more towels from the dryer, the phone rang. She dropped the pieces into the laundry basket and started toward the kitchen, but before reaching the phone, there was a knock at the back door. Looking from door to phone, she wasn't sure which to address first. *Who's knocking this early?*

Grabbing the phone from the counter, she said, "Hold on." Without giving the caller a chance to speak, she moved quickly to open the door. Martha Brantley stood on the back porch, gray as ash. Annie knew something was wrong.

"Come on in. Let me get off the phone," she said, returning to the phone as Martha came into the breakfast room. Noticing on her caller ID that it was Alex, she said, "I can't talk now; Martha just came in. I'll have to call you back."

She stopped in mid-process of hanging up when she heard a shout coming from the phone, "Stop! Don't hang up."

"What is it?" Annie said, as she put the phone back to her ear, slightly annoyed.

"Have you heard? Is your TV on?"

Alex's voice held an unfamiliar desperation. Looking back at Martha, a sensation of doom covered her.

"No. Why?" she asked, afraid to hear the answer. *Oh my God, has there been an accident? Has someone been hurt? Daddy? One of the girls? Dan? Oh please God, not Dan!*

"Turn on your TV," Alex said. But Martha had already gone to the television set in the living room and turned it on. "I'm on my way over. Stay calm."

Annie felt her hands go weak, wet with sweat. She had to know but was afraid to ask. *Has Dan been in an accident? Does everyone know but me? Surely, nothing could have happened to Mom and Dad. They wouldn't make the news. Has some criminal harmed Dan?* She hung up the phone and turned toward the living room, her knees feeling like jelly. As she entered, she saw the image on the screen—the tall building with smoke billowing from a hole on one side.

"What is that? Where is it?"

"It's the World Trade Center in New York. A plane crashed into it," said Martha, tears in her eyes. "Annie, how could that happen? It was a big plane."

Annie felt every hair on her body rise. Her brain refused to process what her eyes saw. The two women stood frozen in front of the screen. Each was silent. For Annie, there was a fleeting relief that Dan had not been shot or in an accident, but he was in New York, and she didn't know where. He could have been in or near the Trade Center. *Dear, God, please don't let him be there.* The tragedy unfolding in front of her eyes was mesmerizing as the magnitude of what had happened emerged in overwhelming proportions. She put her hand over her mouth. Her eyes filled with tears and disbelief.

The phone rang again. This time it was Claire. Retrieving the telephone, she didn't take her eyes from the TV as she listened, then said, "I'm watching, Mom," scarcely able to get the words out. "I'll call you back."

Then it happened. A second plane hit the other tower—right before the horrified eyes of the two women. Both gasped.

"Oh, my God! Martha! What is happening?"

There was no response from Martha as she stood frozen. Annie said no more. Her head turned side to side, trying to deny the image on the screen—her mind raced. *It wasn't an accident. One plane—maybe an accident. Two, there's no way that it was an accident. We've been attacked! Our sacred ground compromised.*

Fear for Dan and fear for the country competed for her comprehension. The voice coming from the television set was shaky, emotional, and unprofessional—speculation mounted. No one wanted to think the unspeakable. *We've been invaded. America has been invaded. What's going to happen next?* Panicked by the threat to the country and traumatized by fear for Dan's safety, Annie never needed to hear his voice more. *Dan, where are you? Please God, he's got to be alright.* She reached for the phone and dialed his cell but got only offensive busy signals.

As the women watched, unable to move, Annie recalled *Pearl Harbor,* a movie she and Dan had seen in June. The image in her head was of terrified people running, bleeding, dying. This wasn't a movie or a recording. It was an unfathomable horror happing in front of her. Although she couldn't see them, people were in trapped in those buildings—maybe Dan. The buildings were on fire, human beings were trying to escape, and she was watching. This was real. It wasn't movie special effects, it was real. Annie was aware that Martha was in the room, and yet, she wasn't aware.

Abruptly, Martha spoke. "I want my children. I've got to get my children." Turning to Annie, she said, "Can I use your car? Mine's in Atlanta for repairs."

"Of course. Go." Annie went to the kitchen and took her spare set of keys from the hook by the refrigerator and handed them to Martha, then returned to the living room. *I should offer to go with her, but I can't. I can't leave the TV.*

As Martha went out the front door, the phone rang again. Annie sprang for it, praying it was Dan. It was Margaret.

"Annie, have you talked to Dan?"

Why didn't I look at the caller ID? I can't talk to her now. "No. I haven't."

"You do know what's happened." Margaret's voice was shrill. Not waiting for a response, she said, "I've tried to call him, but I can't get through. You need to call him."

Silent for a minute, Annie fought an impulse to hang up. Realizing that Margaret did not know that Dan was in New York, she struggled to find the words to respond. *I can't tell her. She'll go into hysterics, and what good would it do for her to know right now?*

"Annie…are you there?"

"I'm sorry. It's just that I'm upset. I have tried to reach him, but I couldn't get through, either. I've really got to go now—someone's at the door. I'll let you know if I talk to him."

Without giving Margaret a chance to say more Annie hung up but stood very still—knees weak and brain mesmerized by the TV screen.

Twenty minutes later, Alex knocked at the front door, but Annie did not move. Receiving no response, Alex opened the unlocked door and leaned into the entry hall.

"Annie," Alex shouted. "Are you there? It's me."

Annie turned and, seeing her sister, went to her. Neither said a word, just wrapped their arms around one another. After embracing for a minute or two, Alex stepped back and said, "Did you see the second plane hit?"

Annie nodded. "Yes. Where were you?"

"In the car. I heard it on the radio. Cole is picking up the girls from school and coming over here. I think Mom is on her way. Have you talked to Dan?"

All Annie could say was, "He's in New York." Her voice cracked as she spoke and tears flooded her face.

Alex put her arms around her younger sister and held her for several minutes, whispering, "He's okay. He wouldn't have been in those buildings." Loosening the embrace, Alex guided Annie to the sofa with one arm still around her shoulders.

Huddled together, the sisters sat with eyes glued to the television. It was as though the world was suddenly paralyzed. Each time the network reran the planes torpedoing the towers, the women flinched as though seeing it for the first time. Within minutes, Claire arrived and was embraced by both daughters. Alex filled her in on the whereabouts of the family members, including Dan, while Annie remained mute.

"Your dad won't close the drug store because he's afraid customers may need their medications, but he said to call if we needed him," Claire said, her face solemn.

As reports of a third plane crashing into the Pentagon were announced, Cole arrived with the three girls. Annie had no reaction to his proximity—the events of the morning having given her temporary immunity. On September 11, 2001, Cole Dalton was not her rapist, nor the father of her unborn child; he was just another family member living in the horror and disbelief of the moment. Ironically, his male presence in the midst of all the women was comforting in that unspeakable moment of fear and anguish. Sunny cried softly, even though she was too young to fully comprehend the magnitude of what was unfolding. She had absorbed the emotional state of the adults and was clinging to her grandmother.

In her fashion, Alex took charge, going to the kitchen to make a pot of coffee. "Does anyone want anything to eat?" she asked. No one did.

Annie sat by the phone, struggling to keep herself together because of the children. She alternately dialed Dan's mobile phone and the New York office of the Bureau. Even though she knew he was not in Atlanta, she tried that number as well, hoping they might have information about his whereabouts. The more she was unable to make contact, the more agitated she became, wondering if more was going on than was being reported. Intellectually, she knew that it was likely she would not hear from Dan for quite a while, but her nervous system wasn't rational.

Then it happened. At 9:50 a.m., just as Alex brought the coffee to the living room, the south tower of the Trade Center began crumbling. It was a moment too surreal to describe.

If not for the TV, the room would have been silent—everyone frozen by the incomprehensible sight taking place in front of their eyes. This is not real. This is not really happening. Tears flowed down Annie's face and chills prickled the skin on her arms.

Putting the coffee down, Alex gasped. Cole and the two older girls went to her where they stood together, watching, horrified. Alex had an arm around Brandi and a hand clutching Cole's. Rhys stood by Cole, both arms wrapped around him and her head against his chest. Sunny remained on the sofa with her grandmother, her face buried against Claire's bosom.

It was Alex who first realized that Annie stood alone in the room, her body trembling, her face drained of color, and her wet eyes not blinking as she stared at the television screen. Breaking free of Cole and Brandi, Alex went over and enveloped Annie with a strong embrace.

"Here, come sit down," Alex said, as she gently guided Annie to a chair.

"I need to talk to Dan."

"I know you do. He'll call soon. He's okay."

"He can't. He would have called, if he could. There's no telling how long it will be before I hear from him—if I do." Her body convulsed as she sobbed uncontrollably.

When the phone rang at 10:15 a.m., Annie was bent over with her face buried in her lap, trying to regain composure. Alex sat on the arm of the chair, rubbing her back; Heidi lay at her feet, seemingly aware of Annie's distress. Everyone jumped when the ringing of the phone pierced the austere mood. Hoping it was Dan, Annie answered before it could ring a second time.

It was Margaret, calling from the home of one of her bridge partners. Annie's heart sank. She cleared her throat, took a deep breath, and said, "No. I still haven't heard from him, but I promise I will let you know when I do. I really want to keep the line open so he can get through." After writing down the number Margaret was calling from, she hung up.

Time seemed to move in slow motion for Annie as she tried repeatedly to reach Dan. Alex sent the girls to Annie's bedroom to watch the VHS tape of Dr. Dolittle. The adults remained in front of the living room TV. Little was said. At 1:35 p.m., the phone rang.

"I hope it's not Margaret, again," said Alex, as Annie lifted the receiver.

This time, it was Dan.

"You know of course," he said.

Drained by relief at the sound of his voice, Annie could hardly speak, but the smile that immediately came across her face told everyone that it was Dan.

"We do. The whole family is here." Her voiced quivered, betraying her fragile state.

"I can't talk but a second. Our land lines are out, and the cell is service overloaded, but I wanted you know that I'm okay."

Annie wanted to beg him to come home, but knew he wouldn't, couldn't, and it would not be fair to ask. "Are we at war?"

"I pray not, angel. I wish I could tell you more, but I can't. I promise I'll call you when I can, but try not to worry. Go home with your parents for a few days. I don't want you alone. I've got to go now. You know I love you."

With that said, the phone went dead.

Annie put the receiver in place and looked around. Everyone was focused on her. "He's okay," she said, tears of relief in her eyes. "Mom, would you call Margaret and tell her that Dan is fine, but communications are terrible with what has happened. Don't tell her he's in New York."

"Honey, she'll want to speak with you. You know she'll want to know details. She'll ask where he is."

"Can you just tell her that I have a splitting headache and can't talk now? Say he's at his office. That's not a lie. He is. He's just not in Atlanta."

The family stayed for the remainder of the day. The girls made themselves sandwiches and one for their father. But Alex, Annie, and Claire couldn't bring themselves to eat. Around four o'clock, Cole left with Sunny and Rhys. Brandi stayed behind with her mother until Frank Brennan arrived at the house a little after six.

Following Dan's instructions, Annie and Heidi went home with the Brennans that evening, leaving Deli food, water, and fresh litter to last several days. Despite attempts by her mother to distract her, Annie stayed glued to a television screen for the next three days. She kept her mobile phone constantly at her side including at the dinner table and on the bed by her pillow. Dan managed to call every day at varying times.

The calls were brief but helped her cope with the overwhelming anxiety.

CHAPTER TWENTY-ONE

In the weeks following the World Trade Center attacks, Dan was rarely home. Anthrax-laced letters mailed to the media and two Senators only days after 9/11 placed an all-time high demand on FBI resources.

When the phone rang on a dreary Friday morning in late October, Annie's heart sank. *He's not coming home again this weekend.*

"Angel, I'm sorry, but know I don't have to tell you how much pressure is on the Bureau right now. The public needs reassurance that this is still a safe country."

"I know. I hear the news every night, and I understand, but it doesn't keep me from desperately missing you."

"It won't last forever, but I know the timing is awful with you having to spend most of your pregnancy alone. Why don't you spend the weekend with Alex? She and Cole always have something going on, and you need to get out."

Annie was silent for a minute, trying to decide whether to stonewall or object. Deciding the former would evoke the least amount of feedback, she said, "I'll think about it."

When they hung up, she sat down on the living room couch and tried not to cry. It wouldn't change anything. For a moment, she was wishing Margaret had persuaded Dan to take the position in the Atlanta law firm. *"Spend the weekend with Alex?" Icicles will grow in hell before that happens.*

Dan wasn't the only one who worried about her spending so much time alone. Claire badgered her frequently about getting out of the empty house and returning to the Brennan home. She had stayed there only four days after the attacks. But Annie refused. She tried to make her mother understand that even though she was lonely, she was more comfortable sleeping in her own bed. As much as Annie loved her parents, they could not fill the gap left when Dan was gone. Fortunately, he was able to call nearly every night, usually after ten o'clock.

Past the morning sickness stage of her pregnancy, Annie was feeling good and gaining weight. To fill her days, she volunteered to help with the annual church bazaar. The committee hoped to raise enough money to purchase new robes for the children's choir. Annie made jewelry to be sold and accepted the job as chairman of promotion and publicity. Any free time left over after household chores and bazaar work, she used to catch up on reading. During the summer, she had been too stressed to concentrate, and the monthly book club selections had accumulated. Staying busy also provided her with an excuse for having not begun preparations for the baby. Claire had nagged about that as well.

"You're going to let the time slip by on you and then be in a panic to get the baby's room ready," she said in a telephone conversation.

"If I don't start until after the holidays, I will have plenty of time," Annie said. Then in a calculated attempt to change the subject, she added, "Are you making German chocolates cakes for the bazaar?"

***

September saw Dan come home only once for barely twenty-four hours. October proved to be little better; however, he was able to stay from late Friday to Sunday evening on the one weekend home. Annie tried to console herself with the idea that military wives would spend months, even a year, without their husbands. When he came home on November 17th, Annie was ecstatic because he could stay until Monday. She did not care how they spent the time, as long as they were together.

"We can have a quiet weekend at home," she said at breakfast on Saturday morning.

"No way. Driving home last night, I thought about how long you've been by yourself in this house. You deserve a night out. I'm taking you to dinner in the city—no argument."

"Well, if you put it that way," she said, folding her napkin. "Should we invite your parents?"

"Not this time. I'm not interested in sharing our time with anyone—including my parents."

They drove to Atlanta in mid-afternoon in order to catch a late matinee of *Serendipity*, a romantic comedy, before dinner. After the movie, they went to one of Dan's favorite bistros.

"Isn't Kate Beckinsale gorgeous?" Annie said, after the server took their order.

"That sounds like a trick question," Dan said, smiling.

"I'm serious. I really like her, especially her British accent."

"She's nice enough. Did you enjoy the film?"

"I did."

"Well. How would you like to see a Broadway show?"

"What are you talking about?"

"I'm asking: how would you like to spend Thanksgiving in New York?"

Annie looked up at him with an eager, albeit puzzled, expression. "Are you serious? How would that work?" She had been dreading how she could get out of the traditional family gathering at her parents' house and was determined not to participate, especially without Dan.

"I thought you might like to fly back with me on Monday. You could spend the week Christmas shopping and sightseeing while I work. I can't guarantee you a lot of attention, but I'm sure we can squeeze in some time together—see a show. With the baby coming in the spring, it might be the last chance for us, the two of us, to have a getaway."

It was the answer to her prayers. Of course she wanted to go—spend time with him—see a Broadway show. Even with the shroud of 9/11 still blanketing the city, the idea of being with Dan and doing her Christmas shopping in New York was thrilling. However, the most extraordinary aspect of the idea was the prospect of leaving Providence for the holiday. *Thank you, God. If we're in New York, I won't have to go through the hell of spending Thanksgiving at Mom and Dad's with Cole—or have to lie to get out of it.*

Thoughts of sitting across a holiday table from Cole, or being seated next to him, had plagued Annie since Halloween. She loved Thanksgiving with the aroma of turkey roasting, yeast rolls rising, and pumpkin pies baking in her mother's kitchen. It was a daylong event in the Brennan family, beginning with food preparation in the morning, followed by the formal dinner served on her grandmother's Haviland. After dinner, the women cleaned-up, while the men clustered in the den to watch football. By mid-afternoon, the women and girls were usually engrossed in a board game or two. No one left before having a light supper of leftovers. Thinking of that much time in the house with Cole terrorized Annie.

"I hate to ask you to miss spending Thanksgiving with your family, but I will have to be in Manhattan whether you come or not," Dan continued.

"Don't worry about that. I don't mind," she replied, eagerly. *Be careful Annie. You might create suspicion if you're too happy about missing the family get-together.* "It won't hurt to skip it this one time. The family will understand," she said.

"I will be working most of the time. Will you be okay on your own?"

"I'll be fine as long as you're there every night, plus you said you could spend some time with me, didn't you?"

"You bet. I will absolutely spend some quality time with you," he said, winking. "I know you've been neglected. It's been a hard time for everyone."

"Are you sure that you want to turn me loose in Bergdorf's and Macy's with a credit card?" she asked with an impish grin on her face.

"I think I can risk it," he said, laying his fork down and reaching across the table for her hand. "I'm more concerned that you'll overextend yourself physically than financially—I know you. Maybe you can shop for the baby."

She flinched internally at the mention of the baby. To disguise the change of mood, she excused herself to go to the restroom.

***

Claire was disappointed when Annie told her about the New York trip, but she was a good sport about it.

"We'll miss you, honey, but I know you want to be with Dan. I want you to have a good time, but please be careful. Your being in New York right now does make me nervous."

When Annie told Alex that she would not be with the family on Thanksgiving, Alex was fully supportive.

"I would skip the forced-family-fun any day of the week for a glam trip to the Big Apple," she told Annie over the phone. "Live it up. You're going to be tied down for a long time, kiddo, after that little one gets here."

Margaret seized news of the trip as an excuse to wrangle some time with the couple before they departed.

"You can leave your car at our house and save the parking fees," Margaret said to Dan, when he called on Sunday afternoon to let her know their plans. They never spent Thanksgiving Day with his family, but they always went to Atlanta on the Sunday after the holiday for lunch at the club with Margaret and Russ. "It just makes sense, darling. Besides, it will give Dad and me a chance to see you. I'll have a nice lunch ready for you tomorrow, and afterward, I can drive you to the airport."

"Make it an early lunch, Mother. We'll need to be at Hartsfield by two," he said.

When he got off the phone, Dan went to find Annie, who was looking through her closet for what to pack. "I hope you don't mind, but I've agreed to lunch at the palace before we take off on Monday. The queen made me an offer that I couldn't refuse, if you know what I mean."

"So, she intimidates you, too," Annie said, smiling.

As Annie and Dan prepared to leave the next morning, she couldn't decide which coat to take on the trip. Dan wanted to reach his parents' house by eleven to give them plenty time for a relaxed lunch, yet check in at the airport by two.

Having finished his packing, which he had down to a science, Dan closed his travel bag and put it on the floor next to his briefcase. Annie was staring at two coats she had hanging on the closet door. One was a standard trench coat style with a zip-out lining, the other a full-length down coat.

"Which one should I take?"

Looking at her bag that was twice as large as his, he said, "I think you'll be fine with the lighter one."

"What if it's really cold in New York?"

With an all-knowing expression, he replied, "Then you'll freeze, I guess."

"You're patronizing me," she said with a slight edge in her tone.

Dan walked to the other side of the bed where she was standing and put his arms around her waist; she resisted, still annoyed with him. "You will be fine. It's not likely to be so cold in New York that your lighter coat with a sweater under it won't suffice, but if there is an unexpected blizzard, I'll buy you a new coat."

She pulled out of his grasp, now fully annoyed. "Maybe I should take them both."

Flicking his hand in surrender, he said, "Good plan, but don't hand them to me to carry when you don't need either one. However, you'd better make up your mind. We've got to get moving if we're going to make it to Atlanta in time to eat the fancy lunch Margaret has made Geraldine prepare."

"You know you can be replaced, don't you?" Annie said, changing her irritated tone to a playful one.

"Is that a promise or a threat?" he said with a smile and grabbed her again by the waist, this time with a firm grip, then kissed her on the forehead.

"It's getting harder to reach around you," he said as he released her. At nearly six months pregnant, her body was clearly broadcasting her condition.

She shot him a pseudo-dirty look, took the trench coat from the door, and pronounced herself ready to go.

"You're not going to have to go through the entire house and check for things you may have forgotten, are you—like an unplugged iron or whether the stove is off?"

"You think you're cute, don't you?" she snapped. "All I have to do is to check to be sure I've covered everything Mom will have to do for Deli while we're gone." The Brennans had picked up Heidi the night before.

As Annie had watched her mother pet the dog, she had thought about Claire's role in the baby's life. *At least I'm not lying to her. This is her grandchild.* The Brennans were the only players on Annie's stage who truly knew their relationship to the unborn child. *How long can I keep this secret?*

CHAPTER TWENTY-TWO

They reached the Cameron house shortly before noon. Margaret greeted them at the door with a hug for each. Russ had come home for lunch and was in his den reading the newspaper. Hearing the doorbell, he laid it aside and came out to welcome them.

"I know you're in a hurry, so let me take your coats, and we'll go straight to the dining room. Geraldine has everything ready," Margaret said.

"The table is beautiful," Annie commented upon entering the dining room. "Is this the Adams' china?" she said, referring to Margaret's prize possession, a set of Sévres, which was allegedly a duplicate of John and Abigail Adams' official White House china. Although the Cameron money came through Dan's paternal family, Margaret considered herself American royalty with direct lineage to the third president and his wife.

"Goodness, no, my dear. This is just some family Meissen. Don't you remember? The Adams' china has blue cornflowers."

"Yeah, sweetheart. This is just some of Mother's old garage sale Meissen," Dan said, sarcastically.

Silly me. How could I not remember that the Adams' china has blue cornflowers?—especially, when she tried to talk me into choosing the modern reproduction as my wedding china. Annie looked around the elegant dining room with its dark-green, silk wallpaper and wide, ornately carved moldings of dark cherry wood. Built-in cabinets, channeling the White House China Room, displayed pieces handed down through several generations, mostly from Margaret's side. In the place of honor was the china with blue cornflowers. The room smelled of polished wood and the stargazer lilies that anchored the floral centerpiece. An antique silk Oriental rug covered most of the hardwood floor. At the north end of the room hung a life-sized portrait of Margaret in a long, blue gown, standing in a formal garden with her King Charles spaniel, Regina, at her feet. The portrait always made Annie feel like she was a peasant at the queen's court, one who had failed to read the protocol manual.

Once they were seated, Geraldine appeared from the kitchen with their lunch of crab casserole, fruit, and muffins. Gingerly, Annie picked up her fork, a piece of heavy sterling, capable of cracking a plate if dropped.

"This is so nice," Annie said, directing her comment to Margaret.

Margaret smiled graciously.

As lunch progressed, the conversation turned in the one direction Annie wished to avoid.

"Annie, dear, my garden circle wants to give you a little shower at the club," Margaret said. "Have you registered with any of the stores?"

Here we go. "Not yet," she replied.

Furrowing her eyebrows, Margaret continued, "You have chosen a theme for the nursery, haven't you?"

Whoops. Dropped the ball on that one too. "Actually, I haven't."

"Annie, you've got to get started. That little fellow will be here before you know it, and you won't have time then to do a proper job of decorating. Be sure to register with Macy's and Saks on your trip."

Annie frowned, trying not to let her mother-in-law get under her skin. *I'd rather register with Target and Kmart. Wouldn't Margaret love referring her friends there?*

Apparently noticing his daughter-in-law's discomfort, Russ intervened before she could respond. "What time does your plane take off?" he asked.

"Half past three," Dan said. "We'd better get moving because we have no idea what to expect with traffic and airport security."

"You haven't finished your dessert," Margaret said. "Certainly, security won't be a problem for you. Can't you just show them your badge?"

Dan's eyes cut around to Annie. "It's a little more complicated than that, Mother, but maybe I can just explain that I'm descended from John and Abigail," he said. Margaret's desire for special treatment had always annoyed him.

Knowing Dan's attitude about claiming privilege, Russ said, "He can't just go around flashing his badge, Margaret. You know Dan doesn't want to call attention to himself."

"Well, what's the point in his being a member of the FBI if he doesn't get some special treatment?" Margaret argued.

Taking her turn diffusing an awkward moment in the conversation, Annie said, "The casserole was delicious, Margaret. I would love to have the recipe."

"I'm glad you liked it, my dear. I'll have Geraldine write it out for you and have it ready when you get back. Now, finish your dessert. You have to eat well to nourish our little guy."

Here we go again—baby equals boy.

They finished dessert with no further stressful comments made. Russ said his goodbyes and headed back to his office as Annie and Dan prepared to leave with Margaret for the airport.

Driving to Hartsfield, Margaret took a final opportunity to remind Annie that she should begin preparations for the baby's room so that shower guests could choose appropriate gifts. Annie assured her that she would give it consideration.

Once Annie and Dan checked in at the airport, cleared security, and arrived at their gate, Dan took a seat at the far end of the waiting area and opened his laptop. Noticing a quizzical expression come across her face, he asked, "Do you mind, if I go over my email before we board?"

"No. Go ahead. I think I'll go over to the newsstand and get something to read and a drink. Can I bring you anything?"

"I'm good.... No, wait a minute. I would like a cold drink," he said, booting up his computer.

He works all the time, she thought.

Browsing through novels at the shop, Annie accidentally collided with an attractive blonde.

"I'm so sorry," the stranger said. "Are you okay?"

"I'm fine," Annie said. "It was my fault. I should be the one apologizing."

Looking down at Annie's six-month baby-bump, the stranger asked, "When is your baby due?"

"Early spring," Annie replied, surprised at how good it felt to tell a stranger.

The woman smiled and said, "Your first?"

She seems genuinely interested. "It's our first," Annie said, nodding. "Do you have children?"

"No," the woman said, a touch of sadness in her voice. "I was pregnant once."

"Oh, I'm sorry." Annie felt instant guilt. Here was a woman who appeared to want a baby, and Annie was still mentally struggling with her pregnancy. *I'm having a baby. I should be grateful. That should be all that matters.*

"It's okay. It was a long time ago." Glancing down at Annie's left hand, she said, "Is your husband excited?"

"He is," Annie said, delicately balancing guilt and maternal pride. She extended her right hand toward the attractive blonde and said, "My name is Annie, Annie Cameron." *Why am I talking to this stranger?*

Taking Annie's hand and shaking it, the woman said, "Well, hello, Annie Cameron. I'm Ansley Sheridan from Jacksonville, Florida. And where are you from?"

"A little town about forty-five minutes from Atlanta, but my husband and I lived in Jacksonville for two years when we were first married."

"Really! What part?"

"San Jose. It was a tall condo building on the river—University Boulevard."

"You're kidding. That's the area I grew up in. What a coincidence."

"Where are you going?"

"New York and I'm a little nervous. I'm going for a performance of the ballet company I danced in eight years ago. It's the first time I've been back."

"You're a ballerina? That's impressive."

"Not really. I wasn't a ballerina, more like a ballet dancer. I was in the corps. Are you going to New York to visit family for the holiday?"

"No. My husband is working on temporary assignment there, and I'm going to spend the week with him—Christmas shopping and sight-seeing. We're hoping to see a Broadway show."

"Sounds really nice. I hope you have a great time."

With that, Ansley smiled and took the book she was holding to the cashier. Annie continued browsing.

Returning to the waiting area, Annie watched Dan as she walked toward him. He was totally immersed in something on his computer screen. *He doesn't seem to know I'm here.*

Sitting down beside him, she placed his soft drink on the small table next to his seat.

Dan looked up and smiled. "Did you find something to read on the plane?" he asked.

"I did. But, I bought more than I can read—one of the sexy romance novels, a novel by the woman who wrote *The Deep End of the Ocean*, and a copy of *People*. I shouldn't be bored." She smiled, and he reached over and patted her knee, but his attention immediately went back to his keyboard.

With less than thirty minutes before boarding, Annie decided not to begin reading. Instead, she amused herself watching the diverse collection of travelers rushing from place to place in the terminal and those seated in the boarding area. On one side of her, there was a young, tattooed couple, who scarcely looked as though they could scrounge up airfare—their belongings in ratty-looking duffel bags. In contrast, on the other side sat a rather well-to-do older couple, dressed in designer clothing and sipping from containers of gourmet coffee.

Directly across from Annie, there was a young woman traveling with a baby girl and a little boy who looked to be about four years old. He was a handful. Annie felt sorry for the frazzled mom as she struggled to restrain the rambunctious child while he climbed over seats and threatened to stray too far. Annie wanted to offer help but feared her altruistic motive might be misinterpreted. *I wonder where the father is. Maybe she's a single mom, or maybe they're on the way to meet the dad.*

As the young woman was about to lose control of the situation, Annie leaned forward and asked, "Can I help you?"

The woman looked up with pleading eyes as though she was about to cry and said, "Would you? I've got to change her diaper before we board, and Charlie is being a bear."

Addressing the errant child, Annie said, "Tell you what, Charlie, you and I will go with Mommy to the bathroom while she changes your sister's diaper, and then maybe she'll let us get you a toy at the store over there."

Toy was the magic word. The restless child immediately beamed and reached up for Annie's hand.

"Be right back," she said to Dan, who nodded, barely noticing.

Her mission was barely accomplished when they were called to board. Passing through the entry to the ramp leading to the plane, a pretty young flight attendant said to Dan, "Nice to see you again, Mr. Cameron." Her sparkling white teeth flashed a broad grin in his direction, as her chestnut hair fell in graceful waves to her shoulders.

"She's attractive," Annie commented, trying to conceal a spark of jealousy. "She seems to know you."

"Does she?" he answered, totally unaffected by the situation and obviously not feeling any need to justify or explain how or why the woman knew his name.

Alex is right. He is the most unaware-of-himself man we know. I could be jealous. I probably am a little, but I know he's faithful. Trusting Dan's fidelity, and how oblivious he was to attention by a pretty woman, made Annie feel even more guilt about the secret she carried. *Am I going to live in the shadow of this secret for the rest of my life?*

Her guilt affected Annie's expression, giving her a tense look. Dan looked at her as he lifted her carry-on into the overhead compartment and asked, "Are you okay?"

Bringing herself back into reality, she said, "Absolutely. I was just thinking about how much I want to do while we're in New York."

Dan smiled and stepped aside for her to take the window seat.

As she slid into her seat, she told herself that she had to stop thinking about the negative and concentrate on the positive. *I can't let one miserable fact ruin all the good. Dan's going to be a fantastic father, and we'll have a great life. Margaret's rich friends can even buy the baby expensive gifts. It's okay.*

CHAPTER TWENTY-THREE

Waking up in a different place was liberating to Annie. The city, the distance from Georgia and everyone she knew, mysteriously lightened the weight of her secret. On Tuesday morning after Dan left for work, she installed her big-city courage and took a cab from the hotel in Times Square to Bloomingdale's, remembering what a wonderland of merchandise was there. *I can do this. I don't need a bodyguard. I'm going to go Christmas shopping.* However, despite her resolve, she let the doorman hail the cab. *I'll do it myself on the way back, but why not take advantage of what's available?* In truth, she dreaded the act of stepping into the street, waving her arms like a mad woman, but assured herself that when she had no choice, she could do it.

The venture proved successful. Not only did she buy gifts for her father and three nieces, she also gained a sense of pride in her independence. Taking advantage of the store's mailing-service, she had the purchases shipped home. After a pleasant lunch in the sixth-floor restaurant at the store, she decided to go to the Metropolitan Museum of Art. Swallowing her fear, she stepped onto Lexington Avenue and with semi-aggression, hailed her first cab ride.

Meandering through the galleries, Annie felt smug about her autonomy. *I can take my time looking.* There was no way to cover the entire museum in one afternoon, so she concentrated on the French Impressionists and the Musical Instruments Gallery where she loved seeing the 18th and 19th century pianos. She regretted not having enough time to look at jewelry exhibits but was determined to check out the museum shop for potential Christmas gifts before leaving.

After buying reproduction, antique bracelets and logo tote bags for Claire and Alex, she left the museum. It was after four, and she wanted to get back to the hotel before dark. She hadn't talked to Dan all day and had no idea what time he would be free.

When she had no luck with hailing a cab at the museum, she decided to take the bus down to 59th Street. There were always a lot of cabs at the south end of Central Park. Annie was so confident about her ability to navigate the city that she was almost cocky, but not to the point of wanting to be on the streets after dark.

Night was falling as she arrived back at the hotel. There was a message from Dan, saying that she should either have dinner in the hotel, or order from room service as he would be late. He asked that she get a sandwich for him.

After taking a shower to remove the city residue from her person, Annie ordered from the room service menu—a bowl of soup and cup of tea, plus a ham sandwich and a soft drink for Dan. When she finished eating, she curled up on the king-size bed to read but scarcely finished a page before falling asleep.

At ten-thirty, Dan's opening the door to the room woke her. Pulling herself together, she stood up to greet him. Hugging her, he asked about her day.

"Veni, vidi, vici," she said. "I had a great day."

Dan grinned at her enthusiasm. She was a like a puppy released from a kennel. "I'm proud of you, but let's not get too carried away. This is still a city with dangers you have to respect."

"I know, I know. Tomorrow, I'm going downtown to Ground Zero."

His face took on a look of concern. "Are you sure you should do that? It's a depressing sight, and there's still a serious problem with the air quality."

"Dan, I've got to see it. Please don't try to stop me."

Since there was no changing her mind, before he left the following morning, Dan spoke with the concierge and arranged for a car to take her to the site.

It was about nine-thirty when Annie arrived at the building where she would observe the tragic scene. Her observation point was located on Barclay Street, about three-hundred and fifty feet from the site. She took the elevator to the top floor with a feeling of anxiety in her stomach.

At the top of the building, she was one of only a handful of people to arrive early. Her view of the site was unobstructed. As she looked down, she gasped silently at the sight of the pile of rubble that had once been the stately buildings. *How could two buildings that stood one-hundred, ten stories high be reduced to that?* As her eyes roamed the ruins, she looked for any identifiable objects, but saw none. *Surely the materials to build the structures would have created a larger mass. Where are the planes?* It was impossible to comprehend how two huge planes could have dissolved into dust and ashes. *How many bodies are still in that mound? I'm looking at where it happened.* Glancing around the surrounding area, she saw that the remaining buildings were frosted with ash.

After only a few minutes, Annie knew she had to leave—the sadness that enveloped her was turning to nausea—her knees were turning to jelly. Realization that the huge pile of rubble was filled with the remains of people was more than she could bear. They went innocently to work on September 11th, oblivious to the horror ahead.

Once back in the car, she asked the driver to cruise around for a few minutes while she calmed her nerves and adjusted her mind. Closing her eyes, she mentally said a prayer for those who died, those who lost loved ones, and a prayer of thanksgiving for the blessings of her life. *Dear God, compared to what all these people have suffered, I have no problems. Thank you for giving me a wonderful husband, a nice home, my loving parents. All I ask is that you please let my baby be healthy.*

Pulling herself together, she told the driver to take her to the artsy district of SoHo. She had to take her mind to another place, which might happen if she concentrated on finding a piece of art for the bare wall in their living room. She knew the galleries on 57th Street would be out of her price range.

Annie had read in a travel guide that bargains could be found in the galleries of SoHo and Tribeca. Although her book made a couple of galleries in Tribeca appear more appealing, she decided Dan would be more comfortable with her shopping in SoHo, given the proximity of the two areas to Ground Zero. It turned out to be the coup of her week.

In a shop specializing in posters, lithographs, and prints, she discovered gold—a vintage LeRoy Neiman poster titled *Big Serve*. The subject was a male tennis player, which made it a perfect choice for Dan. The image was of the back view of a dark-haired competitor in a white tennis outfit—much like one Dan wore at Georgia. The player appeared to be in mid-air, either serving or reaching to make his stroke.

The second she saw it in the shop bin, she knew she had to have it and was relieved to find that it was not expensive. *This is perfect. Dan can hang it in his office or his study at home.* She was so excited about the piece that she wanted to take it with her to look at back at the hotel but decided it would be better to let the shop frame it and ship the finished product to her. *How could I hide it from him, if I took it with me? That would be stupid.* The thrill of her "find" helped dispel some of the gloom cast by the visit to the World Trade Center site.

After eating a slice of pizza from a parlor in the Village, she took a cab back to the hotel, having dismissed the private car driver when he dropped her in SoHo. Annie was exhausted from the emotional and physical stress of the morning. The rest of her shopping list would have to wait until Friday. The only names not checked off were Russ, and the one she did not know how to face.

How am I going to force myself to choose a gift for him? The thought disgusted her. Choosing a gift for Cole would be like choosing a valentine for an ex-husband. The only thing worse was the thought of having to present it. Memories of past Christmases, where the exchange of gifts was coupled with the exchange of hugs, gave her a real nasty feeling. *I'd rather hug a pig, fresh from rolling in manure with a rattler wrapped around its neck, than put my arms around him—or worse yet, have him touch me.* In true Scarlet O'Hara tradition, she convinced herself to delay any further thoughts of Christmas until Friday.

***

Since Dan had to work on Thanksgiving Day, Annie took her time getting up and dressed. She could see the Macy's parade from the hotel window and had no desire to infiltrate the crowd. For all she knew, Dan could be somewhere on the route doing whatever the agents did to boost security. She knew better than to ask him anything about his assignment for the day. Since the parade was the first gathering of the public in large volume since the attacks, all law enforcement agencies were on alert. Annie tried not to think that he could be in harm's way.

Knowing her family was concerned about their trip, she called her parents' house a little after nine. She knew it was too early for the Daltons to have arrived.

"Happy Thanksgiving," Annie said, when her mother answered the phone.

The tone of Claire's reply indicated how happy she was to hear from her younger daughter. "Are you having a good time?"

"I am, Mom. It's been a really good trip for me."

The conversation was short because Claire was in the midst of the dinner preparations, but she stressed how happy she was to have heard from Annie and how much she and Dan would be missed at the table.

Annie thought about calling Margaret and Russ when she hung up from her mother, but decided it was Dan they wanted to speak with on the holiday, and they were likely not home. The Camerons usually celebrated Thanksgiving at the club's holiday buffet with longtime friends.

Shortly after noon, Annie called room service and ordered a salad. She had no desire to go downstairs to the turkey dinner being served in the restaurant. After lunch, she took a nap.

Dan was back at the hotel by six that evening.

"Let's stay here for dinner," Annie said, noticing how tired he looked.

Pulling off his tie, he looked at her with a wide-eyed expression suggesting her words had given him relief. "You don't mind?" he asked.

After Dan showered and put on a pair of tan slacks, fresh white shirt, and a bulky pull-over sweater in light-blue wool, they went down to the hotel restaurant where they found the large dining room unusually quiet.

"I guess everyone came for lunch today," Dan said, looking around at the empty tables as Annie nodded.

After Dan had a glass of wine and Annie was sipping a cup of tea while they waited for their main course, she put her cup down and said, "You know you need to call your mother."

Dan raised an eyebrow, but agreed. "You are right. I'll call when we get back to the room, but don't you let her keep me on the phone for long. Call my cell while I'm talking to her."

"I'll do no such thing. I wouldn't want our child treating me that way on a holiday." She stopped, shocked that she had actually used the words "our child." It had slipped out as effortlessly as swallowing vanilla custard. *I said it.*

On Friday, Annie got up early with Dan. She had a lot to accomplish. Her plan was to be at Saks Fifth Avenue when it opened at ten o'clock. She expected to clear the remaining gift purchases on her list by noon and then treat herself to an elegant lunch at The Plaza. The first part went according to plan. She found a smart handbag for Margaret and a designer belt for Russ. But, she wanted something more for her father-in-law, so she took a cab to Rizzoli's Book Store on 57th Street. Her expertise in hailing cabs was growing stronger each time.

At Rizzoli's she found a coffee-table book on Scotland that she thought Russ would like. It featured St. Andrews golf course, which he loved. Leaving Rizzoli's, she decided to take a sightseeing trip to Bauman's Rare Book Store, not expecting to purchase anything, but wanting to see the store that advertised books costing five figures. On the way, she strolled along 5th Avenue, window-shopping. There was so much to see: intricately carved crystal, Tiffany diamonds, and

Ferragamo shoes. Passing a western-style boutique, she remembered the one gift yet to be purchased.

This would be his store of choice, she thought. *I should go in and buy something. I'm just putting off the inevitable.* Annie knew that she was trapped. Choosing a gift for Cole was not optional. She always bought the Christmas gifts. Dan didn't have time, and she could not ask her mother to buy a gift without inviting questions. This is only the beginning. *You can't avoid it, Annie, so get your act together and do what you have to do.*

She stood at the window for several minutes, debating with herself about going into the store. Finally, taking a deep breath, she opened the heavy door and cautiously entered. The interior smelled of leather with a trace of hay. *Where does the hay smell come from?* Walking to the back of the shop where a staircase led to the mezzanine, she saw the source—a large display populated with life-size, male mannequins dressed in standard cowboy uniforms. The display was bordered by a split-rail fence with a mound of real hay filling in the floor. The fence and the artificial shrubbery in the display were strung with Christmas lights. *Damn, even artificial cowboys have a sexy swagger in boots and a cocked, ten-gallon hat.*

"Can I help you, ma'am?" a solicitous male clerk asked, startling Annie. He was dressed in impeccable western clothing: tight jeans, neatly pressed, and a pretty plaid shirt in primary colors. A bandana surrounded his neck, and a Stetson sat cocked to the right on his head.

He looks about as natural in that outfit as Ray Brantley would look in a tuxedo at the Metropolitan Opera House. It was conventional wisdom that servers and sales people in New York were out-of-work performers. This one looked as though he was ready to audition for the de Mille ballet, *Rodeo.*

"I'm looking for a Christmas gift for my brother-in-law," Annie said.

"Could madam be more specific about what she has in mind?" the obnoxious young man said in a patronizing tone.

What self-respecting cowboy would ever be caught saying that? This fellow definitely brings new meaning to the term "urban cowboy." Looking him straight in the face, she smiled. *I can be just as patronizing as this arrogant jerk.*

"I really haven't decided on anything in particular, but maybe a nice plaid shirt," she said, dialing up her Southern drawl a notch and coating it with sugar.

"Our shirts are on the mezzanine," he said, leading her up the stairs to an array of plaid shirts—some cotton, some flannel, and some of lightweight wool.

"You have a lot to choose from," Annie said.

"Well, maybe we could narrow it down just a little if you tell me what his best colors are."

Cole's best colors? She thought for a minute or two. *That would have to be black and yellow, like a rattlesnake.* "Why don't you just recommend something in a large?" She smiled, enjoying a private, guilty pleasure. *Cole would hate knowing this fellow chose his gift.* Letting this guy pick out his present makes it almost fun, kind of like a server spitting on a customer's food.

Light on his feet, the clerk zipped down the aisle and scooped up about five samples for Annie to choose from.

"I'm sure your friend would love any one of these," he said, spreading the shirts out like a poker hand.

"Sister's husband," Annie said, correcting the clerk. *Cole Dalton is not my friend.*

"Will he be wearing the shirt for work or play?"

"Actually, he might use it for either one. He's what you might call a Georgia cowboy." *This guy has never seen a real horse, much less been on one.* Annie spread the shirts further apart, pretending to be interested. *If he only knew how I don't give a fig about which one I buy.* Taking shirts from the group, one by one, she studied each as if she cared. *It's just a shirt, damn it, Annie. Close your eyes and pick one.* "I'll take the blue," she told the clerk, who was obviously losing patience.

"Excellent choice," he said and picked up the entire group, returning them to their original position, and taking Annie's selection back down to the main floor.

I could have chosen the most atrocious shirt in the store, and he would have said the same thing.

At the register, Annie asked if the store had a mailing service. The young man assured her that they did, plus they could gift wrap the item as well. She immediately took him up on the gift wrap. *Perfect—I won't have to look at the damn thing until Christmas Eve.*

Leaving the western boutique, the thought of baby clothes popped into her head. She had avoided the children's departments in both Bloomingdales and Saks on Tuesday, but now she realized that if she did not buy something in New York for the baby, the family would have questions. *If I can buy for Cole, I can buy for the baby.*

The idea of going to Bauman's was discarded in favor of finding baby things. Bloomingdale's and Saks came to mind. Either would re-quire a cab because she was too tired for more walking. *If I'm going to do this, I'm going to do it big. I have to take a cab, so Saks it is.*

Back at Saks, she got off the elevator on one of the top floors, where the children's clothing was displayed, and felt an instant rush. *I didn't feel this way with Alex at Lenox. She had to drag me, almost kicking and screaming, to the baby department at Neiman's. Now, I feel the urge to buy something for the baby—just one thing.* She was crossing a barrier and didn't want to break the spell.

Wandering through the racks and tables of infant wear, she admired the cute little outfits for both boys and girls, but she found herself so confused that she could not choose. Nearby, a chic young woman with a baby boy in a stroller was shopping. The child appeared to be about six months old. He was a beautiful baby with big greenish-blue eyes and curly blond hair. Annie froze for a moment. *That could be Cole's son—my son.*

Although the sight of the little boy was disconcerting, Annie was strangely drawn to him and began making faces and doing "Patty-

Cake." He responded with outbursts of giggles. She found herself completely caught up in the moment. The mother appeared happy to have someone distract the child while she made her selections. Annie watched as the woman held up adorable little outfits. Making her purchases, the woman tucked the packages into the back of the stroller and smiled at Annie.

"Thank you for distracting Winston while I shopped," she said to Annie.

Winston? What a stuffy name for such a cute little boy. "You're welcome. I enjoyed it."

"When is your baby due?" the stranger asked, looking down at Annie's swollen stomach.

"Early spring," Annie said, happy and proud to be part of the motherhood union.

The woman left, and the clerk turned her attention to Annie. "You know who that was, don't you?" she said.

Should I know? "No, I really don't."

"She's Blake Chandler's wife."

"The actor?"

"The same. She buys all of Winston's clothes here. Now, can I help you now with anything?"

Annie paused. She hadn't made a choice. "Not yet. I'm still looking."

As the clerk turned her attention to another customer, Annie felt a twinge of panic. *I can't go home empty-handed, but, I can't just close my eyes and point, like I did with Cole's gift.* Then she saw it.

In an elaborate display, baby mannequins were clothed in the most beautiful christening gowns that Annie had ever seen. One appeared gender neutral, but suitable for a British princess or a French dauphin. It was made in two pieces, with a long skirt attached to a suit of delicate batiste with exquisite, flat lace trim. There was a double row of white-on-white embroidery down the front and circling the hemline. Five, exquisite mother-of-pearl buttons in the shape of small crosses lined up below the collar. The matching cap was a simple band with matching embroidery motif, attached to a shirred back piece. The garment was a quintessential expression of purity, innocence, and quality.

I bet it's expensive. Of course, it's expensive. This is Saks Fifth Avenue. Feeling the fabric, she felt her heart beating faster. Annie didn't care about the price. This was a moment—a moment when she took charge of her baby. She was going to make the choice for the baby's first important event in life. *My baby is going to be christened as soon as possible, wash away the sins of the father. The gown has to be elegant—it's got to be perfect. I'm going to be the one to pick it out, not Margaret. She can buy anything else, but not my baby's christening dress. It's not her grandchild.* Taking a card out of her purse, she went to a counter where a salesclerk was standing and boldly announced, "I'll have that christening dress on the middle mannequin, please."

CHAPTER TWENTY-FOUR

After buying the gown, Annie's earlier plan to have lunch at The Plaza vanished. Although it was nearly two o'clock, she abandoned both the visit to The Plaza and lunch in general, which spoke volumes as to her state of mind. Having seen the famed hotel featured in a number of movies, she had been anxious to include it among her New York experiences. *I shouldn't go back to the hotel. The christening gown isn't going anywhere. I have the rest of my life to look at it.* The purchase was the only one that Annie had not arranged to have shipped home. She was not letting it out of her control.

Despite the dictates of her practical side, the emotional side won out, and she hailed a cab. With her latent maternal feelings finally released, Annie wanted to savor every precious moment—preferably alone. *I need to have some time to myself. Dan would think I was crazy, and I'm not ready to bring him into this.*

When a cab stopped, she climbed in, handling her package as though it contained fragile china. *I'll pick up a sandwich and take it up to the room. That will give me plenty of time to relax, maybe take a nap, before Dan gets off work.* After instructing the driver as to her destination, she settled back in the cab and daydreamed as the vehicle lurched down 5th Avenue in typical New York fashion. *I'm going to have a baby—my baby—a little person who will call me Mommy—one who I can cuddle and protect.* Looking down at the bulge under her clothing, she thought, *Faith...or Danny...you are going to be so beautiful in your dress and cap.*

The image of the ceremony brought another episode of panic. *Oh my gosh. Godparents!* In her mind she saw the family gathered around the baptismal font at the back of the church, as they had for the baptisms of all of her nieces. *What will we do about godparents? How can we ask Alex to be your godmother and not ask Cole?*

I will die before I let this baby's bastard father be the godfather. She knew that the family, even Dan, would expect Alex and Cole to serve as the child's spiritual parents. Annie was godmother to all three of the Dalton girls, and Dan was Sunny's godfather, even though they were only engaged when Sunny was born. *I can't think about that now. It'll have to wait until after you're born. Your real daddy, the one who's going to raise you, will be off work in a couple of hours, and I won't let bad thoughts ruin this day.*

The night before, Dan had promised Annie that his work would be done by early Friday afternoon, and they would have the rest of the weekend together. "Tomorrow night and Saturday are ours," he had said. "We'll go to the theater tomorrow night and, afterward, have a late dinner in the theater district. Saturday, we'll do whatever you like. But Saturday night, I'm taking you out to an intimate little restaurant for a romantic dinner. I'm warning you now. I'm going to expect a proper reward when we get back to the hotel," he said, with a devilish grin on his face. "The day is yours—but the night is mine."

The idea of a Broadway show was thrilling. Annie had looked at the listings in the newspaper on Tuesday, but it was Dan who got tickets through a Bureau secretary for a new show, *Mamma Mia*.

True to his promise, he was back at the hotel by shortly after four. Annie was dozing. He let her rest while he showered and got ready for their night out.

Annie was excited on the way to the theatre. Although she had no idea what the show was about, she knew that it was based on the music of Abba, and she and Dan both liked the group. Very soon after the opening curtain, the plot struck a dissonant note for Annie when she realized that the premise dealt with a young woman trying to identify which of her mother's three lovers was her father.

I don't know if I can sit through this.

Several times during the production, she fought tears as she empathized with the mother character. *Is that me in twenty years? Will that be Faith or Danny?* At intermission, Dan commented that she was certainly into the show.

"You know me. I'm such a crybaby," she said, trying to brush off the melancholy that had come over her.

By the final curtain, when the mother connects with the true father, Annie was fighting against the story in her mind and carrying on an internal debate. *No way my child's parents are ever going to join for a "happily ever after." But can I hide the truth forever? What kind of person am I?*

At one point during the evening, she looked over at Dan and thought again, *Should I tell him the truth and rip the Band-aide off this festering sore?*

Sensing that she was staring at him, Dan turned his face toward her, smiled and squeezed her leg, affectionately.

Never, she thought, smiling back, *it's far too late—six months too late.*

Saturday, they spent a relaxing day, taking an early sightseeing tour around the city, and returning to rest before going out for the elaborate dinner Dan had planned. After the meal in a cozy little Italian restaurant, complete with violinist, they took a carriage ride around Central Park before returning to the hotel.

Fortunately, the anguish created by *Mamma Mia* and the fleeting frustration of having to buy Cole a gift were the only flaws in an otherwise perfect holiday. Even the trip to Ground Zero, painful though it was, did not mar Annie's enjoyment of the get-a-way. Having the ability to see firsthand the remains of the World Trade Center and say her own prayer for the souls of those who perished was in a way an honor.

As she repacked for the return home on Sunday morning, Dan told her that he would be returning to New York early the next morning. As much as she wanted to spend every minute she could with him, it did not seem fair to make him do the turnaround trip.

"I can go home by myself. There's no need for you to fly Atlanta and drive to Providence, then reverse the process the next morning. As much as I want to be with you, that's just plain silly."

"I don't want you traveling alone, especially in your condition."

"I'm six—five-months pregnant, sweetheart, not crippled or terminally ill." *Good job, Annie. Let the cat of the bag.*

Dan gave no notice of being aware of her near slip-up. "Are you sure?"

"I'm absolutely sure."

***

Back in Providence, Annie found herself thinking about the baby constantly. Silly as it seemed, buying the gown had been a turning point. She wanted to decorate the room, to read books on childcare, and found herself counting the days until the baby was due—the actual date. The only thing that had not changed was her avoidance of talking about the baby with others—all but Molly. With Molly there was no worry about slipping and saying the wrong thing and no guilt about perpetrating a horrendous fraud.

"I've turned a corner," Annie said to Molly in a telephone call the Sunday night she returned to Providence. She was almost glad that Dan had not accompanied her back. She was free to call Molly and talk about the plans she was making.

"You've got to see the christening gown and cap I bought for the baby. I really splurged, but the set is beautiful."

"You sound happy, dearie. I think the trip was good for you."

"It was. Something happened to me. Maybe it was seeing how much others lost on September 11 that made me see that my problem is not so big. I really don't know what it was. But, Molly, I'm ready to fix up the baby's room. I thought about it all the way home on the plane. I think I've decided how to do it without knowing the gender."

"And how would that be, luv?"

"I'm going to carpet the room in a pastel green and paint the walls the same color up to a chair-rail. After the baby's born, I'll wallpaper the upper portion of the walls in an appropriate pattern. The green will go with pink for a girl, or blue for a boy."

"What of the wee one's bed?

"Mom is making a bassinette, which will be fine until I can get a crib. I think I can pick out wallpaper and furniture for both sexes but wait to order the appropriate ones until I know whether it's Faith or Danny."

"I love hearing you happy."

"I am getting there. It's not all perfect, but it's so much better. Let's get together for lunch again. Could you come here one Saturday? Dan's never home these days, and I could use some moral support before the holidays." *I wish I could tell her who the father is, but that knowledge I couldn't trust to a comatose mute.*

***

By Christmas Eve, Annie had kept busy preparing the baby's room. It helped fill the void of Dan's extended absences. Although she didn't buy any baby furniture, she did buy a brass clothes tree on which she displayed the christening gown. With the carpet in and the room painted, she brought the bears in and sat them on the seat of the small bay window. She was thoroughly enjoying the process and felt the full scope of impending motherhood for the first time.

While her spirits had improved since the Thanksgiving trip, the night before Christmas Eve was miserable. Plagued by nightmares, she scarcely slept. Every time she dozed off, Cole appeared. First, he was standing in the doorway of her mother's kitchen, shirt open, belt un-buckled, jeans unfastened—motioning with his index finger for her to come to him. She woke in a cold sweat. Next, he was sitting beside her on the sofa as they opened gifts, presumably at her parents' home. He taunted her, saying, "You're carrying my son. He's going to look just like me—be just like me. Don't think you're going to fool anyone. Dan's going to know."

Finally, she dreamed she was in the backyard, wearing only a brief bikini. She felt naked. There was a playpen on the porch, a baby in it standing up, holding onto the bar around the top. It was a blond-haired boy, and he was crying for his mother. A man was walking up the steps—the swagger unmistakable—Cole. As he reached the playpen, he leaned down and picked up the baby. Annie screamed, "No, no, don't touch him." It was then that she woke with a jolt that nearly knocked Deli off the bed. Drained and shaking, she said to the startled cat, "It's a boy. My baby's a boy."

Getting ready for the annual get-together at her parents' house, she tried her best to put the dreams, and Cole, out of her mind. Only, she couldn't. No matter how she tried to not think about him, the dreams wrapped around her like a shroud. *I can do this. He won't dare try anything with everyone around, and tomorrow it'll be over.*

Dan got home in the early afternoon. She made him a sandwich while she finished baking the Christmas cookies. The gifts were all wrapped, Cole's gift still in the brown box it was shipped in.

As Dan began taking the gifts to the van, he called out to her. "Do you need to wrap the gift in the shipping box?"

"No. It was wrapped by the store. You can take it out of the box. I'll make a tag for you to put on it." She didn't want to touch the gift, if she could avoid it.

***

The Camerons were the first to arrive at the Brennan house. Annie immediately went to the kitchen to help her mother. It was a way to hide. She heard the Daltons arrive. It would have been hard not to hear them with the girls arguing and Alex scolding. Claire was in the living room, directing the placement of the gifts, leaving Annie alone in the kitchen, arranging food on the platters. Her back was to the door, but even amidst the aroma of Claire's homemade yeast rolls baking, she caught smell of the Polo cologne and knew he was in the kitchen. Hoping he would pass on by if she ignored him, she didn't turn before his cold hands encircled her eyes, playfully blindfolding her.

"Merry Christmas, little sister."

CHAPTER TWENTY-FIVE

Annie froze. Words could not describe the sensation she was experiencing. Not only were they in the same room, he had pressed his body against her back, as his cold hands chilled her face and suppressed her sight. Images flashed in her brain, like a video on fast-forward, transporting her back to the moment when those hands held her down, ripped off her bikini, offensively caressed her naked body—violated her.

She could feel him inside her—feel the degradation. Here he was again, smelling of Polo, except that now, instead of blending with his hot, sun-scorched skin, the fragrance combined with the strong leather smell of his cold jacket. Despite layers of clothing between them, Annie felt as naked as she had on the bed—and equally vulnerable.

But, I'm not. He doesn't have me alone and captive. We are in my parents' home; everyone is here—Dan, Alex, the girls. He can't do anything vile to me here. By absorbing her autonomy, vulnerability turned to anger as she fought the impulse to scream. Her hostility peaked when she remembered the knife lying on the counter and felt an empowering desire to thrust it into him. *Of course, I couldn't stab him, but I could throw a cup of Mom's hot cider in his face. Maybe it would burn away the insolent smile I hear in his voice.*

"You need to take your hands off of me," Annie said, with an icy composure that she didn't recognize.

"Is that all you have to say to your favorite brother-in-law?"

"That's all I have to say to my only brother-in-law, other than this is a fairly large house, and you should have no trouble staying the hell away from me." Her venomous tone failed to assuage his audacity.

"My, my, you're in a testy mood, Muff," he said, moving his hands down to her shoulders. "Are your pre-partum hormones giving you a bad time?"

Curling in her lips, her back still to him, she squeezed her eyes shut and took a deep breath, determined to both keep her composure and to deter his harassment.

Slowly and deliberately, she said, "Cole…take…your hands…off of me. Considering where you are, you don't want to push your luck." Her tone was low, like a cat's guttural growl, unequivocally warning a foe to stay clear.

"Okay, okay. Simmer down, Muff. Far be it from me to be one to rankle a pregnant lady." Having said that, he removed his hands and reached around her for a piece of the meat she was arranging, brushing against her in the process. It was unmistakably his way of signaling that he was not intimidated by her hostility.

When she knew from the trailing away of his cologne that he was gone, she crossed herself and whispered, "Thank you, God." The tension in her body subsided, but she was left weak and trembling. *Pull yourself together, Annie. You don't have the luxury of crying. Giving in to emotion is not an option.* She put both hands on the counter for support and stiffened her body, her eyes closed. *Think of something else. Think of the beautiful christening gown. Think of hugging Dan this afternoon.*

Despite her best efforts, she felt a line of moisture slinking down her cheek. Noticing an onion on the counter, she reached over and immediately cut it open. *This will justify the tears, but I've got to pull it together. It's going to be a long night. Damn, it's going to be a long life.*

The rest of the evening went as well as she could have expected with the next tension arising when Cole opened the gift from Annie and Dan. True to his arrogant nature, he blew her a kiss to express his appreciation. She looked away and pretended not to see the gesture, thus avoiding the necessity of responding in kind. After all presents were exchanged, Annie and Alex adjourned to the kitchen, with the two older nieces, to begin the cleanup. Claire excused herself to go upstairs and change for church.

As Annie cleared away the buffet dishes, she could hear Cole and Dan laughing. *No doubt Cole has told Dan one of his raunchy jokes. Dan wouldn't find him so funny if he knew what the bastard did to me.* It was all she could do to hide her anger. Brandi was helping Annie clear the dishes, while Rhys was drying the dishes that Alex washed. Watching Brandi gather the soiled plates, Annie's mood was temporarily meliorated. *She's innocent. He's her father, and she loves him, with no knowledge of what he is capable of. How could I ever destroy her idea of who her father is? Alex would be crushed, but she's tough—a survivor. She might even find someone worthy of her. But the girls only have one father. He can't be replaced. I just pray he never does it to another woman.*

With the Brennan house back in order, the families began to end the evening. The Camerons and Brennans were attending midnight services, but the Daltons opted out. As they said their goodbyes in the wide entry hall, Alex prompted the girls to give their grandparents, Aunt Annie, and Uncle Dan a hug and final thank-you. She also hugged Annie, then Dan, and wished them a Merry Christmas. The moment Annie dreaded all night had arrived. Could she avoid contact with Cole without appearing to blatantly snub him?

As Alex backed away from Dan, Annie stepped forward. Reaching up, she put her arms around Cole's shoulders and gave what appeared to be a warm hug. However, both Annie and Cole knew it was anything but warm—more like a "don's" kiss of death. Her arms were stiff, and she used her swollen belly as an excuse to keep her distance. Cole responded as though there were nothing unusual about the encounter. He then reached out and shook Dan's hand, wishing them both well for the remainder of the holiday.

It's over. I made it, Annie thought as all headed for their respective vehicles.

CHAPTER TWENTY-SIX

The weeks following Christmas passed rather well for Annie. She actually enjoyed the baby shower that Margaret's friends gave at the Piedmont Driving Club. As expected, the luncheon food was excellent and the gifts lavish, including many sterling silver baby items, generous gift certificates, and a luxurious, British pram from Margaret, which was Annie's favorite. Several of the guests commented that they would have loved to pick out cute little outfits for the baby, if only they had known the gender.

Annie had to bite her tongue to keep from saying, "Well, all you had to do was ask Margaret. She would tell you it's a boy." *Alex wouldn't have hesitated to say it,* she thought, which made her smile.

A week after the Atlanta baby shower, Claire called Annie and told her that some of the women at the Providence church also wanted to give a shower.

"St. Mary's Altar Guild wants to give a shower for the baby."

"I don't know, Mom. It's sweet of them, but I'm not too keen on having another party, and I really don't want to listen to more horror stories about how difficult giving birth is."

"Annie, you can't be rude. One day, it will be you telling those stories. Besides, Alice and Phoebe have already begun making plans. They just need you to give them a date and a list of who you want to invite. They are planning to use the fellowship hall, so you can invite as many of your friends as you like."

"I don't want to do this, Mom. But I guess I have no choice. Just tell me when I have to show up, but please don't let them schedule it for a Friday, Saturday or Sunday. Dan never knows when he can come home for the weekend, and I'm not giving up any time with him."

"Is he going to be home when you have the baby?" Claire asked with an edge to her voice.

"He's going to try his best, but I'll be okay if he's not." *Slim chance of his being home, since he thinks the baby is due in March.* The reminder of her lie about the due date brought on the familiar internal conflict. *What am I going to do if this baby is early?* "If this party has to happen, I'd prefer it sooner than later." The fear of an early birth was giving Annie cold chills. *If I have a ten-pound baby six weeks before my due date, what questions will that create?*

After hanging up the phone, Annie sat down at the dining room table with her face buried in her hands and prayed aloud. *"Please, God, please, don't send the baby early. I'll try so hard not to ask anything else if you will just grant this one prayer."* It had become her mantra as her due date grew closer. *I hope God listens to squeaky wheels.*

Two weeks later, the women of the Guild filled the church hall, together with Annie's local friends and her family. The room was decorated with crepe paper streamers in pink and blue, a life-size stork, and multiple balloons. On the long serving tables, plates of finger sandwiches filled with chicken salad, pimento cheese, and country ham alternated with plates of homemade cookies. There was a large basket of potato chips, with a bowl of onion dip, and two bowls brimming with punch made of ginger ale poured over lime sherbet. In the center of the hall, a round table held a three-tiered cake, decorated with sugar roses and miniature, plastic toys in pastel colors. The hostesses had even set up a CD system playing "Brahms Lullaby."

"It's not the Atlanta country club, but the ladies certainly went all out for our town sweetheart," Alex said flippantly.

"I'm not the town sweetheart," Annie snapped.

"Couldn't prove it by me. All I've heard is 'what a sweet girl that Annie Cameron is,' and 'we're all so thrilled that she and that darling husband of hers are finally getting their family,'" Alex said, sarcastically mimicking an anonymous commentator.

Annie wrinkled her face. "Makes you sick, doesn't it?"

"Pretty much, but they made great cookies. Want some more?"

"No, I've had plenty, but you go ahead."

"Think I will. I'll need a king-size sugar boost to get through the silly games and syrupy gift-opening ritual."

By the time Annie finished opening gifts, she had enough baby towels, blankets, baby toiletries, and sleepwear to take care of the first six months of the baby's life. In addition, the Guild gave her a state-of-the-art car seat. Claire gave her a nice, wooden highchair, and Alex gave an electric swing that converted from bed to chair.

"Trust me, kiddo, you can't imagine how much you're going to love that thing until the baby is cranky and you're exhausted," Alex said, as Annie thanked her.

Finally, Margaret contributed a stuffed rocking horse—a large horse. When grouped together, the gifts took up a substantial area of the room.

As the party was breaking up, Annie looked at the array of gifts and said, "I'll never get all this in my van." That was her first mistake of the evening.

"Not a problem," Alex asserted. "I'll send Cole over with a truck in the morning, and he can bring them all to your house. You'll be home tomorrow, won't you?"

Annie was speechless. Because of the pregnant pause, everyone turned to look at her—waiting for her to respond. *This is not going to happen. He is not going to come to my house with me alone—not that he's likely to attempt to rape me again with my body shaped like a pear on steroids, but I'm still not going to be alone with him. Think fast. What can I say?*

"That's a great idea, Alex," Margaret said, breaking the silence. "Annie doesn't need to carry any of these heavy things with Dan out of town."

Thanks a lot, Margaret. If I try to say I don't want to trouble Cole, Alex will just insist. I know her. What am I going to say? What?

"Alex," Annie said and paused, stalling for a little more time to think. "Can I call you about that tomorrow? I was just trying to remember, but I'm fairly sure that I have a doctor's appointment in Atlanta. Can we just leave the large things here at the church until day after tomorrow?" *Damn, I'm good at this. Who knew, when I was the one who always told the truth, that I could become such a gifted liar? I should run for office.*

CHAPTER TWENTY-SEVEN

Before the baby shower, it had seemed like a good idea to invite Martha to share a ride to the party, but on the way home Annie regretted her decision. They had barely fastened seatbelts when Martha launched into a marathon monologue.

"Wasn't it just a wonderful party?" Martha asked, as the van crunched across the graveled parking lot. "Y'all got so many nice presents."

I'm in no mood for useless chit-chat. Wanting to avoid being engaged in a conversation, particularly about the gifts, Annie adjusted the vent on the heater. "It's really cold tonight." Her brain was focused on how to come up with a plan that would keep Alex from sending Cole to the house, and she wanted no distractions.

"Believe me, hon, I was one relieved chickadee when Alex came up with the idea of having Cole get the big stuff home for you."

It might have been a relief for you, Martha, but it has created a nightmare for me.

"Do you know that from the second I saw all those packages, I started worrying about how me and you was going to make all that stuff fit in this van? I couldn't think of anything else. That Alex is just so smart. Right off, she thought about sending Cole to help you."

Annie rolled her eyes, confident that Martha could not see her face in the dark. *Oh, yes. Alex is so smart,* she thought in mental mockery. *So smart to send the fox back to the chicken coop. There's no way that's going to happen—no way.*

"Annie, have you been listening to me, girl? You've haven't said a word," Martha said, and then paused for a minute. "Oh, I know—you're thinkin' about the baby. You've been waiting so long to be a mama.

It's going to be so much fun dressing him up in those cute little jammies. I bet Dan's excited too—probably more than he'll admit."

Why doesn't she shut up? She is making me crazy, but I'd better say something to her.

"Dan is really excited. But tell me, how are your kids doing?" That ought to distract her.

"That's sweet of you to ask. My baby girl is fine, but Raylene is gettin' downright ornery, must be the puberty thing coming on. I don't know if I'll make it through without killing her. And the boys—don't even ask me 'bout the boys. They keep me durn near busier than a cat trying to cover his business on a marble floor. I declare, Annie, those are the messiest creatures that God ever thought about giving breath."

"Really," Annie said, trying to be polite.

"Let me tell you, right now, five young'uns gets a mama a free pass to heaven—'specially when their daddy's on the road all the time. Wish'd I'd known sooner that near 'bout every time Ray Brantley hung his pants on the bedpost, I'd git knocked-up. Don't' you go lettin' Dan keep you pregnant, now that he got the hang of it."

Spare me, God, please. Annie cringed at the course commentary. *Thank goodness, we're home.*

As Annie pulled up the Brantley driveway, Martha offered to stay in the van and go with Annie to her house so that she could help unload the gifts. Annie quickly declined.

"I'll be fine. I'll probably wait until tomorrow morning to take everything in. I'm in kind of a hurry right now. Dan's supposed to call." Actually, that was not accurate. Dan had told her that she should call him when she got home.

"Then run along, sweetie. It must be nice to have a man who calls when he's on the road—Ray Brantley never calls lest he needs me to do something for him."

Poor, dumb Martha, Annie thought, watching Martha get out of the van.

CHAPTER TWENTY-EIGHT

As soon as she was in the house, Annie called Dan. During the brief conversation, she forgot about the dilemma with Alex and Cole, but it didn't take long to reappear after she said goodnight. *What am I going to do? I've got to come up with some excuse that won't look like I'm avoiding him.* Sitting on the side of her bed, she racked her brain for a solution, but only became more and more stressed. *I'm too tired to figure this out now; I'll just have to think about it tomorrow.*

Putting it out of her mind was easier said than done. All night, she tossed and turned, sleeping intermittently and waking with a sudden feeling of panic. But by morning, she had come up with a plan. After taking a shower, and getting dressed, she took her little Bible from the bedside table and went downstairs to prepare breakfast. *I need all the strength I can get. Maybe eating some ham and eggs will compensate for my lack of sleep.*

After the dishes and utensils were washed and put away, she braced herself for what she had to do. Before retrieving her address book from a kitchen drawer, she picked up the Bible and held it up to her heart for a moment. Laying the Bible back on the counter, she flipped through the address book and found the needed number. As she keyed the number into her phone, she drew more and more tense.

As the phone rang on the other end of the line, she again picked up the Bible and mentally repeated a prayer of desperation. *God, please, give me strength, please.* Part of her hoped he would not answer the phone—but he did. Before speaking, she leaned against the kitchen wall for support.

Gripping the receiver and the Bible as though her life depended on it, she paused, and then said, "This is Annie." Swallowing hard, she quickly prayed, *Please, God. Are you listening? Give me the strength to get through this.*

The call must have caught him off guard, because before he could respond, she continued, "You—you, don't say anything—just listen—very carefully." Clenching the Bible, she pressed her back harder against the wall and said, "I don't like you, but my sister and my nieces do. Therefore, I'm stuck with you. But I'm putting you on notice right now. There are going to be rules, and you'd better stick to them."

"Well, good morning to you too, Miss Muffet."

"Shut up. I have no interest in your smart-assed impertinence." *That was good, Annie. You can do it.* "My rules are: first, you will never come to my home without advance notice and my approval; second, you will keep as much distance between us at all family gatherings as can be managed—without being obvious; and third, you will not touch me unless absolutely necessary to avoid arousing curiosity from others—and then it had better be brief and non-personal."

For a second or two, there was silence on the phone. Finally, Cole asked, "You done?"

"For now, but I may add more later. Do you understand?"

In typical cocky manner, he said, "Well, let me see. I think I do—all but one thing."

"Which is?"

"Wasn't I a good fuck?"

Annie slammed down the phone and slid her body down the wall until she was sitting on the floor, tears flooding her face.

The phone rang almost instantly, but Annie didn't move. *I can't talk to anyone, not now.* After six rings, the answering machine picked up, but the caller hung up. She breathed a sigh of relief—not knowing who had called. Then it rang again, following the same pattern—six rings, hang-up. Finally, when it rang for the fourth time, she pulled herself up from the floor and looked at the caller ID. *Damn him, damn him.* Gingerly, she picked up the receiver, but didn't speak.

"Muff, it's about damn time you picked up. I know you're there, and don't you dare hang up. We need to talk."

Annie said nothing. *Why don't I hang up?* Something compelled her to stay on the line. *Poison, he's lethal poison.* Her head told her to hang up, but some mysterious force compelled her to listen. Somehow, as long as she didn't speak, she felt safe.

"Apparently you're mad at me about something, and I guess it's about last summer. But you have to admit, I got you primed for Dan. Your belly's the proof of that."

I hate him—I hate him—the damn-cocky son-of-a-bitch—but he doesn't seem to suspect that I'm carrying his child.

"Listen up, little sister, we're gonna spend a lot of time in the same places over this lifetime because I ain't goin' nowhere. So, you're gonna have to deal with it. Like it or not, I gave you probably the best fuck you ever had, but for some reason, it's made you mad at me."

I hate him, I hate him, I hate him, Annie's brain was screaming. *I can't find words vile enough to express how much I hate him.*

"Well, there ain't nothin' I can do about that. But I know you ain't interested in Danny boy knowin' about it, otherwise, somebody would of said something by now. I admit I don't want Lexi to know, not that she'd believe that it was my fault—but there we are."

Annie was frozen. Her heart was pounding; her knees were going weak. She felt almost as though either the room was spinning or she was spinning. She could smell the faint remnant of the ham she had fried earlier, and it made her nauseous. *I'm going to pass out. I'm going to fall on this floor, and no one will know.* She slid back down the wall, once again to a sitting position. *You can't pass out if you're sitting. I can't pass out.*

Cole was still talking. "If it helps you lighten up some, I can promise, without a speck of doubt, that your virtue is safe with me. You weren't that fuckin' good."

Leaning her head back against the wall, she pushed the button of the telephone, and turned him off, having never said a word.

It took a week for Annie to shake the brutality of Cole's words, but the call had accomplished her goal. He did not deliver the shower gifts to her house. Two days after the call, one of his employees rang the doorbell. The company truck was filled with the gifts. Of course, Cole didn't give her any notice—that would have extracted a larger bite of his ego than he was capable of relinquishing. Although she was annoyed with his inconsideration, she was relieved to not hear his voice again and to have the matter settled.

As each day of February passed, Annie's anxiety over a premature birth decreased. Molly provided comfort, telling her, in one of their weekly telephone conversations, to avoid as much physical activity as possible.

"You might stay abed as much as you can, luv. Try not to disturb the little one, and maybe she'll not disturb you, at least not before your due date."

"If I can just get through the month, I'll be okay."

"You might not be able to stall the little one that long. What is the date that we calculated?"

"You calculated February 24th, using forty weeks from the date my last period began. But, according to my calculation, it's February 18th, using two-hundred, sixty-six days from the date I believe I conceived."

"All you can do is stay quiet, and let God take care of it, Annie. There's no use fretting over what you can't control."

CHAPTER TWENTY-NINE

February 17, 2002, Annie woke with a sharp pain in her lower body, like none she had ever felt. It was only minutes after midnight. "This is it," she whispered in the darkness of her bedroom. "I'm in labor."

There had been pains in the month before that felt similar, like pain combined with a pulling sensation, but none of the magnitude she was feeling. Heidi was on the floor next to her bed. Sitting up, she turned on the light and looked down at the dog. "I'm having a baby girl. This is it."

Reaching for the phone, she dialed her parents. The plan they had made in case it happened while Dan was away would have to go in motion. Claire answered, and Annie could tell she was barely conscious.

"Mom, it's Annie. I think you'd better send Dad over."

"Oh, honey! Are you in labor?"

"Considering I've never done this before, I can't be sure, but it sure feels different."

"Have you timed your pains?"

"There's one coming on now. I don't know how long it's been. Please, tell Dad to hurry."

Frank Brennan must have broken the sound barrier, because he arrived before the fifth contraction started. Annie had her Bible in one hand and her travel clock propped up in her lap.

"The pains are about ten minutes apart. I think we have time to make it to Atlanta," Annie said, her voice a little shaky.

"Mother's in the car. We'll make it, baby. Where's your bag?" Frank's hair hadn't been combed. He had barely taken time to throw on clothes.

As they walked out of the house, Claire got out of the car and went to Annie, putting her arms around her daughter's shoulders.

"Have you called Dan?" she asked.

Annie nodded. "He's making arrangements to fly home, but I don't know how long it's going to take him."

"I hope he gets here in time," Claire said, as Annie backed into the backseat of the Brennan car. There were blankets and a pillow waiting for her, and Frank had left the motor running to keep the car warm.

He put her bag in the trunk and got in the driver's seat. As they pulled out, Claire twisted around to keep an eye on Annie, who was clutching the pillow tight to her abdomen.

"Take deep breaths, honey," Claire said. "Are you sure you want to try to make it to Atlanta?"

Annie was in the throes of a contraction and could only nod. As the pain subsided, she said, "I really want Dr. Windsor to deliver the baby, Mom. I called her service."

It was the longest drive to Atlanta that Annie had ever experienced. During the course of the forty-minute trip, she had five contractions, each increasing in intensity. She did not talk. If her parents said anything, she was too absorbed in her situation to listen. Between pains, her only thought was the fact that she was actually about to give birth.

When they pulled into the hospital's emergency room entrance, Claire jumped out of the car, nearly running into the building. The waiting room was empty, and only one in-take clerk was on duty. The clerk immediately dispatched an orderly with a wheelchair to the car.

Once she passed the doorway of the hospital, Annie breathed a sigh of relief. Although a hospital was not her favorite place, in this instance, she was happy to be there.

The attendant took her directly up to the maternity floor, leaving her parents to answer the bureaucratic questions at reception. Annie had given Claire her wallet with insurance cards and identification. The ride through the sanitized corridors was a blur, bringing back a fleeting memory of the abortion clinic months before.

A young nurse took charge of Annie once she arrived in the delivery area. The woman was gentle and sympathetic, helping Annie through the prep procedure.

Throughout the pregnancy, Annie resigned herself to the idea of going through the delivery alone. There was no need to whine about Dan's availability because there was nothing he could do about it. She had told herself she didn't need him. But at that moment, she wanted him there.

Soon after Annie was prepped and placed in a labor room, Dr. Windsor appeared. Through her pain clouded vision, she welcomed the sight of the woman who could take care of everything. With tears in her eyes, Annie looked up at the doctor and said, "Thank you for coming."

Dr. Windsor smiled and patted Annie's arm. "Of course I'm here, Annie. You didn't think I would let you have this baby without me, did you?"

Annie's labor waxed and waned over the next four hours. Her mother had come in to serve as her Lamaze coach. Both were growing tired. At a few minutes before six, the door opened, and in walked Dan.

The weight of the world lifted from Annie's shoulders. She could take anything with him there. "You made it," she said, weakly, smiling with tears in her eyes.

"You damn right I made it. Cost me a fortune in cabbie tips, plus a little abuse of authority, but I'm here." He leaned over and kissed her, taking her hand and holding it tight—his paper hospital gown crackling as he moved. "Now, let's finish what you've started."

Thirty minutes later, Daniel Russell Cameron, IV arrived.

Weighing in at eight pounds, two ounces and measuring twenty-one inches long, the general consensus was that Annie had miscalculated her due date. No one seemed to be at all curious as to how such a miscalculation could have occurred.

"Babies work on their own timetables," Claire said. Science just thinks they have it figured out. If it were all that scientific, we would know when our teeth were coming and in and falling out."

Annie was astounded at how she felt when the nurse put Danny in her arms for the first time. *I know women have been having babies since Eve, but this feeling is so overwhelming that I can't believe it happens every day.* Mesmerized by her delicate little baby, she was hardly aware of even Dan at her side, but thankful he was. She took the tiny hand and Danny's fingers curled around her index finger. Each little digit was perfectly formed with a miniature nail at the end. Blond fuzz covered the top of his head and blue eyes gazed up at her. Annie was so enraptured with her precious gift that she ignored the fact that his coloring matched Cole's.

By the time young Danny was twelve hours old, most of the family had been to the hospital to greet the newest member. The only one absent was Cole, for which Annie was grateful. There had been no further contact between them after the ugly phone call following the baby shower. Whether obeying her rules, or by circumstance, he told Alex he had critical business matters to transact when she told him she was taking the girls to the hospital to see Annie and the baby.

Alex arrived with all three girls and a large flower arrangement containing stargazer lilies and roses that filled the room with fragrance. "Well, didn't you go and upstage me, little sister—a boy on your first try. I hope you know that Cole Dalton is pea-green."

Annie felt the blood in her veins go cold. *He's jealous over his own child. Stop it! Don't think about him.*

Not to be outdone, Margaret immediately ordered an arrangement of exotic tropical flowers, including orange birds-of-paradise, white orchids, pink ginger, and red anthuriums. Before the day was out, numerous flowers had arrived, and Annie's room looked like the viewing room at a mortuary.

When Dan walked in the room after being gone for a cup of coffee, he looked around and said, "Is this a hospital or funeral home?"

Annie laughed. "I know what you mean. I'm afraid to go to sleep because if I wake up among all these flowers, I may think I'm dead."

By the time the last of the family left, it was nearly dinner time. Annie had dozed off and on during the day despite the visitors. With them gone, she and Dan finally had the opportunity to share an intimate moment. Reaching into the pocket of his jacket, Dan pulled out a small box and handed it to her.

"What's this?" she asked.

"Open it and find out."

Inside the box was a heavy gold bracelet. Hanging from one of the links was a heart-shaped charm on which was engraved "Annie and Dan" in script.

Tears filled her eyes. "It's beautiful."

Dan smiled, took the bracelet out of the box and wrapped it around her wrist. "I'll have the other side engraved with his name and the date."

She raised her arms up to him and he leaned forward so that she could hug him. "I can't believe you did that."

"You didn't think I would let you give me the greatest gift a woman can give a man and not mark the day with something special, did you?"

After kissing her again, he walked over to where the baby was sleeping in the neonatal crib.

"Is it just me, or is he the most beautiful baby you have ever seen?" Annie asked, as Dan stood by the crib, looking down at the sleeping baby.

Smiling with obvious paternal pride, he said, "Absolutely. You did a magnificent job, angel."

She wanted to say, "We did a magnificent job," but the words wouldn't come out. The euphoria of the moment had given away to reality. *How can I do this to him? I should have put him first. Was I really protecting Alex and the girls? Or, was I afraid that he would reject me? Reject the baby?*

"Are you okay, honey?" Dan asked. Annie's face was obviously strained.

"I'm fine," she said and smiled at him. "I just had a little cramp in my stomach."

He walked back to her bedside and took her hand. "Can I get you anything?"

"No, I'm fine." *Lies, lies, lies. All I seem to do is lie.*

Giving her hand a squeeze, he settled himself in the chair between her bed and the crib, where he stayed for the remainder of the evening until a nurse came in at 9:00 p.m. to shoo him out.

"You've got to give your wife some time to rest. She's had a busy day," the elderly woman said.

At first he protested, but Annie insisted that he go to his parents' house and get some sleep. "You need to go," Annie told him. "You've been dozing in the chair for the past hour. Besides, I doubt that I'll be awake much longer."

Reluctantly, Dan accepted the instructions. Standing up, he moved closer to the bed, leaned over, and kissed Annie on the forehead as he prepared to leave. "Don't run off before I get back," he said, and winked.

"I'll try not to," she responded and blew him a kiss.

As Dan walked out the door, Annie moved the telephone from the bedside table to her side and pushed the button to lower the angle of the bed.

"Molly, it's me, Annie. I had the baby. He's the most beautiful baby in the world. I'm so happy."

PART II

By late March of 2006, Danny was a precocious four-year-old. Annie doted on him to the exclusion of the rest of her interests. She stopped making jewelry for the boutique soon after he was born and shied away from any activities that did not include the child. Although she neglected Dan, he seemed too busy to notice.

His career continued to consume much of his time and attention, even though it had settled down considerably since the demands of 2001. He traveled less but got home late most evenings and often worked Saturdays. If he noticed that Annie was obsessed with Danny, he had not said anything.

Annie seldom allowed her thoughts to stray in the direction of Danny's paternity. Although the boy's hair stayed blond like Cole's, and he had eyes the color of a changing sea, one minute blue, the next green, no one had commented on how little he resembled Dan. In fact, to Annie's consternation, Margaret was constantly finding similarities between Dan and the child. It was like salt in a sore that Margaret would point out mannerisms or expressions that she attributed to the Cameron clan.

When Margaret arrived bearing more gifts for her grandson than in the bag of a department store Santa, Annie choked on her guilt and resentment, but allowed her mother-in-law to spoil the child. Annie's motives were not all altruistic. Danny was becoming spoiled, and she could point the finger at Margaret's generosity to divert attention from her own indulgence. Nonetheless, it was hard listening to Margaret's gushing about what a little Cameron her boy was.

"If she knew he isn't her grandchild," she told Molly one day on a rare lunch date in Atlanta, "he would never see her again."

Annie had registered Danny for a preschool program in the city the previous fall. He went only two mornings a week. If she had not wanted to give him every educational advantage, she would never have let him go for the six hours each week. The day he started seemed like the first step toward his emancipation, sending Annie into depression. To reduce her stress, she volunteered at the school and justified her action on a theory that driving back and forth twice each day was not practical. Since she had to fill the time, it was a valid excuse, albeit a thinly disguised attempt to conceal the fact that she couldn't quite cut the proverbial umbilical cord.

Going to Atlanta also provided her an opportunity to see Molly more often. Usually, they had lunch with Danny included, but once in a while, Annie would leave Danny in the extended care for an adult lunch. On rare occasions, she and Danny met Dan for lunch, which was always a special treat. Passing near her parents' house on the way home, they frequently stopped for a visit. One day at the beginning of March, Alex was there for lunch as well.

It was a pretty day, with the sun shining on the Brennan backyard. Danny went out to play with Charlie, his grandparents' black cocker spaniel. As the door closed, Alex asked Annie, "When was the last time you and Dan went out on a date?"

Annie thought for a second, but before she could answer, Alex said, "You can't even remember, can you?"

"Of course I can. We went out to dinner Valentine's," Annie said in a defensive tone.

"And before that?"

"I don't know…maybe our anniversary."

"Annie, that was nearly a year ago. You need to get out more—pay attention to your husband," Alex said. "Why don't you and Dan go slumming with Cole and me this weekend? You might surprise yourself and have a good time."

A roadhouse, pool, beer, and Cole—no, not my idea of a fun evening.

"Of course if you guys think it's too far beneath you—"

"Of course not," Annie interrupted, frowning. *Well, partly,* she thought, but said, "It's Danny. He's gotten to be such a handful. I never know when he's going to go to sleep at night, so it's hard to leave him with a sitter."

Alex made a face, implying her disgust with Annie's statement. "That's BS and you know it. Mom and Dad would love to have him spend the night here. Right, Mom?"

Claire smiled. "Dad and I always love having Danny around."

"But you haven't been feeling well since you had that bout with the flu, Mom," Annie protested. "I don't want to impose on you."

"Annie Cameron, you're obsessed with that child," Alex continued. "You need to think about having some quality time with your husband. What you need is another baby."

No way. I can't have another baby. If we try again, and I don't conceive, Dan might want to go through testing again. He might be sterile. I'm not buying that lottery ticket. Besides, Danny needs all my attention.

"Dan and I have quality time together. It just so happens that he enjoys including Danny." Annie was still careful to avoid saying "his son," even though more than four years had passed, and for most of the time, she blocked memories of Cole.

But Alex was determined. "If you're really worried about imposing on Mom and Dad, one of the girls would be glad to help. Rhys can stay over. It'll give her something to do."

"Come on, Alex. Why would a high school senior want to take care of a four-year-old on a Saturday night?"

"Because she doesn't have another damn thing to do. She's grounded because of coming home at 2:00 a.m. last weekend from a date with that Carson kid. Cole was livid. He restricted her for a month and threatened to do worse if it ever happens again. She had me nearly out of my mind with pictures of her lying in a ditch somewhere, bleeding to death."

Considering Cole's libido, I'm not surprised that he was upset— probably afraid she was going to follow in her mother's footsteps and make him a grandfather before she graduates from high school. I doubt that an auto accident is what worried him.

"It will keep her from moping around the house and fighting with her sisters."

"Will you leave the other girls alone?"

"They are fine. Brandi's sixteen—a little immature, but she babysits all the time. They'll be fine. They know how to reach us if there's an emergency, and no one is going to come around the house with Cole's dogs in the yard.

"I can't believe that Rhys will be in college this fall. With Brandi going next year, your nest will be almost empty. Doesn't that scare you?" *I can't imagine Danny going away. It's not fair. You have them, give them your heart, and then they leave you.*

"A little, but Brandi's such a homebody that she may do community college and live at home. Stop changing the subject. You're stonewalling. What time can you meet us at Blackie's Saturday night? They've got a new cook and the ribs are great. There's a pretty good band, too. Cole and I always have a blast."

I bet you do, but don't just assume that we will come. There's no way that sounds like a good idea to me. "I can't say yes until I check with Dan. He might have to work Saturday, which could make him too tired to go out," Annie said, stonewalling to keep Alex from asserting more pressure.

With a snap of her fingers, Alex came back with, "No problem, I'll check with Dan. He won't tell me no."

Damn it, Alex. Nobody tells you no, except maybe Cole. "That's not necessary. I'll ask him and let you know," Annie said, with a note of finality in her tone.

After dinner that night, fearful of Alex getting to him first, Annie told Dan about the invitation. His reaction shocked her. Although in the early days of their marriage, they had gone to the tavern with the

Daltons, it had been years—long before Danny. However, to her cha-grin, he was all for the idea.

It wasn't that Annie objected to shooting pool and country line danc-ing, but she was in no way interested in spending an evening with Cole. Time had mellowed, but not erased, the hostility she felt toward him. Since Danny's birth, there had been no excessive contact. He followed her rules and managed to avoid intimate moments. At family gather-ings, Cole focused on either the men of the family or the children.

As much as Annie hated to admit it, he was great with Danny—probably too great. Danny loved Uncle Cole and ran to him whenever the opportunity arose. On one such occasion, Dan made the comment, "It looks like Danny prefers Uncle Cole to his dad." It wasn't said pet-ulantly, rather in the spirit of humor, but it wasn't funny to Annie.

"Maybe you should get an assignment closer to home, so that he sees you more," Alex had quipped. She meant no harm, but Annie took it personally.

Damn her. Can she ever keep her mouth shut? Dan feels guilty enough about how much he's gone. He doesn't need her to rub it in.

The moment passed, but looking at Danny, Annie wished his hair would turn darker. It had stayed light blond, which others thought came from the Brennan family. She believed otherwise. Annie lived in fear that as he grew older, the boy would resemble Cole more and more. His eyes were becoming greener every year, and he tanned easily, which was a gene he could have inherited from either man. During the two-year physical, the pediatrician told her that he was likely to grow to over six feet. Cole was six-two, while Dan was barely five-eleven. She told no one. Like a puppy, Danny had big feet for his age, thereby reinforc-ing the idea that he was destined to be tall.

***

As they got ready to meet Alex and Cole that Saturday evening, An-nie was in a bad mood. Her mother had picked Danny up so that Annie could dress in peace, but she was still fretting over what to wear. "I really don't want to do this," she said to Dan, as she laid several pairs of jeans out on the bed. "I know you agreed to go just out of courtesy. It's not your thing."

"I'm kind of looking forward to it. Two beers and my neck will turn red."

"Right," she said. "A year of Jeff Foxworthy lessons wouldn't turn your blue blood to red."

He grabbed her around the waist and pulled her close. "Just you wait 'til we get home tonight. I'll show you who's a redneck and who's a blue blood." With that, he kissed the top of Annie's forehead, turned her around toward the closet, and playfully slapped her rear. "Get ready, woman, we're gonna have a hot time tonight."

Annie couldn't help but laugh. *Mr. Black Suit, White Shirt, and Striped Tie is putting on a plaid shirt, faded jeans, boots, and a cowboy hat. How unnatural is that?*

When she finally settled on a pair of "mommy jeans" and a full-cut white shirt with a red bandana-print scarf, she announced she was ready to conquer cowboy country.

"Where's your hat?" Dan asked as they started for the door.

"I'm not wearing one of those ridiculous things."

"Oh, yes you are. We are going first-class country. You'll never be in the spirit without the headgear."

"I have no desire to be in the spirit, only to survive the experience."

"You're not going to be a spoilsport. March yourself upstairs and get a hat, or I'll do it for you," he said, trying to sound stern, while smiling.

CHAPTER THIRTY-ONE

The Camerons arrived at Blackie's Bar and Grill a little before seven. The Daltons were already at a pool table. As Annie and Dan walked in, Cole spotted them and raised his beer mug in the air, signaling them to the next room over, where their booth was. Alex was leaning over the table, sizing up her shot in a game of 8-ball. She needed to set up for the next shot by getting the proper spin on the ball.

"Come on, sugar, put the right English on the ball," Cole shouted to her.

"I'm not listening to you. You'll screw me over," Alex shouted back, without looking up. She chalked the end of her stick, then drew it back and took the shot. The cue ball soared across the table, striking the target ball with just enough speed and spin to sink the 11 ball, and then to bounce off the rail, thereby setting up her next shot. From that point, she ran the table to Cole's chagrin.

"Luck, that's all it is—luck," Cole grumbled, as they walked over to the booth where Dan and Annie had already seated themselves. "Let me get you guys a beer, while Lexi gloats. Have to let her win occasionally so she'll keep coming out here."

"I hope you guys don't believe a word he's saying," Alex quipped. His ego is so inflated that he can't stand to lose, especially to a woman and even worse—to his wife."

I have no trouble believing that, Annie thought.

"You have to make allowances for us men, Alex. We haven't gotten over the idea that you women have the vote, yet," Dan said, smiling as he reached his fist out to rap knuckles with Cole.

Alex leaned over the table and gave Annie a hug. "Love the hats," she said, pointing to Dan and adding, "How did you get him to dress the part?"

"Actually, it was the other way around. He made me wear this thing," Annie said, taking the hat off as she spoke.

Cole sauntered back out to the bar area. When he returned, he had four tall mugs of draft beer that he slid to the center of the table, ignoring the overflow that sloshed over the rims. "I told Lurleen to order us up a couple of slabs of ribs."

Annie's eyes followed the mugs, watching the small puddles of beer collect on the wood. Alex immediately reached for the metal container at the end of the table, pulling out several napkins and blotting up the stray beer.

"You are so damned sloppy, Cole. Can't you watch what you're doing?" Alex chided.

"Love you too, darlin'," he said, grabbing her chin and kissing her on the mouth, before sliding down in the booth.

Annie hid her irritation by looking around at the cheap pictures of horses and cowboys on the walls of the room.

Settling down on the seat, Cole looked across at Dan and said, "Long time, no see, Danny boy. You catchin' all the bad guys?"

"Doing my best," Dan responded as he reached for two of the mugs and passed one to Annie.

As the small talk continued, Annie fiddled with her mug of beer. She had no intention of drinking it. Beer was never her drink of choice, plus she was not consuming alcohol with Cole on the premises.

"Drink up, Muff," Cole said.

You just have to call me Muff, don't you, you bastard? I bet you would love for me to get drunk, she thought. "I'd better stick to soft drinks. I'm driving," she said, forcing a smile.

"Honey, a sip or two of beer won't put you in jeopardy," Dan said.

Thanks a lot, sweetheart. You're a real big help. "I'm really more in the mood for a Coke," she said, looking up at Dan. "Would you mind getting me one, pretty please?" She looked up at him with the expression of a pleading child.

Patting her on the hand, Dan got up and started for the bar. When he returned with Annie's cold drink, the band had begun playing in the next room and more patrons were beginning to collect. Several new couples came into the food service area and filled booths near Annie's group. The singles tended to congregate at the bar. With additional people, plus the music, the noise made it harder and harder to carry on conversation. Looking at her watch, Annie said, "I'm going outside and call Mom to check on Danny."

"Will you sit down and relax," Alex chided. "Danny is fine. Mom and Dad raised two children, and Brandi's there. Give it a rest."

Annie ignored her, pushing at Dan to move out of her way.

"He's okay, sweetheart. Alex is right," Dan said as he grabbed her hand.

Annie pulled it away, trying to resist the impulse to snap at both of them. "I won't be but a minute. You guys do whatever, and I'll be right back."

"Might as well let her go, man," Cole interjected. "You can't change the mind of a Brennan woman. I oughta know."

Your help, I don't need, Annie thought as she walked away from the booth.

Danny was fine, of course. Annie returned to the table just as the food arrived. After biting into a rib, she had to admit that it was good—meaty and tender. The sauce was amazing. Dan had finished his beer and began drinking the one meant for her as he ate. *He's really enjoying himself. He deserves to have some fun. I'll just have to get through this. Cole can't do a thing to me with Dan and Alex around.* Annie had to admit that it would have actually been fun if she had not been sitting across the table from Cole.

Wiping her face and fingers, Annie said to Alex, "You were right. The ribs here are delicious."

Scrunching up her dirty napkins and dropping them on her plate, Alex announced that she wanted to dance. The waitress had barely completed clearing away the dishes. Jerking Cole's shirt to get his attention, she commanded, "Come on. Dance with me."

"One more beer and I'll be ready to do whatever you like," he said.

"I'm not that patient. Get your you-know-what off that bench and dance with me, or I'll find some cowboy who will."

Oh my gosh. She is on fire tonight.

"Careful, darlin'. You're talking to your lord and master."

I'm going to be sick. Annie reached into her purse for a tissue to hide her disgust.

"Okay then, I'll be careful," Alex replied. "Get up off your ass and dance with me—lord and master."

At that, Dan and Cole burst into laughter.

"I guess she told you, Cole," Dan said.

"What can I say? I tried my heavy hand, and as usual, it got slapped." With that response, Cole got up and grabbed Alex so hard she lost her balance and fell into him. "You wanna dance, woman? Let's do it."

Once they were away from the table, Annie looked at Dan and said, "We don't have to stay if you don't want to."

He reached over and patted her knee. "I'm actually having a good time," he said, smiling. "Would you like to dance?"

Annie looked at him for a moment. *He's really enjoying himself.* "You bet. I'd love to dance," she said, squeezing the hand he extended.

CHAPTER THIRTY-TWO

Although the dance floor was filled with couples, Cole and Alex dominated.

"You have to give it to Cole, he knows his way around the floor," Dan said, as he took Annie in his arms.

"I suppose he does," she forced herself to reply. *He knows his way around a lot of places.*

When the song ended, the band leader invited the crowd to join in a line-dance as they began to play "Achy Breaky Heart." The lead singer bore a loose resemblance to Billy Ray Cyrus. Dan and Annie were about to head back to the booth when Alex grabbed Dan by the arm.

"Whoa. Where do you think you're going?"

Dan smiled. "I'm line-dance challenged. I think we'd better sit this one out."

"Bullshit. Anyone can do the Achy Breaky. Don't you dare sit down."

"We, or at least I, don't know the steps," Dan protested.

"Just follow us. You'll catch on in no time."

Dan shrugged, but acquiesced, accepting that it was useless to fight Alex.

Amazing himself, he caught on to the routine quickly and seemed to get a kick out of his newfound talent. Annie knew the steps well, having danced it in her senior year of high school when the Cyrus record first came out. By the end of the song, they were all laughing and having a great time, even Annie, despite herself.

Following "Achy Breaky Heart," the band changed tempo with the Cyrus look-a-like singing Keith Urban's hit "Making Memories of Us." Dan took Annie's hand and started to turn her around in dance hold.

Alex stopped him, "Let's swap partners," she said. "We need a little variety to spice things up."

Damn, damn, damn. Despite her best efforts, Annie frowned. *How do I get out of this?*

Before Annie could open her mouth to protest, Alex was dragging Dan across the floor, and Cole had grabbed her hand.

"Great idea," Cole said, taking a firm hold, as he pulled her close.

Annie stiffened, words failing her.

"Relax," he whispered in her ear. "I'm not going to assault you with forty witnesses watching."

"There are many types of rape," she replied. "And you're capable of every one."

She was trapped, again. Create a scene, and too many questions would arise. Alex would dig and dig to find out why she objected to dancing with Cole. Even Dan would wonder. She had no choice but to tough it out. Even if she feigned illness, she might not be believed.

To make matters worse, the lyrics of the ballad were like alcohol on a raw wound. *If only I were in Dan's arms, I would love dancing to this song. I could just melt against him. Think about Dan*, she told herself. *Don't think that this is Cole Dalton holding me with an iron grip. No wonder I couldn't fight him off, he's strong as a bear with muscles like stone.*

She tried her best to keep her body from having full contact with his, but it was a futile effort. Whether by accident or design, when he whirled her around, he swayed in such a manner that torsos met and memories ignited. He was a blur of the sexy young man she had secretly lusted after, the tender father to his daughters, the savage animal who stripped away her dignity and damned her soul—and, he was the father of her child.

Feeling her body tense, Cole whispered, "Just relax and dance with me. You might actually enjoy it, and it's about damn time you got over the spur you've got up your ass."

"Never," she said. "And why don't you change your cologne? That one makes me nauseated."

"Couldn't do that, Muff. Alex loves it. Says it turns her on."

The song seemed like it would never come to an end. No matter how hard she tried to blank out her mind, images of his naked body, her useless resistance, and his insolent attitude kept reappearing. After the final series of turns, ending in a deep dip, he leaned over her and said, "Was it as good for you as it was for me?"

"I don't think you want to hear the answer to that question," she said, walking briskly in front of him back to the table.

Once back in the booth, Annie moved herself to the corner, wedged between the seat and the wall. It felt more secure having two solid surfaces to lean against. She finished the last of her Coke, while Dan finished the last of his second mug of beer. As the waitress passed, Cole waved her down and asked for a couple of pitchers of beer.

"We're a little dry here, Lurleen. You've been neglecting us."

"I'd never do that, sugar," she replied with a wink. "I'll have you refills in a shake."

She'd better be careful who she winks at, or she might get more than she bargained for, Annie thought. *Or, maybe, she's already been there, done that. I wouldn't put it past Cole to hide a mistress in plain sight.*

"Penny for your thoughts," Alex said, startling Annie.

"They're not worth it. You'd want your money back."

The sound system screeched about that time, making it impossible to converse for a minute or two. When it was rectified, Alex seemed to have forgotten her question.

"Don't you guys have a big anniversary coming up in about a month?" Alex asked, changing the subject.

"Tenth," Dan said, smiling and reaching for Annie's hand.

"Have you made any plans yet?" Alex continued.

Before Annie could say no, Dan blocked her with, "As a matter of fact, I have."

Annie looked at him with a puzzled expression.

"I haven't told Annie yet, but I've planned a second honeymoon to Paris."

Annie couldn't believe what she was hearing. She was touched by his thoughtfulness but also horrified. *I can't leave Danny. I can't get on an airplane without him. What if something happened and I never came home? The plane could crash. Who would love him?*

"That is so romantic, Dan. My sister is a lucky gal." Alex turned to Annie. "Aren't you thrilled?"

What do I say now? "This catches me totally off guard. Of course, it's so sweet, but Dan, have you thought about Danny? It's not just the two of us anymore."

"Well, that's certainly no problem," Alex said, before Dan could respond. "Danny will stay with us. The girls would love it, and Cole would adore having a son for a while. How long did you plan to stay?"

Cole having a son? Over my dead body. He's not having my child. Sperm donors—felon sperm donors—don't get paternal privileges.

"That sounds great, Alex," Dan said. "Don't you agree, angel?"

Annie hesitated, trying to find the right response. "I'm stunned. I don't know what to say. We couldn't impose on you like that, Alex. A four-year-old, especially a boy, is a handful. He would invade your house like a cyclone."

"Nonsense. Uncle Cole can keep him in line. You guys deserve some time to yourselves. I don't think you've had a child-free holiday since Danny was born. We can keep him a month if you like."

Cole keep my child in line? He'll roast in hell first. He better not ever lay a hand on Danny. I would tear his eyes out of the sockets.

"No, no. We won't be gone that long. I'm thinking about ten days to two weeks. Enough time to do Paris up right and to touch down on the Rivera." Turning to Annie, Dan said, "Remember when we were in France on our honeymoon, you said you wanted to visit Provence to see where Monet lived?" He squeezed her hand. "I promised you then that I'd bring you back. It's about time I made good on that promise."

Caught between fear of leaving her child and fear of offending her devoted husband, she struggled to respond. *His eyes are like a cocker spaniel, so gentle, so trusting and hopeful. How can I disappoint him?* "This is too much for me to absorb tonight. We'll talk about it and get back to you, Alex. But thank you for making such a generous offer."

"Annie Cameron, you've got to cut the cord. You can't hover over that child forever. Go to Paris with this hunk of a husband of yours and make another baby."

Annie's face burned but was camouflaged by the dimly lit room.

The discussion ended at that point when the band began playing one of Alex's favorite songs. Her desire to get in the groove exceeded her desire to lecture her sister.

When the evening ended, Annie had to admit that for the most part, it had been fun. Alex and Cole did keep people laughing. They verbally boxed back and forth, but it all appeared to be in good fun and kept Dan amused, but not always Annie. As they said their goodnights, Alex hugged Dan and told him how glad she was to have him as a brother. Annie had no choice but to hug Cole as well. As she put her arms around his shoulders, he leaned forward and whispered, "It wasn't as bad as going to the dentist was it, darlin'?"

"It was fun. I had a good time," Annie said, loud enough for Dan and Alex to hear.

Once behind the steering wheel, headed home, all she could think was, *I can't go to Europe. That's all there is to it. I can't go.*

The trip wasn't mentioned during the drive home, but once they were in their room, preparing for bed, Annie decided she had to clear the air.

"Dan, it is so sweet of you to want to take me back to Paris, but we can't leave Danny here. Maybe we should postpone the trip until he's older, unless you would consider taking him with us?"

Dan didn't say anything for a minute or two. His back was to Annie. When he turned around, she saw from his body language and facial expression that he was not happy with what she said.

"No, Annie. I would not consider taking Danny with us. I love him as much as you do, but right now, I need my wife, not my son's mother."

"But, that's the same thing."

"No, Annie. It's not. I don't think you realize how wrapped up you've become in Danny. I feel like a guest in this house. I know I'm away a lot, but I need a fair share of your attention."

Annie looked at him, stunned. She felt a sinking feeling in her stomach.

"I'm not going to beg you, or even discuss it more than to say: our marriage needs this trip."

CHAPTER THIRTY-THREE

Upon opening the door of her condo a few days after the Camerons' date with the Daltons, Molly embraced Annie with a hearty hug and ushered her inside. Molly was off work for Good Friday. The smell of fresh flowers and baking bread permeated the atmosphere and combined with the sound of Chopin playing softly in the background to create a warm and inviting ambiance.

"Would you have a cuppa tea, luv? 'Tis freshly brewed."

"I would," Annie answered, much of her stress already evaporating in the tranquility of the setting.

Molly disappeared into the kitchen as Annie settled down in an over-stuffed chair and looked around the room. Houseplants thrived on the sill of the large window behind the couch. The African violets were in full bloom. The older woman obviously had a way with plants. Angus, Molly's red tabby, languished in the sunlight beaming in on the back of the sofa and caused Annie to think of Deli who also liked to nap in the path of sun rays.

When Molly returned with two cups of tea, Annie spilled out all the details of her dilemma. Finishing the story, she said, "He implied... no...he clearly spelled out that our marriage is in trouble. What am I going to do? I'm terrified of leaving Danny, and there's no way I could leave him with my sister's family."

Molly listened intently, letting her talk, uninterrupted, but reached over and put her hand on top of Annie's.

"Oh, Molly, I might as well tell you…. 'Adam Henry,' Danny's father, is my brother-in-law," Annie blurted out in a flow of tears.

"I had figured as much, child," Molly responded. "There's no one I could imagine you would otherwise protect."

"Molly, Danny looks more and more like the rogue all the time. If he spends two weeks with them, I may come home to a mini-Cole. The child already thinks his uncle is awesome because he jokes around so much and takes Danny out with the farm animals—the horses, the dogs, the cows. Danny says Cole has promised to teach him how to ride a big horse and how to build a campfire. My son will be shooting pool and drinking beer by the time we get back. And what if, after spending so much time with Danny, Cole notices all their similarities and does the math?"

"Nonsense, dearie. Every little tyke loves horses and dogs and all the things that a farm has. It's not genetic, it hormonal. I know how you be feeling about the bastard, but it's been a long time, and he's not done anything else, now has he?"

"Wasn't what he did enough?"

"I'm not defending him, child. I'm trying to help you work this out. You've told me that the man is good with his own, right?"

With some reluctance, Annie agreed.

"Then, you must go, luv. Your Dan is a good husband. Many 'tis the lass who would kill for one like him, and even the virtue of a saint can be tried by a tempting filly. Dan wants to take you to Paris. Go, darlin'."

"And let Danny stay with Cole?"

"You know, 'tis hate the bastard that I do. But this is your marriage, luv."

***

It took all the courage Annie could muster to make the phone call accepting Alex's offer. Once done, she turned her efforts toward overcoming her fear that tragedy was lurking in the air over the Atlantic. Molly had suggested that she research commercial aircraft statistics. The Internet proved to be a Godsend. By the time they arrived at Harts-field International in early June, bound for Charles De Gaulle, Annie was nearly as confident as anyone in the terminal. The hardest part had been saying goodbye to Danny, but her departure didn't appear to faze him. He was so excited about staying with Aunt Alex and Uncle Cole that he hardly stood still long enough for Annie to kiss him goodbye.

Watching Dan, as they waited to board the plane, Annie was thankful that she had been able to work through her anxieties. *Danny's fine. He's going to have a blast at the farm. The girls will spoil him rotten, and he won't even know I'm gone. How much damage can Cole do in two weeks? Most of the time, he won't be home.*

***

Paris was all that Annie and Dan had hoped for. They stayed in a quaint, little hotel near the Arc de Triomphe. They strolled along the Champs-Elysées, the Latin Quarter, the Left Bank, and consumed sumptuous French cuisine. They spent an entire day at Versailles, finally touring Marie Antoinette's cottage. One night, they dined at the top of the Eiffel Tower and at Moulin Rouge on another. But for Annie, the highlight of Paris was cruising on the Seine after dark. She insisted that they repeat the excursion several times and always on one of the boats with an open-air deck on top. Cuddled under Dan's arm, she soaked in the moist air and the view of the brilliant Paris lights, as the boat glided on the water. It was a perfect prelude to a romantic evening.

CHAPTER THIRTY-FOUR

On one of their last days in the city, Annie told Dan that she was planning a surprise for him, provided he followed her instructions. "If you obey my every command, without question, you will be rewarded in a manner you will remember for a lifetime," she said to him, with a mischievous smile on her face. They were walking along a side street populated with small boutiques, flower shops and art galleries.

As they passed a recessed boutique, Annie lingered, gazing at the window display. "Stop," she demanded.

Dan was three paces ahead of her. He turned with the typical husband's expression indicating "what now?"

She beckoned him back to where she stood, and said, "I feel wicked."

Dan had failed to notice that they were in front of a lingerie shop.

"You feel wicked? Define that, please."

"No questions, remember? Let's go in. Pretend I'm your mistress, and you are buying me something extremely expensive and wickedly sexy for a very naughty night."

Dan started laughing. "I don't know who you are right now, or what you've done with my wife, but I like the sound of it. But I warn you, if I go in there and buy you something wickedly expensive for a naughty night, you're going to pay up, big time."

"Just do as you're told. I think you'll like what I have in mind."

"If it involves trashy underwear and orgies, I'm all in."

In the shop, Annie played her role. She behaved as though Dan was her sugar daddy. She made him choose an outfit, which she could tell embarrassed him, but he was a good sport and went along with her charade. From an array of forms displaying various undergarments and provocative nightwear, Dan chose a black-lace bra and a wisp of a lace skirt attached to a thong bikini. As he paid, he did not look at the clerk. His face had acquired a pink glow.

"You weren't blushing in there, were you?" Annie teased as they left the boutique.

"Damned right, I was blushing. You damned-well better make this worth my while," he said, smiling at her. "I felt like Adam taking that bite from the apple." He grabbed her hand and jerked her to his side, then whispered in her ear, "I can assure you, Mrs. Cameron, I'm getting my money's worth tonight, with interest."

That evening began with dinner and another cruise on the Seine. Throughout both, Annie acted mysteriously mischievous. On returning to the hotel, she lit candles around the suite and instructed Dan to order a bottle of champagne. He ordered two. She set up her portable CD player with a disc of music for lovers, slipped into the bathroom for a shower, and changed into a silky peignoir under which she wore the risqué lingerie purchased that afternoon. When she came out, Dan was sitting on a love seat in the suite, sipping champagne. He wore the jeans and shirt of the day, but now, the shirt was unbuttoned, hanging loose and exposing his toned torso. He had a glass of champagne waiting for her on a Louis IV table by the small couch.

"No one's driving tonight," he said, handing her the glass. "You better be dressed appropriately under that."

"That's for me to know, and you to find out," she said, taking a sip from the flute. "But, first, you have to dance with me."

"Drink up, and we'll dance," he said, standing up.

Annie drank the contents of the glass like a pro. Dan then refilled it but left it on the table while he took her in his arms.

"You smell good," he said.

"You like it?"

"I do," he responded in a whisper as he held her tight, and they undulated in unison to the rhythm of "When a Man Loves a Woman." Intermittently, he would turn, causing her negligee to flare in the breeze created. As the turn slowed, he would swirl her down in a flourish that combined with the champagne to give her a rush, as her long hair brushed the floor. Effortlessly, he would then pull her back upright and press her against his chest to resume the swaying in place. As the sexual tension increased, with one hand, he slowly began to remove her peignoir.

"You're overdressed," he whispered, close to her ear.

As it fell to the floor, she stood in front of him, back-lit by the soft glow of candlelight and clad only in the abbreviated panties and bra. She continued moving her hips in sync with the music, as his eyes traced the outline of her body with the look of a hungry animal.

"Now…that's more like it," he said, almost under his breath, and put his hand around her waist, pulling her against him. With his free hand, he took each of hers and placed them behind his neck. She felt herself surrender—he was in full control.

One hand held her nearly naked body with a firm grip, while his other artfully stroked her smooth skin, all the time swaying to the sensual music. It was intimacy at its peak.

Annie moved deeper and deeper into a hypnotic state enhanced by the effects of the champagne. She thought of nothing past the feel of his hands roaming her body, his groin pressed against the skimpy lace, as the two bodies followed the pulsating rhythm of the music. She was ready for him—ready for him to take her fully—to be his in the most carnal and primitive way. Annie hungered to merge with him in an inextricable connection. In response to his stroke, her body arched, and his mouth was on the base of her neck. As a track ended, he slid his hand slowly down her back and gently over her derriere, slipping the lace down to fully expose her. As it fell to the floor, she stepped away in a cat-like move. When she was free of the panties, Dan swept her up and carried her masterfully to his bed.

***

Annie woke the next morning, Dan's arm and leg sprawled over her—both of them still nude. Although his limbs were pressing heavily on her, she didn't care. She was remembering every moment of the night before and realizing that they had broken a barrier. She was finally free to be the wife she was before Cole violated her. *Thank you, God. Thank you for giving me the courage to let myself go. Thank you for giving me Dan. I love him so much.*

The rest of the trip was marred only by a little bad weather in Provenance, but nothing could really spoil what Annie had found in Paris. She called home daily to be sure that Danny was doing well and was consistently told that he was having a blast.

"I rode Sunny's pony all by myself," he spouted out on one call. "Uncle Cole says that I'm a natural horseman. Can I have a pony at my house, Mommy?"

Each time she heard his little voice, a brief longing to be home occurred, but once the moment passed, she was able to put Danny out of her mind and concentrate completely on Dan and their activities.

Talking to Danny the day before they were scheduled to fly home, Annie gave him what she thought was the good news. His response was unsettling.

"You don't have to come home tomorrow, Mommy. You and Daddy stay there. I'm going fishing with Uncle Cole and Sunny tomorrow."

His words sank in her heart like a stone in water. He doesn't need me. I thought he would be excited that we are coming home, but he's telling me to stay—and he means it. He would rather go fishing with Cole than see me and Dan.

When Alex took the phone, she said, "He's having a blast, Annie. Why don't you just let him stay over one more night and give yourself a chance to get over the jet lag?"

"Stay with you another night?" Annie asked. "I can't do that Alex. I'm dying to see him."

Dan came from behind her and took the phone away. Speaking into the receiver, he said, "I think we better pick him up on our way home, Alex. Annie's been a real trooper for the entire two weeks. I'm proud of her, but she misses him and deserves to see him as soon as possible. Put him back on the phone."

When Danny was back on the line, Dan said, "Listen up, little buddy, Mom and I are going to pick you up on our way home from the airport tomorrow evening. Be sure you have all your things packed to go home."

"But Daddy—"

"Hold it, little man. You can go back over to Uncle Cole and Aunt Alex's sometime real soon, but you're going home with us tomorrow night. Your mom and I miss you. Are you clear with that?"

The phone was silent. Dan's tone had been no-nonsense firm. Finally, in a small voice, Danny said, "Yes, sir."

"That's my guy. I think you're going to be happy to see us. Your mom found some neat toy stores over here."

"Did she buy me something?"

"You bet, but I'm not telling you anything more. You'll have to wait until we pick you up."

When Dan hung up the phone, Annie wiped a tear away and said, "That was unabashed bribery."

"Works on Cameron men every time. You ought to know. How do you think you got me into that sexy shop?"

"You want to know a secret?"

Dan nodded.

"There's a little part of me that hates to go home. It's not that I don't miss Danny desperately, but it has been pretty great over here."

Dan took her in his arms and held her close to his chest as she slid her arms around his back. Neither of them spoke.

CHAPTER THIRTY-FIVE

Annie and Dan returned from Paris with Annie pregnant—a smile on Dan's face, and a strong shot of adrenalin to their marriage. Of course, they didn't know they were expecting until more than two weeks after arriving in Providence. When Annie missed her period, she initially took little notice, attributing the deviation in her cycle to the effects of foreign travel. It did not occur to her that she could be pregnant since she had been on birth control pills, a practice she had insisted on since Danny's birth.

It must be because of the change in diet, water and time zones. I can't be pregnant. My body chemistry must be confused. My period will start soon.

After a week had passed, the thought of another pregnancy caused her heart to beat a little faster. *Is it possible? Could I be pregnant? I know I missed taking the pill several times, but we had unprotected sex without me getting pregnant before. Surely, this is not possible.* She burrowed down in the corner of the living room sofa, hugging a throw pillow, with a smile on her face, and daydreamed about what it would be like if she were going to have another baby—Dan's baby.

Over the past four years, whenever friends and family suggested they have a second child, Annie perpetually resisted the idea. She insisted that one child was plenty to care for with Dan gone so much.

"I have my hands full, and there's nothing wrong with raising an only child. Look at Dan, he doesn't have siblings." In truth, her denial was just another thread in the fabric of her coverup. She wanted another baby but was afraid to risk exposing Dan as being sterile. They didn't discuss it, but he didn't seem to mind that she claimed one child was enough, or that she stayed on birth control.

I don't get pregnant. There's probably some other explanation. Leaving her cozy spot on the couch, she retrieved her birth control pills from the bathroom and found nine left. *I didn't realize I missed that many.* She smiled to herself. *Don't get your hopes up, Annie. It's still not likely.* Looking at the clock, she decided that if she hurried, she could make it to Walmart and back before Danny would have to be picked up at preschool. Not bothering with makeup, she combed her hair, pulled on a pair of jeans and T-shirt, and left.

By the time she had to pick up Danny, she had repeated the ritual of five years before with the same result, but a very different attitude. Every home pregnancy test Walmart sold said "positive." Beside herself with joy, she wanted to call Dan and blurt out the news but decided to wait until later that night. *Thank goodness, he's not traveling. I couldn't wait.*

All afternoon, she was in a great mood. When she picked up Danny, she gave him a tremendous hug.

"Mommy, you're hurting me. You hug me too hard," Danny complained.

"I'm sorry, sweetheart. Mommy just feels so good. Let's go for a Slurpee." Life was on a roll, and she wanted to celebrate, even if it was just with a convenience store beverage.

"Yeah," he responded with a big grin.

That night, she made spaghetti and fruit salad for dinner. Dan had been getting home on time more often since they returned. He walked in at seven on the dot, and Danny ran to meet him.

It was hard for Annie to keep her secret through dinner, and she tried to avoid eye contact out of fear her silly expression would let on that something was amiss.

After dinner, Dan bathed Danny, while she cleaned up the dishes. By eight, he had the child in bed and was reading a story. Annie was so excited, she could hardly contain herself. She hoped Danny would fall asleep quickly, and he did, shortly after they both heard his prayers and kissed him goodnight. He had played hard that afternoon.

As they went into their room to watch TV before retiring for the night, Annie pulled Dan around to face her.

"What's up?" he asked, casually.

"I've got to talk to you," she said, trying to make her tone sound serious.

"The floor's all yours."

"Do you know what you did to me?" Frowning, she spoke in as harsh a tone as she could garner.

Puzzled, Dan responded, "No, but I think you're about to tell me."

"You," she said, punching him in the chest with her index finger, "made me," pointing to her chest, "pregnant." She tried not to smile.

His face lit up like a candle with its wick on fire. "You've got to be kidding me. You're pregnant?"

"According to five early detection tests, I am. What have you got to say for yourself, Daniel Cameron?"

"How about, 'Congratulations—way to go, Dan'?"

"Are you not shameless?" she asked, an involuntary smile creeping across her face.

"Absolutely, you little foxy devil, come here," he said, as he reached out to grab her. "I'll show you how shameless I am." He snatched her close and gave her a passionate kiss on the mouth.

***

When Annie told the rest of the family, no one was more excited about the news than Alex, who took full credit. "If I hadn't insisted that you take that trip to Paris, you wouldn't be pregnant now," she crowed. "This is exactly what you and Dan need. Is he happy?"

"Of course."

"I knew he would be. I don't know why you waited so long to try again. It's always easier after you've had one. Brandi is proof of that."

"Things happen the way they're supposed to—at least, most of the time," Annie replied.

***

For Annie, the second pregnancy was all the first should have been. She relished aspects she avoided before, shopping for the nursery, buying baby clothes, and even choosing names early on. But, she refused to allow them to tell her the sex of the baby when she had her sonogram. When the family made comparisons of her change in attitude, she tossed them off as first-time paranoia with Danny.

Embracing her second pregnancy with the joy of a child with a new bicycle, Annie soaked up impending motherhood to the fullest. Without the horrendous secret to hide, she basked in her condition. Sometimes while doing her chores or shopping, she would look down at her bulging baby-bump and feel all warm and fuzzy about how it came about. If there was any flaw in her life, it was only a tiny fear that the child, particularly if it was another boy, would look a great deal like Dan and evoke comparisons that she would rather not discuss. But, she refused to let even that thought dampen her excitement. *I'm going to enjoy what I missed out on with Danny.*

It was no secret, nor any surprise, that Annie hoped for a girl. She felt guilty and tried to say that all she wanted was a healthy child, which was true, but there was an overwhelming desire to have a little girl to dress in lacy ruffles and patent leather shoes. That's so superficial, Annie. *Stop it. A healthy baby is all you need. I will not pray for a girl. That is wrong. It doesn't matter.* But no matter how many lectures she gave herself, the truth was, Annie Cameron wanted a daughter.

***

Sometimes, the stars do align in the order mortals request, and Annie got lucky. That night in Paris, Dan's little Xs beat his Ys to the finish line. Máire Faith was born on March 1, 2008—every bit a Cameron with Dan's dark hair and eyes. Another charm was added to Annie's bracelet.

CHAPTER THIRTY-SIX

By the time fall of 2008 arrived, Annie was in the groove of juggling two children, her household chores, and volunteer work at the church. She usually had it under control, but a rainy day toppled the best of routines. On the third Friday in September, it had rained all day, bringing out the worst in Danny. He had been a handful since he got home from kindergarten. Although Annie did not believe in spanking, he had tested her patience to the point where she had given it serious consideration. It seemed that every time she needed to give Faith attention, Danny acted up—throwing toys, terrorizing the cat, and making about as much noise as he knew how. By the time Dan got home, the house was a wreck, and Annie was on mommy-overload, struggling to get dinner made.

"He's been horrible," she complained to Dan as he walked in the kitchen with Danny perched on his back, piggyback fashion. "He cut Deli's whiskers off."

"Was that painful?" Dan asked, frowning.

"The vet said it wouldn't have hurt her, but she's like a drunk now. Her balance is all screwed up." Pointing to Danny, Annie said, "He was like a wild man today."

"Is that true, son?" Dan asked, putting the child down on the floor.

Danny hung his head with a look of pure innocence.

"Well, I don't think you have to answer. Get yourself over there and tell Mommy you're sorry and give her a kiss—and don't you cut any more whiskers, cat or dog."

Without hesitation, Danny ran across the kitchen to Annie, apologized and reached his short arms up to give her a hug and kiss.

"Now, run play while Daddy helps Mommy with dinner," Dan said.

Danny turned sharply on his heels and scooted out of the kitchen without a hint of protest.

"How do you do that? Do you secretly beat him when I'm not around?" Annie asked as she pulled her electric mixer out to mash the potatoes.

Dan laughed and held up both hands as though surrendering.

"You do realize that it really annoys me that I've been nearly ready to kill him all afternoon, but you walk in, snap your fingers, and he's meek as a lamb."

"What can I say? Some of us are naturals," he teased, then put his arm around her waist and gave her a kiss on the cheek.

With Dan in charge of the children, Annie finished making the meal. After they ate, she cleaned the kitchen, while he bathed Danny.

Faith had just gone to sleep when the doorbell rang. The three of them were watching the Disney Channel, Danny having talked his dad into extending his bedtime by thirty minutes. It was nearly half past eight and still raining outside. Dan turned to Annie, with a bewildered expression, and asked, "Are you expecting anyone?"

"No. Who would want to go out on a night like this?"

He got up and went to the door, while she watched from the living room couch.

Opening the door, Dan recognized Father Blake, their parish rector. "Stephen, what are you doing here on a miserable night like this?"

Upon hearing the rector's name, Annie immediately stood up and began moving in their direction—a puzzled look on her face.

"I'm glad you're home, Dan. I wasn't sure I would find you here," the priest said, pausing to wrap the Velcro strap around his wet umbrella and propping it up by the door before stepping inside the front hall. "There's no easy way to say what I have to say." He paused, looking past Dan at Annie as she approached. "Annie, I have some difficult news."

Annie froze, as she heard his words. A weakness flooded her body—the color leaving her face. "Is it Mother—or Daddy?" she asked, her voice distorted by the fear of what she was about to hear.

"Neither, Annie…. It's Alex."

Annie frowned, slightly relieved, as she did not expect tragedy where her sister was concerned. "Alex. What do you mean it's Alex?"

"There was an accident—an automobile accident on the highway."

Panic returned, pulsating through Annie's gut. "Where is she? Is she hurt?" The words shot from Annie like sparks from a firecracker. "I'll get my coat. Dan, can you get the baby? We have to go." Barely taking a breath, she shouted to Danny over the sounds of the television, "Danny, turn the TV off, we have to go."

Reverend Blake stepped forward and reached out, taking both of her hands in his. Dan had moved behind her, holding her shoulders. Annie's eyes grew large, and she began twisting her head from side to side in denial of what she was about to hear.

"Annie, there's no need to hurry—Alex is gone," he said, in a soothing, ministerial tone while holding her hands tightly.

Annie gasped and started to crumble toward the floor, the two men keeping her from falling. All the strength left her legs. She could barely walk with their assistance, as Dan guided them to the dining room and away from Danny in the living room.

"No…. It's not true. They can save her. Doctors do miraculous things. They can fly her somewhere…to specialists."

"They can't, Annie. She died instantly."

"How do you know? Where was she? What about Mother and Daddy, do they know? Do the girls know?"

"Slow down, honey; let Stephen talk," Dan said, his voice soothing and patient, his hands holding her shoulders.

"I don't know a lot—just that she was coming back from Columbia on I-20. She had gone over yesterday to help Brandi settle in and was on her way back. Apparently, Alex lost control of her car on the wet road. No other vehicle was involved."

"She always drove that flashy little sports car too fast," Annie sobbed. "Where was Cole? Why wasn't he with her? Why did he let her go by herself?"

"I don't know, Annie. He's broken-up—all I got from him was that Brandi was homesick at college, and Alex just wanted to make a quick trip to boost her morale."

"How did you find out?" Dan asked.

"Sheriff Summers got in touch with me as soon as he got the call from the Georgia State Patrol. He asked me to help him notify Cole. The wife and I met him at the farm. Myrtice stayed out there with Cole and Sunny while I came to talk to you. Cole asked me to tell you, Claire, and Frank. I thought it best to come here first."

"You were right," Dan said. "We'll go with you to Frank and Claire's." Squeezing Annie's shoulders, he asked, "Are you okay, honey?"

Crying quietly, she nodded.

"I'll call Martha and Ray and ask them to take care of Faith and Danny until my parents can get here," Dan said, and went to the phone while the priest put his arms around Annie's shoulders, keeping her steady.

CHAPTER THIRTY-SEVEN

The next few days were a blur for Annie. It was hard to separate one day or time from another. Meeting her parents and breaking the news was agonizing, as was greeting the two older girls when they arrived home. Cole had not contacted his older daughters until after Annie, Dan, and the Brennans got to the farm. Claire couldn't speak—Frank was ashen and said little. Dan took over as spokesman for the family that night. He offered to drive to the colleges to pick up Rhys and Brandi, but once she calmed down, Rhys insisted on driving. She said flying would probably take longer, and she wanted to be with Brandi when her younger sister was told.

"We can get there faster if I drive, Uncle Dan. Paul will come with me." She and Paul Jefferson had been dating since she started school at Chapel Hill. "We can pick up Brandi in South Carolina. Don't call her, I'll tell her when we get there. She shouldn't be alone when she finds out. She's already so unstable," Rhys said, her voice shaking.

When the older girls got to Providence, Rhys took charge, putting up a brave front for her sisters. Cole withdrew emotionally. He took care of necessary arrangements but pulled away from everyone other- wise. Whenever present, it was obvious that his mind and spirit were absent. The look in his eyes was vacant. Annie felt he was being selfish, indulging his grief while neglecting the needs of the girls. Stifling her own sorrow, she tried to fill the gap.

The funeral service was sedate in the traditional Episcopalian man- ner. After the service, it seemed that the entire town convened at the Dalton farm. Annie thought the stream of hugs, tears, and black dresses would never end. Margaret and Russ stayed at the house with the children, and for once, Margaret was quiet and inconspicuous. Even Molly came for the viewing and stayed overnight in Providence for the funeral. Annie wanted a chance to be alone with Molly to pour out her pent-up grief but was not afforded the luxury.

Food was everywhere, primarily arranged by the church women: platters of fried chicken, hams, potato salad, green bean casseroles and an array of pies and cakes. Annie ate very little. She was numb. She scarcely covered her bitterness toward Cole. *Why didn't he drive Alex to Columbia?* Annie needed to blame someone, and he was such a good candidate. But intellectually, Annie knew it wasn't his fault. Despite her resentment and judgmental attitude toward him, there were fleeting moments when she felt a modicum of sympathy for the first time in seven years. No matter what his sins, he had loved Alex. Annie could see that.

Sunny, like her father, withdrew as much as possible. The twelve-year-old was lost. Rhys was the only one of the girls who appeared to be coping and assumed the role of family hostess and anchor. Paul proved to be a likeable young man and a good source of support for her. Brandi cried constantly and blamed herself for causing Alex to be on the road that night. Annie wanted to take Sunny to her house but knew the Daltons needed to be together. It was a common grief, but each had to face it on a different level.

After the last of the guests had left the farm the evening of the funeral, Annie was preparing to go home when Rhys brought her an envelope.

"This was addressed to you, Aunt Annie. Dad found it when he went through Mom's papers. She wrote letters to all of us," Rhys said.

It was a standard-size, sealed envelope of heavy paper stock. The only thing written on it was "Annie" in Alex's unmistakable handwriting. Annie's hand trembled as she accepted the last remnant of her sister.

"I think I'll wait to read this until I get home, honey," she said, tucking it in her purse. I don't think I can handle anything else right now without breaking down.

Later that night, after the children had gone to sleep and Dan was in the shower, Annie took the letter from her purse. With her in-laws back in Atlanta, the house was quiet but for the sound of water.

Holding the envelope in her hand, she looked at it for a moment before taking a brass letter opener from her bedroom desk. There were three pages written in the familiar hand.

June 10, 2003

My dearest little sister,

If you're reading this, and I hope you never have to, I am gone. You're probably surprised that I have actually written a letter since my literary skills are limited to grocery lists and signing Christmas cards, but I guess my hormones are racing because I felt the call to put feelings on paper that I have never expressed. I may tear this up before the ink is dry, but here goes.

Annie, there are so many things I want to tell you that I should have told you in person, but never did. Next to my children and Cole, I love you more than anyone, with all due respect to our parents. I have been hard on you over the years, jealous of you for sure, but always protective and proud. You were what I tried to be—honest, sincere, and loyal. And you were what I could never be—level-headed, conscientious, conservative, and educated. I hated the pedestal you occupied, but wouldn't have changed it for anything, which brings me to the purpose of this letter.

Because you're reading this, my girls have lost their mother, and Cole has lost his wife. Obviously, you can't be a wife to Cole (don't think I would like that idea and know Dan wouldn't), but you can be the surrogate mother to my precious girls. They adore you. Help them through the loss of me and all the obstacles and temptations of growing up. Annie, you have to stand in for me, and I know you will because you could never let anyone down. Don't let Cole stand in your way. Make sure that they finish college. I always envied your education. It made you more complete somehow. Cole has fought education all these years because he made it without one, but it gives you another level of respect. Please make sure the girls graduate. Fight Cole if you have to. I know you can. He comes on tough, but he's not. That's his cover-up.

Keep them in church. Cole will never go without me. Be there for them to talk to. Help them shop for clothes and makeup and all the things a man, particularly Cole, can never understand. Maybe your good taste will rub off on them. Most of all, please give them the love I won't be there to give.

Annie, you have always been the younger, smaller and more fragile Brennan girl, but I know you're tough, a steel magnolia. You have a core that is rock solid, probably more so than mine. I'm a fraud, Annie. I have lived a life of fear that I could never admit. Fear that I would lose Cole. I don't know if he has been faithful to me. I'm scared to know. I seemed hard as nails, but it was a façade. You are the one with an inner strength that would sustain an apocalypse.

Annie, Cole will need you desperately, not that he would ever admit it. He loves the girls, and in his way, he is a great father; but he's not on their age or gender wavelength. Over the past few years, I have sensed a tension between the two of you. I don't know what he did to offend you, and maybe I'm afraid to know. However, if there is a problem, I have no doubt that Cole caused it. But, Annie, he is a good man. His childhood was so different from ours. He didn't have loving parents or any type of security. My God, you know that he was only thirteen when his mother killed his drunk, abusive father in self-defense. You know that if the Bannisters hadn't taken Cole in, he would have probably ended up in prison, like one of his brothers.

You don't know how hard it was for Cole to come into the Brennan family. Mom and Dad treated him so bad in the beginning. You know how mad they were when he got me pregnant. They didn't even want me to date him. It didn't help that you married God's gift to parents. Cole had to live with Dan's perfection. I know it's not Dan's fault that he was born into the "lucky sperm club," and truly, there is no finer man anywhere than Dan Cameron. But it was hard for Cole to walk in his shadow. He knows that Mother and Daddy respect and adore Dan, while he's "the other son-in-law from the wrong side of the tracks." All I ask is that you be there for him. Let him know that he is still part of the Brennan clan. It's the only family he has. Don't let him pull away, or pull the girls away from my family.

Annie, please put your arms around my girls and tell them it's going to be all right. They will see me again. I will make sure of that.

I am depending on you and trusting you with the dearest things I have. If something should happen to you, God forbid, you know that I would be there for Dan and Danny.

Never doubt or forget how much I loved you,

    Alex

By the time Annie had reached the end of the letter, it was wet with tears. Dan came in the bedroom as she put the letter on the bed. She had to preserve it. It was all she had left of Alex. All the memories of childhood came flooding back. "Alex always looked out for me. She didn't want me to follow in her footsteps. She wanted me to excel."

"This is the worst, angel. You'll always miss her, but time will ease the pain." Dan said quietly, putting his hands on her shoulders.

"She cared so much for me, Dan. I don't think I knew how much."

"May I read the letter?"

"Of course."

As he read, Annie could see that the letter was burrowing deep into his emotions as well. When he was done, he laid it back on the bed.

"She left you with a gigantic task to accomplish, angel. She was right. The girls do need you, especially Sunny."

"I'll do what I can, but I don't know if I can be everything Alex wanted me to be."

"You can. I know you, and so did Alex. You'll take care of them."

"I want to blame someone, Dan. I want it to be someone's fault, so I can hate them. I want it to be Cole's fault. Why wasn't he with her? Why did he let her drive up there by herself?"

"It wasn't anyone's fault. Alex did what she wanted. Cole couldn't be with her all the time. She wanted to help Brandi, and nothing could have stopped her. No one could have known what would happen."

"Intellectually, I know you're right, but emotionally—I need someone to be angry with. I need to scream at someone—hit someone." Annie began to shake. She reached across the bed for a throw pillow and pulled it close to her stomach, tears drenching her face. "Alex is gone. I'm never going to see her again." Dan sat down beside her and pulled her close, cradling her head against his chest.

"Give it time, angel," he said, as he brushed away the hair that had fallen down on her wet face. "Give yourself a chance to heal. Right now, it's raw, but trust me, honey, you will feel better. You've got to believe that she's still here, watching over you, the girls, and Cole."

"What are the girls going to do without a mother?" Annie sobbed. "Poor Sunny. Thirteen years old with no mother. She's going to go through her teen years with no one but Cole. There's no way, with as rough and crude as he is, that he can give her what a young girl needs."

"You're here for her," he said, reaching for tissues on the bedside table.

Taking the tissues from him, Annie sat up and wiped her face. "You know Brandi blames herself for Alex going to Columbia? Cole doesn't have enough sensitivity to get her counseling."

"You may be right. It will be up to you to make sure that Cole gets her help."

CHAPTER THIRTY-EIGHT

In the days and weeks that followed the funeral, Annie put her feelings toward Cole aside and reached out to the family. She convinced him to arrange counseling for all of the girls. Considering his remote demeanor, she thought he needed therapy as well, but with his macho attitude, she knew he would never talk to a "shrink." If truth be told, Annie did not care whether he got help and took a little pleasure in knowing that he was suffering.

When the older girls threatened to quit college to stay with Sunny, Annie vehemently insisted they stay in school. "Your mom wanted all of you to graduate. Don't let her down," she said. "I'm here for Sunny. I'll keep a close watch on her. You concentrate on your classes. If I think at any time that she needs you, I will call. Your job right now is to set an example for your little sister and do what your mom wanted."

Reluctantly, Brandi and Rhys gave in to Annie and returned to their respective schools. Brandi made it through the term with constant support from Rhys and Annie, plus help from a therapist in Columbia. The following term, she transferred to Chapel Hill to be with Rhys.

Alex's death left Annie with her hands full. The girls were just part of it. Claire was not handling the loss well and resisted the efforts of everyone to comfort her. When Claire began spending days without getting dressed and dropped out of her social activities, Annie convinced Frank to take her to Atlanta for grief counseling. It took several months, but the counseling finally helped Claire adjust to her loss.

"There is no pain greater for a woman than losing a child. I've heard that all my life, and now I know how true it is," Claire said, over and over.

"I know, Mom, but you have to pull yourself together for Dad. He's hurting too," Annie said one morning while visiting her mother.

"It's unnatural, Annie. Children are supposed to bury their parents, not the other way around."

"I know," Annie said, trying to be patient as she watched Faith and Danny playing in the yard with Charlie. They ran and laughed as the black cocker chased them and retrieved his ball each time it was tossed. Seeing her children, she knew the depth of despair her mother was experiencing. *I would lose my mind if anything happened to either of them.* Searching for words to comfort Claire, she said, "The rest of us need you, Mom, especially Sunny. Alex doesn't want you to throw your life away. She wants you to help the girls." Annie couldn't bring herself to refer to Alex in past tense, especially with Claire.

Annie became the backbone of the family. Staying strong for the others helped her cope with her own grief. But, even when time had healed a portion of the pain, there were random moments when sorrow would strike. It was not triggered by talking about Alex, or even seeing photographs. It occurred in those moments of joy, confusion, or sadness when she wanted to share her feelings, ask for advice, or cry on Alex's shoulder. She would catch herself reaching for the telephone to "tell Alex," and the realization would strike. She felt it also when looking in the eyes of the girls, particularly Sunny—so young, so innocent.

One morning, months after the funeral, Annie drove to the cemetery and sat on the cold ground by the grave, talking out loud to Alex. "I know it wasn't your fault, but you left me with more than I think I can handle. Please, wherever you are, help me." Tears rolled down her face as cool air blew through the surrounding trees, drying the tears nearly as fast as they appeared.

***

As time went by, Sunny spent more and more time at the Cameron house. Annie wasn't sure whether it was because she craved a mother figure, enjoyed feeling needed, or that life with Cole was less than pleasant. Annie didn't probe.

"She'll tell me if she needs to," Annie said to Claire, one Sunday morning after church. Sunny had gone to retrieve Danny and Faith from their Sunday school classrooms. "I want her to feel comfortable at our house—to feel totally at home. There's no telling what Cole is like when no one is around."

"I heard that he's been seeing a waitress from that roadhouse out on the highway," Claire said.

"Probably just sleeping with her, Mom. I don't see him getting serious about another woman. Cole is unaware of everyone but himself. Instant gratification is his motto."

"I'm not sure about that," Claire responded. "Men are helpless and need a woman. Look at all the old geezers here in Providence who jumped into another marriage before the grass had grown over the graves of their wives."

Thinking for a minute, Annie said, "Maybe—women do seem to handle being alone better."

Spending so much time together, Sunny became more like Annie's older daughter. Annie attended the school events, helped with homework, and listened to the young teen's struggle to navigate the turbulent waters of adolescent love. As she matured, a beautiful teenager emerged with compelling blue eyes and streaked hair that grew lighter in the summer as her skin grew darker. When they went shopping in Atlanta, clerks assumed she was Annie's daughter, especially when Danny was with them. He and Sunny were a matched set, except for Danny's blue-green eyes. Dark-haired Faith was the odd one of the group.

About all Cole did for his daughter was sign her report card and support her financially. Annie took care of everything else. When Sunny won the lead in a school play, Annie heard her call Cole to invite him to attend.

"It's this Friday night, Dad, in the auditorium. I'll leave you a ticket at the box office."

236 · JUDITH ERWIN

Hanging up, Sunny turned to Annie with a big smile. "He's said he's going to try real hard to come."

It was obvious how much the child craved her father's attention.

Friday night, Annie and Dan were in the audience with the children, but there was no sign of Cole.

"I can't believe he didn't show up," Annie said to Dan at intermission. "What am I going to tell her?"

"He may have had to work late."

"Oh please, spare me. You're here, and you're not even her father. He's the boss. He can set his hours anyway he wants to. There's no excuse. He's just a despicable, self-centered jerk—probably out with some floozy."

"It's his loss, sweetheart," Dan said, putting an arm around her shoulder as if to calm her. "Cole has never rowed in sync with the rest of the crew."

By the fall of 2009, Sunny was staying with Annie when Dan was out of town and many times when he wasn't. She told her father that Annie needed help with the children. Cole never complained. If Annie and Dan had a date night, Sunny was their on-call sitter. The guest room became her room. Annie let her redecorate it with posters and teenage paraphernalia. After being introduced to the Celtic Thunder by Molly, Sunny became obsessed with the Irish singers, abandoning her former crush on Joe Jonas. She hung posters of Keith Harkin on her wall and played their music constantly. She was convinced that Dan looked like Ryan Kelly.

For Molly's birthday, Annie bought tickets to a Celtic Thunder concert for the four of them. Leaving the Fox Theatre in Atlanta after the show, Sunny walked out saying, "You've got to agree with me now, Aunt Annie, Uncle Dan looks exactly like Ryan."

Molly nodded in agreement, but Dan protested, a little embarrassed with the comparison. "No way. He's much better looking and much younger. Besides, I'm not Irish."

"You're Scottish, and Scots are Celtic too," Annie said, enjoying the attention Dan was receiving. "He might be a distant cousin."

Following an after-theater dessert, they dropped Molly at her condo and headed back to Providence.

"Aunt Annie, play 'Raggle Taggle Gypsy' again, please." Dan had bought Sunny a CD and a DVD of the show, along with the program and a T-shirt. The disc had been playing since they got in the car.

"Sweetie, aren't you tired of it? You have that song on your other CD. I've heard it. Uncle Dan may not love the group as much as you do."

"She's fine," Dan said, patting Annie on the leg. "I like having her so happy."

"Where do you want us to take you?" Annie asked. "Your house or ours?"

"I want to go home to my room at your house, if that's okay."

"You know it's fine with us, but I thought you might like to go home since you haven't been there all week."

"It's fine. Dad's probably not even home."

Sunny seldom mentioned her father. Annie suspected that Cole was drinking, maybe too much. He had always enjoyed his beer and seemed able to handle it. However, Annie wondered if it was spiraling out of control. There had been no further mention of his actually dating, despite any number of single women in Providence who threw themselves at him.

When the subject came up in conversation with her mother or friends, Annie's only comment was, "You know a man's sex appeal goes up in direct proportion to the number of zeros to the left of the decimal point on his bank balance." She believed that he took his sexual gratification whenever it was convenient and from whomever he pleased. But she wasn't interested in wasting effort exploring his lifestyle as long as her nieces were properly provided for. In some ways, she was quite happy that he didn't interfere in her relationship with Sunny.

Annie was the second mother, so much so that one day when Sunny was looking after Faith, she called Annie "Mom." Catching herself, she said, "I'm sorry, I meant Aunt Annie."

"No need to apologize. I'm flattered that you made the slip, but Alex will always be your mom, sweetie."

"I know, but Aunt Annie, sometimes I can't remember what she looked like. It scares me. I have to go find her picture. It seems like she's been gone forever, but it hasn't been that long." Sunny picked up Faith and started into the house to get the child a drink.

As she walked away, Annie watched, thinking how much she loved the girl. *Cole doesn't deserve her.*

CHAPTER THIRTY-NINE

When Rhys and Brandi came home, they tried to act as Sunny's advisors. Although she was always glad to see them, she ignored unsolicited advice. The visits became less and less frequent, as they were moving into adulthood with sparse time left over for a kid sister. Cole provided a credit card and little else. When, in his awkward way, he attempted to thank Annie for being there for Sunny, she deflected his gratitude by saying, "We all need one another."

One afternoon as Sunny played with Faith, Annie commented, "I don't know what I would do without you, honey. You are such a help with Faith."

Sunny looked up smiling and said, "I love taking care of her, Aunt Annie. It's like playing dolls with a real doll. I hope I can marry a man like Uncle Dan and have a little girl just like Faith."

"Maybe Ryan Kelly and Keith Harkin will still be available when you're older," Annie said, and they both laughed.

Sunny tried to teach Faith some dance moves to a Michael Jackson song, and the toddler did her best to mimic her cousin's moves, shaking her little hips almost in time with the beat. Watching Sunny brought back memories of Alex. *She's your daughter, Alex. Can you see her dancing? She moves just like you did. You would be so proud of her.*

Brandi and Rhys called Annie often, but they needed her far less than Sunny. Brandi was recovering from her guilt over her mother's death, but still leaned on Rhys. While the sisters sharing a dorm room had been a good idea initially, after a year, Rhys was ready to break free.

"It's just too much togetherness, Aunt Annie. I need my space, and she needs to stop clinging to me."

"I'll talk to her, honey. Do you want me to come over there?"

"No. We'll be home for Christmas, and we can deal with it then."

During the holidays, Rhys announced that she was moving in with Paul when the new term began in January. Brandi was devastated, but Cole was livid. In a rare call to Annie, he sought backup.

"Talk to her, Annie. I have better luck getting through to the damn mules. She makes me want to beat some sense into her. Alex could have handled it, if she was here."

"She's twenty-one years old, Cole. You can't stop her."

"The hell I can't. I can damn sure quit paying her bills. She thinks she's a grown-up, then she can fucking well support herself—or let Paul take care of her if he wants to shack up."

"You don't want to do that. Why would you want to jeopardize her education? You know that's not the solution—that's not what Alex would want."

The phone was silent. She had played the trump card, and she knew it. He might have argued with Alex in life, but in death, she ruled supreme.

Backing down, he said in a last-ditch defense, "What the hell good is her fucking education if she gets knocked up?"

I have to be good and bite my tongue, but, oh how I want to say, "Like you knocked up Alex and raped me?" Fighting her momentary resentment, Annie said, "I doubt that she will get pregnant. Kids today are pretty savvy about contraception. And don't you know that the more you oppose it, the more appealing it becomes? Rhys is a mature young woman. She'll be alright. Paul seems to be a nice young man and crazy about her. It's probably better that they live together, rather than get married at this point."

Again, the phone was silent for a minute before he responded. "Yeah, I guess you're right." He wasn't happy, but he gave up arguing.

Further encounters with Cole were minimal, even though Sunny spent the majority of her time with the Camerons. While maintaining a workable routine was a constant chore, Annie felt life had a good rhythm. Alex had been right, two children may have taken more time and work, but she was able to better balance her attention between the children and Dan because she was no longer an obsessive parent. Leaving Faith and Danny with Sunny, her parents, or a paid babysitter for "date nights," or to meet Dan out of town for an occasional "stolen" weekend, became normal. The FBI still kept him away more than she liked, but they had adjusted to the routine.

However, by late spring of 2010, Annie began to have an uneasy feeling about Sunny. As a teenager, she should have been busy with high school activities and friends. But something was holding her back. She seemed to lose her steam. She stopped participating in the activities she had loved—swimming, dancing, and playing tennis with Dan. He had taught her well, and she loved to beat him. But by June, Annie knew something was wrong. Sunny seemed to catch every cold that came along and complained of unexplained joint pain.

CHAPTER FORTY

"Mom, Sunny's still sleeping," Danny said, coming into the kitchen one Saturday morning in midsummer.

"She's probably tired, honey," Annie said absent mindedly, as she stirred her pancake batter.

"But I need someone to play video games with."

"Try your little sister," Dan said, from the kitchen table where he was having coffee and reading the newspaper.

Danny wrinkled his nose in a gesture of disdain. "Daddy...you know she's too little to play my video games."

"I can play," said Faith, coming in the kitchen from the den where she had been watching cartoons.

"I'm not playing one of your silly baby games," said Danny, becoming frustrated.

"Well, figure something else out to do until Sunny wakes up," Dan said, looking up at the boy. "Why don't you and Faith watch cartoons?"

Thinking about it for a minute, Danny said, "I don't like cartoons."

The room became very quiet. The only sound was the humming of the microwave cooking bacon. *Don't tell me we're going to start the day with him acting out,* Annie thought, pausing midway through adding strawberries to the batter.

Dan tipped his head slightly, raised his right eyebrow, and gave Danny a look that said, "You don't want to go there." It didn't go unnoticed.

Deciding not to press the issue, Danny said, "Can I go out and ride my bike?"

Dan nodded, and Danny left the kitchen.

The tension neutralized, Annie resumed breakfast preparation, but with a frown on her face. "Dan, I've been meaning to talk to you about Sunny. She has me worried. She sleeps later and later."

"Maybe she stays up watching TV in her room later than you know."

"I don't think so. I've also noticed that she turns down invitations from her friends to go to a movie or sleep over. She just doesn't seem to have her usual energy. When was the last time the two of you played tennis?"

Folding the newspaper, he said, "I guess I haven't been paying attention, but it has been a while."

"It's hard to put a finger on it, but her color isn't quite right. It has a slightly grayish cast. Fifteen-year-olds are supposed to be high energy, but Sunny's in slow motion."

"Have you talked with her about it?" he asked, putting the newspaper on the end of the kitchen counter.

"She says she just tired and doesn't want to see a doctor, but I don't like it. I just feel that something's going on."

"You know you're a little paranoid, but if you're worried, why don't you give Cole a call? Or, better yet, when the folks are here tomorrow, I'll ask Dad what he thinks."

***

Late the next afternoon, Dan and his dad enjoyed catching up over a cold beer while Dan grilled chicken. The children swam in the pool. Margaret was in the kitchen with Annie, keeping her company while she finished making scalloped potatoes and coleslaw. Everyone seemed to be enjoying the summer activity. Faith had learned to swim earlier in the summer and did well for a two-year-old, but Annie insisted that she wear her water wings just to be safe. Sunny swam the length of the pool and back once, and then settled on the steps where Danny enjoyed tormenting her with his cannonball jumps. After about ten minutes, she left the pool, poured a glass of lemonade from the pitcher Annie put out for them, and lay back on one of the chaise lounge chairs in the shade of the patio canopy.

Picking up his beer, Russ moved over to the chair next to her. "How are you doing, gal?"

Smiling at him, Sunny said, "I'm good. It's summer—no school."

Russ smiled back and then said, "Dan tells me you've been tired a lot lately."

"I'm fine. Just a little lazy, that's all."

"Mind if I look at your eyes and hands?" Russ said, putting his beer down next to his chair.

"I'm really fine," she answered, trying to avoid the subject, "but I don't mind." She extended her hands out for him. They were icy cold, despite the ninety-degree temperature.

Russ looked at her nails, then leaned forward and pulled her lower eyelids down. As he checked her, he noticed that she had two large bruises—one on her right thigh and the other at her waist.

"So, I'm okay, right?"

Russ smiled. "I think you may need some vitamins. You could be anemic. I'll talk to Annie about bringing you to Atlanta for a checkup."

"I'm fine, Grandpa Russ."

"I'm sure you are, honey, but let's keep you that way, okay?"

When the children went in the house to change from their wet bathing suits, Russ advised Annie to make an appointment for Sunny with a specialist. "I don't like her color or the lethargy. It may be just a vitamin deficiency, but I would like to see her have blood work done."

The next morning, Annie made a call to Cole. When he answered, she went right to the point. "Cole, this is Annie. I'm calling because I'm worried about Sunny. She doesn't seem herself, and Russ thinks she should get a checkup in Atlanta." Her tone was cool and indifferent. Interaction with him was still objectionable, but unavoidable since Alex's death. Their conversations were always brief, neither wasting words on idle pleasantries.

"She's fine, Muff. If you think she's sick, run her by Doc Martin's."

"Doc Martin is an old, country doctor. Russ specifically said we should take her to a specialist. He should know what he's talking about."

"Excuse me, sugar. I should have realized that a powerful and brilliant Cameron had spoken. Did the earth shake?"

"Is that really necessary?"

"Probably not, but I'm really jammed up right now and don't think there's anything wrong with little Sissy, but if you want to take her, I'll give you my insurance card."

"Fine." *Jerk,* she thought, fighting the impulse to slam the phone down.

***

Hearing Annie had made the appointment, Sunny protested.

"I'm fine, Aunt Annie. I don't need to go to a doctor. I've just been so busy that I haven't been getting enough sleep."

"Well, I can't sleep if I don't get you in for tests, sweetheart. I don't care what you say, you're not yourself, and you're losing weight. Your mom trusted me to look after you."

CHAPTER FORTY-ONE

The first appointment with Dr. Weitz was preliminary. While Annie hoped he would reassure them that there was no cause to worry—he didn't.

"Her red and white cell counts are not good," the doctor said, without looking up from the clipboard holding Sunny's lab results.

His words and tone sent cold chills through Annie. "What are we talking about?" she asked, thankful that Sunny was still in the examining room with the nurse.

"I'd rather not speculate at this point. It could be a number of things. There'll need to be more labs—perhaps a bone marrow study."

Annie cringed at the words "bone marrow." *Oh, no.* she thought, *not that—he suspects leukemia.* She couldn't bring herself to press further; her knees felt weak and her hands clammy. *What am I going to say to Sunny? What am I going to say to Cole?*

Struggling to stay composed, she finally asked, "What should I tell her?"

"I wouldn't say anything to alarm her. We'll repeat the same blood work in a week. If the results are not better, then I will recommend the bone marrow extraction."

Hold on Annie. You can't lose it now. Sunny's waiting. I can't respond to him. If I speak, I'll break down, and I can't do that.

The doctor stood, which Annie took as a signal to leave. She slid the strap of her purse over her shoulder and rose. The only communication she could manage was a slight nod and a weak, "Thank you."

In the waiting room, Sunny broke into a smile when she saw Annie. As they left the office, neither spoke about the exam until they reached the parking lot.

"Well, am I going to live?" the teenager said facetiously.

Oh my gosh, she's so naïve. She has no idea how sick she may be.

"No more than seventy or eighty years," Annie said, her stomach turning inside out.

"Does he think I have mono or something?" Sunny asked as she climbed in the van.

"You know doctors. They won't tell you what they're thinking until they're sure. But he wants you to have another blood test in about a week. He said it takes a couple of tests to make a reliable diagnosis," Annie said, as she gingerly touched the hot steering wheel.

Sunny made a face. "Well, that's crazy. Doc Martin always tells you right off what's wrong. If these Atlanta doctors are so smart, they ought to be able to figure it out even faster."

Annie smiled. "You would think." In her mind, she was dreading the call to Cole. *Maybe, I'll wait until I have more information. I might not have to ever mention the bone marrow test if the blood work is good next week. He probably wouldn't understand anyway, and it's not certain Sunny has anything serious...but who am I kidding? Her symptoms are bad.*

After talking it over with Dan, Annie decided to tell Cole that the situation could be serious and that he should go with them to the next appointment. He opted out, again with a shabby excuse of having a conference with his bankers about a building project.

As Annie sat in the richly appointed office, waiting for the doctor to come in with the results of Sunny's second blood test, she struggled to stay optimistic. When he finally walked in with the chart in his hand, she tried to read his face before hearing his words. *He's not making eye contact. It's not good news.*

"Mrs. Cameron, I wish that I had better news."

Oh, God. I knew it. I knew it.

"Sunny's red and white cells have not improved. If anything, they've moved further in the wrong direction, which leads to the conclusion that something very serious is going on."

Annie sat mute, clutching the arms of the chair.

"The bone marrow test is essential at this point. I'm sorry."

A tear crept down Annie's face as she managed to say, "I understand."

"Do you want me to tell her?"

Annie shook her head. As much as she didn't want to tell Sunny, she knew she could break the news in a more compassionate manner than this clinical man of medicine.

I've got to tell her that she will have bone marrow extracted from her hip bone. Alex, wherever you are, please help me. Please pull every string you have up there to help us.

***

When Annie told her what the doctors would do, Sunny was devastated. She tried to act brave, but terror drained the color from her blue eyes, leaving them paler than usual. As they left the clinic, she said, "Aunt Annie, I think I would like to go home. I kind of want to be alone." She never asked what the test was for.

As much as Annie hated to let the child shoulder her anxiety alone, she respected her wishes. *Cole is a loose cannon. There's no telling how he will react to this.*

"I understand, sweetheart. I'll call your dad and tell him what the doctor said."

"No, that's okay. I'll tell him."

Dropping Sunny at the farm, Annie was sick to her stomach, but knew that the scared teenager did not need to have the confusion of two rowdy children. *Cole Dalton, you better come home early. You've let that child down enough. You don't deserve her.*

In a state of depression, Annie went through the motions of picking up the children from her mother's, avoiding mention of the medical tests. As she drove home, Danny and Faith lessened her gloomy mood with their innocent exuberance.

After getting the children settled, she went to the kitchen to begin preparing dinner. However, the ritual brought Sunny back to her thoughts. *She's always here, entertaining Faith or helping me cook. This is a nightmare. Please God, don't let her have something they can't cure.*

Annie had hardly begun cooking when the phone rang. *I'm not in the mood for chit-chat right now.* She started to ignore the call, but then thought that it might be Dan, so she answered.

"Annie, give me the straight stuff about this appointment today." It was Cole.

Nice of you to remember, she thought. "I don't have anything definite to tell you. The doctor has ordered a bone marrow biopsy. She has to go into the hospital the first of next week for the procedure."

Cole was silent.

"Where are you?" Annie asked.

"Headed home."

"Sunny's there. She wanted to be alone, but someone should be there with her."

"I know. She sent me a text but didn't say anything about the appointment. This is pretty serious, isn't it, Annie?"

"It is, but we've got to hold on to the idea that it could be something simple. Do you want to take her on Monday?"

"No. You take her. I'll try to meet you there. I'll let you know."

I'll never understand that man. Annie stared at the phone for a minute after hanging up. *I know he loves her. Why doesn't he insist on being the one to take her? He's the only parent she has.*

Annie never heard more from Cole. She sent him an email that gave him the specifics of the appointment and left it to him to show up or not.

Sunny didn't speak on the trip to the hospital, and Annie didn't try to make conversation. Dan met them there and waited with Annie when Sunny was taken in for the procedure.

"I'm scared, Dan," Annie said, trembling, as Sunny was rolled away on the gurney. "She's my other daughter."

"I know, angel," Dan said as he reached over and took her hand. "She's going to be fine."

"I wish I could believe that, but I have a bad feeling about this."

"Don't borrow trouble. Remember last year when you were sure that Danny's heat rash was measles?"

"That didn't compare with this. When I took her in, I thought the doctor would say she had mono, but he didn't. She is so scared, Dan, and so am I."

"Of course you are, honey," he said, and reached around her shoulders, pulling her close. "I feel almost as close to her as you do. She's a great kid and already had a bad break losing her mom. It isn't fair."

"God can't let this happen. Where is Cole? This is his daughter."

"Honey, I'm not sure Cole can handle this. Remember how he was when Alex died? He can't express his fears or his grief. Try not to judge him too harshly."

You don't know him like I do. As Annie laid her head on Dan's shoulder, Russ walked up.

"Dad, what are you doing here?" Dan stood up and extended his right hand to his father, while putting his left around the older man's shoulder in a man-hug.

"I checked on Sunny with Weitz's office. They told me about the bone marrow test."

Turning from Dan, Russ leaned over and hugged Annie, noticing that her eyes were red and swollen. "She's in good hands, sweetheart. John Weitz is tops in his field. Try not to worry. He just wants to rule out any serious possibilities."

"It's leukemia they're testing for, Russ." It was the first time that Annie had verbalized the term. She feared that saying it would make it a reality.

"Wait to panic until they finish the tests, sweetheart. I won't lie to you. That is one of the things that they are hoping to rule out."

Dan nodded, and stroked her hair.

"Let's go down to the cafeteria," Russ said. "She'll be in there for a while. They're not going to let her go home until most of the medication has worn off. You look like you need a cup of coffee. Come on, Dan. Let's get her out of this place for a few minutes."

When Sunny was finally released, Annie drove her back to the Cameron house, with Dan following in the SUV. Cole had not shown up at the hospital. Nothing was said on the drive as Sunny drifted in and out of sleep. Looking at her in the back seat, Annie's heart ached. The girl had lost a significant amount of weight. *She needs her mother, especially with a bastard like Cole for a father. She knows I love her, but I'm not Alex. Where the hell is Cole? How can he desert her like this?*

When they got back to Providence, Dan helped Sunny to her room. Annie brought her a glass of iced tea and tried to get her to eat some soup, but she refused. "I'm not really hungry right now, Aunt Annie."

When Annie went back downstairs, Dan was making the two of them turkey sandwiches. "Do you want me to go pick up the kids at your parents' house?" he asked.

"I'm thinking about leaving them there tonight. What do you think?"

"That's probably a good idea. They take over here, and it's probably best that Sunny get some sleep."

"What should I tell Mom?"

"I would just tell her that everyone is tired from the long day. I wouldn't alarm her. Besides, until the test results come back, we don't know anything."

"They're testing for leukemia, Dan. She has all the symptoms. I looked it up. Did you see how pitiful she looks?"

He nodded. "What are you going to do about Cole?"

"I'm so disgusted that he didn't show up at the hospital today. I know she was brokenhearted. He's her father. Would you miss being there, if it were Faith?" Answering her own question, she said, "No, you would not. Nothing could keep you from being there if it were one of our children."

Dan reached over and put his arm around her shoulder, pulling her close. "You're just a little bulldog, aren't you?"

They finished the sandwiches, and Annie called her mother. It was a brief conversation. Dan got on the phone to caution Danny to behave himself and go to bed on time.

Annie never spoke to Cole.

CHAPTER FORTY-TWO

It took nearly a week before the test results were back. Dr. Weitz's office called and set up an appointment for a consultation with the doctor about the findings. Annie knew it wasn't good news. "They would have told us over the phone if it was good news," she told Dan. "We have to go in tomorrow."

"Have you told Cole?"

"Not yet. I've got to call him. He better show up this time."

He did. The next day, Cole, Dan, and Annie were sitting in the mahogany-paneled office of the hematologist, listening to him explain that Sunny had been diagnosed with Idiopathic Aplastic Anemia.

"She doesn't have Leukemia," Annie said.

"No. But, I'm afraid, it's just as dangerous," said Dr. Weitz.

Cole spoke up. "Are you saying she could die?"

"Let's don't talk like that, Mr. Dalton. I will tell you that this is an extremely serious condition. Left untreated, your daughter would probably die. But at her age, with treatment, she should have an eighty-percent chance of survival."

Cole was ashen, Annie speechless. Only Dan was truly in sync with what was being said.

"What is the treatment and how soon can you begin it?" Dan asked—neither Annie nor Cole appearing able to react.

"The preferred treatment is a bone marrow transplant, and the sooner it is started, the better her chances."

"Then let's get it started," Cole said, speaking for the first time.

"That is exactly what we want to do, Mr. Dalton, but I'm afraid it's complicated. We have to find a suitable match for your daughter."

"I'm right here. Take whatever you need," Cole said, standing up, his voice resolute.

"I wish it could be that simple. Siblings are the primary candidates to be bone marrow donors, but even siblings have only a one-in-four chance of matching. Do you have other children?"

"Sunny has two older sisters—but what about my marrow? I'm her father."

"Mr. Dalton, you've not been paying attention."

Annie's eyes moved from the doctor to Cole. *No, no. This is not good. He's losing his patience with Cole—and that's not a good way to handle him.*

The only one standing, Cole's face was growing redder by the second, his green eyes wild, like those of a trapped, feral cat.

I've seen that look on his face once before, Annie thought—and shuddered.

Apparently recognizing that he was dealing with a volatile situation, Dr. Weitz softened his approach.

"If testing your daughters does not produce a suitable donor, we will, of course, test you and any other close relatives. But you must understand that like her sisters, Sunny's HLA factors were derived equally from each of her parents. You provided only half of the critical elements."

Annie held her breath. *Calm down, Cole, please. This man is here to help Sunny, don't go off on him.* She looked at Dan, wondering if he would intervene to cool Cole down. He was frowning, and looked poised to speak, but before he had the chance, Cole sat back down, his expression remaining confrontational.

"Bring Sunny's sisters here for testing as soon as you can. Time is of the essence," Dr. Weitz said, ignoring Cole's demeanor.

"How invasive is the procedure for the donor," Annie asked. It was only the second time she had spoken since they arrived.

"There's relatively little discomfort for the donor."

"And for Sunny?" It was Cole who asked, his tone still abrupt.

"There are certainly more issues for the recipient. Before we can inject the donor marrow, the patient's marrow has to be destroyed with chemotherapy. There is some risk, but the success rate is very high. My nurse can provide you with some literature that should answer all your questions."

An image of the abortion clinic flashed across Annie's mind. *Where did that come from?* she thought. *Is God reminding me that I almost killed Danny? What am I going to do if neither of the girls match?* She felt the palms of her hands grow moist and the blood drain from her face. *Danny may be the only one who can save Sunny.*

Dr. Weitz stood, indicating the consultation was over. Dan thanked him for his time. Annie could only nod. Cole said nothing. As the three left the office, Cole walked ahead without looking back.

"Cole, wait," Anne called out to him. He stopped, turned around, but said nothing, his face still red, but some of the fire gone from his eyes.

"Are you going to get in touch with the girls?" Annie asked.

"Yeah," he replied in a tone suggesting he was not interested in discussion.

"Do you want me to call them?"

"I'll take care of it."

"And Sunny?"

"I'll take care of it," he said, making it clear Annie was excluded. Saying no more, he walked briskly away.

When they got to the car, Dan opened the passenger door for her. Annie paused, looking up at him, she asked, "How do you think he will tell her?"

"I think he will handle it in his way, sweetheart. She's his daughter."

***

For several agonizing days, Annie heard nothing. When she sent Sunny a text asking how she was feeling, the short reply stated simply that she was fine. On Saturday, the phone rang as she was giving the children their breakfast. Dan had gone to pick up a gallon of milk.

"Aunt Annie, this is Rhys."

Annie could tell her niece was crying.

"Brandi and I are home with Dad and Sunny. He just told us about…." At that point, her voice broke up completely.

"I know, honey," Annie said, her chin trembling. "Has your dad told Sunny?"

"She knew when we got here. He just called us Tuesday and told us to come home this weekend—that he needed to discuss something with us," Rhys said, pulling her voice together. "Are we going to lose Sunny, too?"

"No. Don't even think that. Did your dad tell you about bone marrow testing?"

"He told us that Brandi and I should do the test."

"Are you okay with that?" Annie felt tears sliding down her face.

"Of course—I'm praying that I'm a match."

"How is Sunny?"

"Not good. That's why I called. Dad called her doctor, and we're taking her to the hospital. Sunny wants you to come."

CHAPTER FORTY-THREE

When Annie and Dan reached the hospital, Sunny was running a high temperature, and access to her room was limited. Cole and Rhys were with her, while Brandi was alone in the small waiting room across the hall.

"Are you okay?" Annie asked as she hugged Brandi.

"No," she answered. "Dad and Rhys are in her room. They won't let but two people in at one time. You have to put on a paper gown, a mask, and the gloves that are in a box by the door." Beginning to cry, she struggled to speak. "She's so sick, Aunt Annie."

"Have they told you anything?"

"They say she has a bacterial infection and may have some internal bleeding. I'm so scared."

"Of course you are, honey. But these are the best doctors. They'll take care of her." *I wish I could believe what I'm saying.*

"She wants to see you. She's been asking Dad when you're coming. I'll text Rhys and tell her you're here."

When Rhys came out, she was pale and drawn; her mascara smudged. Both Annie and Dan embraced her, and then Annie went into the room. The sight of Sunny lying motionless on the bed with monitors, oxygen, and IV lines attached was nearly unbearable. The room was quiet except for the bleeping of a cardiac monitor. As Annie approached the bed, the slight rustle of the paper gown caused the teenager to open her eyes slightly. Seeing Annie, she lifted a hand. Thankful for the mask she wore that hid at least part of her face, Annie took the hand, being careful to avoid the clip that held a medical tracking device attached to her index finger. At the touch of Annie's hand, a tiny smile appeared on Sunny's pale face.

How could she have gotten so much worse so fast?

"Don't try to talk, sweetheart. Just rest. We're all here. Uncle Dan is in the waiting room."

Sunny nodded slightly, a tear slipping down her face. Cole stood in the corner of the room, stoic. He barely acknowledged Annie's presence.

At least he's here.

Annie stayed in the room until Sunny fell asleep, and then left to allow one of the sisters to go in.

Back in the waiting room, she said to Dan, "She's so sick. Mom and Dad have to be told, but I don't think I can find the words."

"Call and tell them Sunny's in the hospital. They'll come, and we will tell them together."

Taking a deep breath, she fished her phone from her purse. "Darn it. I forgot to charge my battery." The frustration brought more tears.

"Here, honey. Use mine."

The Brennans arrived less than an hour after Annie called. As they stood in the area designated for family, Annie and Dan tried to explain Sunny's illness.

"She's going to be all right, isn't she?" Claire asked, with fear in her eyes.

"We have every reason to be optimistic," Dan said. "Dad told me that early treatment is almost always successful. So let's not panic."

"But what if neither Brandi nor Rhys is a match?" Claire asked. Her expression begged for reassurance. Frank stood behind her, his hands grasping her shoulders for both his support and hers.

"God won't let that happen," Annie said, tears backing up in her eyes.

Blood tests were run on both sisters that afternoon, as well as all the adult blood relatives. An hour or so after the blood was drawn, Claire and Frank were in Sunny's room. Cole had gone to the hospital snack shop for a cup of coffee; Rhys went with him. Annie and Dan stayed in the family waiting room with Brandi.

"How long does it take for them to get the results of the tests?" Brandi asked, as she twisted the red scarf in her lap into a tight string.

"I don't know," Annie said. "It's Saturday night. We may not know until Monday."

She had hardly finished speaking when Dr. Weitz walked up. Looking around, he asked, "Where's Mr. Dalton?"

"He's on his way back up. I texted him when I saw you coming," Dan said.

Obviously lacking patience, the doctor said, "I'll look in on another patient and come back when he's here." He then walked down the hall.

"Why couldn't he just wait for Dad?" Brandi asked.

"Doctors are busy, honey. I'm sure he'll be right back," Annie said, trying to bridle her own anxiety.

Within minutes of missing the physician, Cole walked into the waiting room, Rhys behind him.

"You just missed the doctor," Brandi said.

"Where is he?" Cole asked, with an angry expression on his face.

"He'll be right back. He's gone to see another patient," Dan responded.

"Why the hell couldn't he wait for me?"

No one spoke.

Rhys went to the chair next to Brandi and sat, putting an arm around her sister. As they waited for the doctor to return, Cole paced the room like a caged animal.

Damn it, Cole. Why can't you just sit down? You're getting on everyone's nerves.

Dr. Weitz finally returned, clipboard in hand. Annie stood up. Cole met him at the edge of the room.

"I'm sorry, Mr. Dalton, but we didn't find a match," the gray-haired man said.

The words fell like a boulder of granite. No one spoke except Cole, who uttered a single profanity under his breath. Tears flooded Brandi's face. Dan was solemn—Annie and Rhys, glassy-eyed.

"We'll begin a search of the data base for a potential donor. I'm afraid it may take some time before we come up with a suitable enough match, but we might get lucky. We'll keep you informed. In the meantime, we'll begin an alternative treatment. Of course, we'll continue the aggressive antibiotics to treat the bacterial infection." With that said, he turned and walked away, not waiting for any questions.

Annie was silent. Cole left the room without speaking, while Rhys and Brandi huddled together in the corner. Brandi's scarf was wet from her tears.

"Don't give up, Annie," Dan whispered. "They do find matches through the system," Her head was pressed against his chest, tears and makeup soiling his shirt.

This room is freezing, Annie thought, as she fought to regain control of her emotions. I've got to talk to Molly. She had discussed Sunny's prognosis with Molly the day after receiving the diagnosis. Pulling away from Dan, but continuing to hold one hand, she said, "I think I need a cup of coffee. Can you stay here with the girls?"

He nodded.

"Does anyone want me to bring a drink back?" she asked, looking toward the sisters. Both shook their heads negatively.

"I'm fine," Dan said, as she pulled her hand from his.

Annie walked to where the elevators were. A bank of courtesy phones was adjacent to the public restrooms nearby. She sat down in front of a phone, her hand trembling as she punched in Molly's number.

Molly scarcely said "hello" before Annie blurted out, "It's me, Annie. I'm at Emory. Sunny was admitted this afternoon, and it's bad." Her voice was on the edge of hysteria. "They've tested everyone. No one matches."

"Calm down, luv," Molly said in a compassionate tone. "You've got to hold on to your faith. It can't be God's will that anything should happen to that girl."

"You know that Danny could match. He could save her life."

"Let them test him then, luv. 'Tis only a blood test, and he's her cousin."

"You know he is Sunny's brother, not her cousin. They have the same four grandparents."

Annie didn't know that Dan had come after her, having changed his mind about the coffee. Turning the corner, he overheard her last statement to Molly and froze, the color leaving his face. As Annie continued speaking, Dan was motionless for a few seconds, then turned around and went back to the waiting room.

CHAPTER FORTY-FOUR

When Annie returned, she was too absorbed in her emotions to notice that Dan had become withdrawn.

Later, as they drove to Providence, Dan was unusually quiet, but since Annie didn't feel like talking, she was relieved. At midnight, the house was dark and deadly quiet. The children were staying the night with the Brantleys.

Dan immediately went to the den and made himself a drink. Annie headed upstairs to get ready for bed. She had just removed her jewelry when he walked to the bedroom door, making no attempt to truly enter.

"We need to talk," he said. There was an unfamiliar edge to his tone.

"I'm really tired, honey. Could we do it tomorrow?"

"No—I don't think that we can."

All of a sudden, her radar went on full alert. *What does he want to talk about?*

"I'll come straight to the point, Annie. I overhead you say something earlier tonight that I need explained."

Annie felt the color leave her face. Oh, my God. Surely he didn't hear my conversation with Molly.

"I don't know who you were talking to. I did not intend to intrude. I was trying to catch you at the elevator to ask you to get me a cup of coffee. But you weren't waiting for an elevator, Annie, you were on the phone."

Annie was speechless, racking her brain to remember exactly what she said to Molly.

"I don't know what you mean," she lied.

"Cut the dumb act, Annie. You know exactly what I mean." His voice was cold, all the usual warmth and tenderness absent. "Who were you talking to?"

Becoming defensive, she said, "You can drop your FBI persona. I'm not one of your suspects." Panicked, she stalled for time to think of what to say. *How much did he hear?* Her world was teetering.

"You know damn well that I'm asking as a husband, not as an agent. But I'll tell you, the agent in me recognizes an attempt to dodge when the question nails the target."

The expression in his eyes was like none Annie had seen before—icy black replacing the usual warm brown.

"Who the hell is 'Sunny's brother, not her cousin,' Annie?"

He heard me. Oh, dear, God, he heard me say that? What do I do? What do I say? She had no words. They wouldn't come out. She couldn't even say the wrong thing. She lapsed into a fit of hysterical tears.

"You will forgive me, Annie," he said, sarcastically. "There's just one connotation I can attach to those words." Spewing venom, he said, "Is Danny Cole Dalton's son?"

She didn't say anything. She couldn't. She stood frozen by the bed.

"You don't need to say anything. I have my answer. There's just one more question, and I hope you have the decency to be honest. How long did the affair last? Is it still active?"

The repugnance of an affair with Cole spawned strength in Annie.

"There was no affair. There was never an affair," she said, matching his bitter tone. The thought unleashed her words. "You can hate me all you want. You can believe anything you want, but there was never an affair. I was never unfaithful to you."

"So what then?—immaculate conception or artificial insemination? Is Faith his too? If I couldn't make you pregnant, did you take on your fantasy lover?"

"No—no—no," she responded, her eyes wide. "If I tell you the truth, you've got to give me your word that you won't do anything—that you won't say anything." Annie was hysterical. "You've got to give me your word, Dan."

"I don't think I have to do anything. I don't know who you are. I've spent the past fifteen years sleeping with a woman who just became a total stranger to me. Who the hell are you?"

"I'm me, Dan. Please. I'm Annie. Something happened. I made a decision. I don't know if it was right or wrong. I still don't know, but I did the best I could. I've had to live in the shadow of secrets for ten years." At that point, she threw the bracelet and watch she had been holding as hard as she could across the room. "I never wanted to lie to you. I never wanted to."

"Well, that's very comforting. You never wanted me to believe that I had a son who wasn't mine. How am I supposed to feel toward him now?"

"You can't stop loving Danny just because he isn't your son. It's not his fault. None of this is his fault. He loves you. And you know damn well, Daniel Cameron—you know—Faith is your daughter. Don't you dare go there. How could you even say those words? And you know what? Danny could be your son. He could be."

"Funny, that's not what I heard you say. By the way, who the hell were you talking to, and who all knows?"

"No one—no one, except Molly O'Brien. That's who I was talking to."

"Well, why didn't I figure that out? I should turn in my badge," he said, shaking his head.

"Dan, on all you hold sacred, you've got to promise me that you won't do anything if I tell you."

"Maybe I don't want to know. Maybe it's just better if I go." He turned to walk away.

"He raped me!"

CHAPTER FORTY-FIVE

Dan stopped, turned, and looked at her—an inscrutable expression on his face. Neither of them spoke for a minute or two. Annie was trembling so much she could barely breathe. It was Dan who finally broke the silence.

"And I should believe that—why?" he said, his head cocked, his tone challenging.

"Because it's the truth. I am telling the truth."

"And, you just never thought to mention this to me until tonight?"

"I couldn't. What can I say? I just couldn't."

"Why, Annie? Why couldn't you tell me? Did you think I would kill him?"

"I thought a lot of things, but not that. I did think you would have him arrested."

"And why wouldn't that be a good idea? Assuming what you now say is true."

"He was my sister's husband. He was the father of her children."

"He was a criminal."

Annie moved closer to Dan, but he stiffened, dodging her advance. "Is that your FBI inculcation? Everything is black or white, right or wrong. How can you think it's that simple?"

"Truth is simple, Annie," he said, looking directly in her eyes. "It's the lies that are complicated."

"No it isn't. I always thought it was, but I found out—it isn't." She moved back to the bed and sat down. "I can't change anything I did. I can't go back to the day it happened and tell you the truth. I can't make Danny your flesh and blood because I want him to be. I can't fix it, Dan, I can't. But if you tell anyone—anyone, think about how much it will hurt Danny, Sunny, Rhys, Brandi. Can you do that? Can you break their hearts even more?"

"This is going nowhere. I don't want to hear anymore—not tonight."

"He never touched me again, at least not in that way. You have got to believe that."

"Annie, I find out that you have been lying to me for ten years, and now you expect me to believe you. Your credibility is blown. As I recall, the story is that at one time, you were pretty hot for Cole. How do I know you didn't finally get the chance to fulfill your adolescent fantasy? I'm sorry, but everything I thought I knew about you has been vaporized. It's going to take some time to wrap my head around this. I'm looking at you, and you're a stranger."

"You don't believe that. I'm no stranger; I'm the girl who has worshiped you since the first time I saw you in tennis shorts on the University of Georgia court. I'm the same—almost the same. Cole may have had sex with me, but I wasn't there. I've never made love to anyone but you. Somewhere deep inside, you know that's true." Her words slid from her lips like the warning growl of an angry dog. Her eyes glared defiantly with the passion of her conviction.

Dan stood in the doorway, obviously bewildered, his head moving from side to side as he gazed down at the carpet, refusing to continue eye contact.

"I tried to have an abortion."

"Well, there's just no end to your revelations, is there?" he said, raising his head to look at her. "You actually considered aborting Danny?"

"I didn't know what to do." She pulled a pillow to her stomach, which was aching from the totality of her stress. "He could be your son. You know how hard we were trying to have a baby then. You made love to me the night before it happened. You got me pregnant with Faith. He could be yours."

"Seems like it would have been easy enough for you to find out."

"I've been too scared to find out. I didn't want to know because I couldn't stand letting you believe he's yours if I knew for sure that he wasn't. It was only sort of a lie if I didn't have the DNA testing."

"There's no sort of lie, Annie, like there's no sort of dead. You either tell the truth or you don't. I assume Cole is aware that he's Danny's father. It would explain why he paid so much attention to Danny for a while."

Annie shook her head. "He doesn't know."

Without saying more, Dan walked into the room and toward their closet.

"No. No one knows but Molly," Annie continued.

Once in the closet, he took the travel bag that stayed packed for urgent calls from the Bureau, then turned to walk out of the room.

"Please don't leave," Annie begged.

"I've got to have space."

"Are you going to divorce me?" More tears were building.

"Annie, I have no idea what I'm going to do. All I know is that I've got to have some time to sort this out."

"Couldn't you do that here?"

"No. Absolutely not."

"What am I going to tell everyone—the children?"

"You'll think of something. Apparently, you're real good at that. Tell them anything you like. Tell them I was called in by the Bureau. At this moment, I just don't care."

"That was cruel." She covered her face with her hands.

"Maybe so, but right now, I'm just not in the mood to be kind."

"Will you sign for Danny to be the donor if he is a match?"

"Get his father to sign," he said, walking down the stairs.

"That was low, Dan, really low," Annie called out.

Turning back toward her, he said, "You know I'll sign. I won't jeopardize Sunny's life. Get the paperwork to the office, and I'll do whatever is necessary."

"Will I know where you are?"

"I'll have to figure that out."

CHAPTER FORTY-SIX

Annie hardly slept after Dan left that night. She never changed to her nightclothes nor turned down the bed. Lying in the fetal position on the top of the bedspread with one hand clutching the small pillow tightly to her stomach, the other holding her well-worn Bible, she alternately cried and prayed. "Please let him find a way to forgive me, not because I deserve it, but for Danny and Faith. Please God—they need him so much. Danny needs him. Please don't let our marriage come apart. I'll do anything."

At 6:00 a.m., she gave up on sleep and took a shower, shampooed her hair, and put on fresh clothing. Food was out of the question, so she sipped a glass of milk, hoping it would provide enough nourishment to keep her functioning.

After putting on makeup, she walked over to the Brantley house to check on the children. If not for Sunny's condition, her bloodshot eyes and swollen face would have given rise to questions, but neither Martha nor Ray commented. Martha gave her a hug and insisted that Faith and Danny stay with them. Annie gave in with little resistance, despite the plans she and Dan had made to take the children to their grandparents in Atlanta. She was relieved that she would not be facing Russ and Margaret.

Knowing they would attend early services at St. Lukes and afterward go for breakfast, she called just before nine and left a message cancelling. *I can't face them regardless of whether Dan has told them anything. One question from them and I would melt down faster than ice cream in the oven.*

As she drove back to the hospital, she contemplated her next move. *I have to tell Cole that Danny might be the key to saving Sunny. What if he wants Danny to know he's his father? At that thought, Annie felt a lurch in her stomach. What if Danny isn't a match? Then, I've ruined everything for nothing? Neither one of her sisters was a match.*

Before leaving for the hospital, Annie had called Molly and spilled out the details of what happened the night before, including the part about Dan leaving.

"I can stay the day or two with you, luv," Molly said.

"You are so kind to offer, but I'll be okay. There's too much to think about for me to grieve right now. I've got to put Sunny first. I screwed up my marriage, and I'll have to live with it. I don't think Dan will forgive me. I'm just afraid of what he's going to do where the children are concerned, especially Danny."

"'Tis going to be alright, child. He loves you and that little boy. Once he gets the matter settled in his head, he'll be back. You might need just the bit of counseling, but 'twill be all right. Of that, I'm sure."

When Annie arrived at the hospital, Cole was the only one there. It was a perfect time to have a conversation. Sunny was sleeping comfortably, her fever down as a result of the aggressive antibiotic treatment.

"Let's walk down the hall," she said, quietly. "We have to talk."

"I don't need any lectures from you right now, Annie."

"It's not to lecture you. I have something really important to tell you."

Without saying anything further, he walked toward the door and held it for her to pass. The waiting room was deserted, giving them the privacy Annie needed.

"What's this about?" Cole asked as Annie sat down in the far corner of the room.

"I may have a donor for Sunny," she said, skipping any preliminary explanation.

"Yeah.... Who would that be?"

"Your son."

He looked at her, his head cocked to one side, one eyebrow raised. "Knock it off, Annie, I don't have a son."

"I think you do. Have you forgotten that you raped me on May 29, 2001?"

"I remember fucking you somewhere around then, but I never raped you, darlin', and I hope it's not Danny that you're thinking is my kid."

"Don't even go there with me. You know you raped me. You came to my house, unannounced, forced me down, ripped my bikini off, and violated me. That's rape!"

"Whoa. Hold on here a minute. I never came to your house unannounced. Alex called you and told you I was coming. You met me, sugar, with nothing covering that little ass of yours but an invitation to take it. You don't put the cheese in the cage with the rat and expect him not to nibble."

Annie's eyes grew larger as she said, "Alex did not call me. I had no idea you were coming. I would never have been dressed like that if I had known you were coming." She stared at him, trying to assess whether there was any veracity in what he had said. *Oh, God.... He can't be telling the truth.*

"Well, darlin', you're wrong on two counts, much as I would gladly eat ground glass and chase it with gasoline to find another potential donor," he said. "Skipping the part about me raping you, Danny's in no way my boy. It just ain't possible."

"Think about it, Cole. He looks just like you."

"He looks just like you. Believe me, sweet pea, my little swimmers had nothing to do with making that little rascal. I'd be proud to claim him if they did, but, as I said, 'It just ain't possible.'"

"Danny was born nine months later, or can't you count?" Annie said, her eyes flashing with the conviction of her belief.

"Simmer down, Muff. Don't you know I had one of those vasectomy jobs after Sunny was born?"

Annie couldn't speak for a moment. Staring at him in disbelief, she said, "Are you sure?" *That was a dumb question.*

"Fairly sure. I was the one that got cut. Never had any reason to believe it didn't work. Didn't use a raincoat with Alex for another fourteen years, and there's no more cowboys or cowgirls in my corral."

Annie was speechless. *How did I not know that? Sunny was born in 1994. Where was I? Athens. I was in school when she was born.*

"I appreciate the offer." His voice softened as he spoke. "I really do, Annie. I'm sorry if there was a misunderstanding a long time ago. I thought you just liked it a little rough—that you wanted to do me but couldn't come out and admit it—the Alex and Dan thing and all. But I can tell you, I really didn't know you weren't expecting me."

Tears started pouring down Annie's cheeks. "I don't know what to say. I've screwed my entire life up over a misunderstanding, if you are telling me the truth."

"Why would I lie?"

"To stay out of prison."

"I'm not lying, Annie. Hell, I'll give you all the DNA you want. No skin off my ass. You want scientific proof, Muff, I'm game. If you thought the boy was mine, go home to Lord Cameron tonight knowing that unless you screwed someone else, which I seriously doubt, that pup is a pure-blood and heir to the Cameron kingdom."

Annie walked across the room to the window. She didn't want to look at him. "Everything was for nothing—all the lies I've told. My God, Cole, I almost aborted Danny. Why didn't you stop when I said no? If only you had just listened to me."

"I was an ass. But, believe it as you like, I never thought I was raping you—never considered that for a second. I wouldn't have done it. I may be a fuckin' bastard—but not that low."

Her eyes were filled with tears; her knees and hands weak. "I need to hate you. I've hated you with every inch of my being for ten years. Now, I'm confused. I was just beginning to think there was some kind of a twisted reason for it all—that Danny was needed to save Sunny. But that's even gone. What am I supposed to feel now?"

"Just go home to Dan and your perfect little world and forget it. It never happened."

"There's no Dan to go home to."

"You told him?"

"I had to tell him. He overheard a conversation I was having with Molly O'Brien, and he confronted me."

"Holy shit. I guess he wants to kill me."

"I don't know. He left. I don't even know where he is. I'm scared to call his parents, because if he hasn't told them, I'm not going to." Completely agitated, she began shuffling around in her purse. "I've got to go now. I can't let Sunny see me like this. Tell her that I forgot something I had to do for Martha. Tell her that I'll be back later."

As she reached the doorway, Annie paused, turned, and then said, "I said no, Cole. No matter what you think or thought, you raped me. You committed the crime, but I suffered the consequences." Before he could respond, she walked away.

CHAPTER FORTY-SEVEN

Annie left the hospital with her mind frozen. *I could have avoided all the anguish and preserved my marriage with one test.* Hardly aware of her destination, she drove from the hospital parking deck toward Molly's condo.

Opening the door, Molly said, "Oh my, Annie. 'Tis dreadful that you look, child."

"I talked to Cole...." It was all Annie could say before a torrent of tears overcame her, and she began shaking.

Molly reached out, putting an arm around her shoulders, she guided Annie inside. "Come, come, child. I've a pot of soup on the cooker. Let's have a bowl, and you tell me what's happened."

In the kitchen, Molly ran cold water over a paper towel and handed it to Annie, who sat at the bar. While Molly ladled the thick potato soup into bowls, and poured two cups of tea, Annie blotted her face and gathered her composure.

"What's the bastard done to upset you so, luv?"

Annie recited the conversation, nearly word for word, pausing only to swallow soup. When she finished, Molly sighed and said, "I think we need a bit of the Irish spirits." Taking a bottle of whiskey from a kitchen cabinet, she poured a dollop in her tea cup, and then offered the bottle to Annie, who smiled, but declined.

After sipping her fortified tea, Molly said, "But the question 'tis: do you believe him, luv?"

"I think I do. You know how much I've hated him. He's rude, crude, and despicable, but he's too arrogant to lie. Alex was flighty. She could have forgotten to call me—and he did agree to a paternity test."

Molly reached over and put her hand on Annie's. "'Tis a blessing, child—the son-of-a-bitch is not our boy's dad."

"I know. I was so sure...I should have listened to you and done a...." Annie's emotions began to take over again.

"Don't think about that. Take the joy and leave the rest be."

"What would I do without you?" Annie said, squeezing Molly's hand.

After they finished eating and cleared away the dishes, Molly wrote down the location of a DNA lab. Later that day, Annie discretely passed the information along to Cole.

***

On Sunday night, overcome by exhaustion, Annie slept, albeit fitfully. She woke several times with Cole's words echoing in her head: *"I had one of those vasectomy jobs." He was telling the truth; I know he was.*

On Monday, Annie fought depression. She had prayed Dan would call, but he didn't. *He's not going to forgive me. He hates me. But, I can't give in to grief. The kids need me; the family needs me.*

After breakfast, she picked up Danny from the Brantleys, but left Faith with Martha. She explained to the child how he would be tested in Atlanta to see if he could help Sunny.

Once she and Danny were underway, her mind drifted back to Cole. *Will he follow through with the testing? He said, "No skin off my ass. You want scientific proof, Muff, I'm game." But what if he doesn't go? I can't make him. I'll never be sure until I see the proof.*

Breaking her train of thought, Danny said for the fifth time since leaving Providence, "I don't want them to stick me with a needle." His voice grew more anxious each time.

"It will be over in the blink of an eye. If you're brave, I'll take you to a big mall and buy you a new game." *Dan would disapprove of bribery, but, it's not a bribe, it's a reward.* She glanced over at Danny in the passenger seat. *What a gift from God to know he is truly Dan's— never to worry about his discovering a terrible secret.*

"Mom."

Danny's voice interrupted her thoughts again.

"Are we going to see Daddy in Atlanta?"

"Not today, sweetheart. He's busy." *What am I going to tell them if Dan doesn't come back? Who am I kidding? He's not coming back. Molly calls him a decent man, but decent and forgiving are not synonymous. He can't accept my deceiving him.*

Danny sneezed, changing her focus again. *I'd better give him a reason for doing the DNA test or he may describe it to someone and raise questions.*

"On our way to see Sunny's doctor, we're going to make a quick stop at another doctor's office so they can check your throat to be sure you don't have any germs," she said. *Will I ever stop lying?*

"Are they going to give me a shot?"

"No, no. The nurse will just put a cotton swab in your mouth. It won't hurt at all." *I hope Cole goes today. He promised. Please go, Cole. You owe me that much.*

Cole kept the promise.

***

By Monday evening, they officially knew that Danny was not a match for Sunny. The news brought mixed emotions to Annie. She was glad Danny would not have to go through the transplant procedure and pleased that no doubt was cast on Cole's revelation, but she was dismayed that Sunny remained without a donor.

The DNA results took seventeen days to arrive. When they finally came, the report excluded Cole from the pool of men who could be Danny's father. Although anticlimactic, the documentation was nonetheless a relief. For the first time, Annie looked at her son without doubt or guilt. *He is Dan's son, all Dan's.*

The afternoon she received the notification, Annie placed the call, her hand once again trembling as she dialed. *Will he hang up when he hears my voice? That's silly, he can see my number on caller ID. If he doesn't want to talk to me, he doesn't have to answer.*

Dan answered, his cool tone sending chills through Annie on two levels—but he agreed to meet with her for lunch without asking her purpose.

They met in a small, out-of-the-way bistro in Atlanta. Annie arrived first and was seated at a table facing the door. She had full view of the restaurant and could see him as soon as he entered. In his usual fashion, he walked in at noon as agreed. When he approached the table, Annie's heart raced. *He looks tired. I wish I could hug him.* She remained seated until he reached the table.

While his greeting was cordial, it was arm's length as in a business rather than personal relationship. "Do you mind?" he asked, motioning for her to move to the opposite side of the table to allow him to be seated with his back to the wall.

As he brushed by, she could smell the Aqua De Gio, and a flurry of desire produced by the smell and the brief contact ripped through her. *Oh, God, I love him so much. Be cool, Annie. Keep it together. Don't spook him. He's like a cat; he could sprint away in a second.*

Once seated, he picked up the menu and asked, "How is Sunny?"

"She's home."

"I know."

Annie looked surprised.

"I called the hospital to check on her and was told she had gone home. Since I haven't received any paperwork from you, I assume Danny wasn't a match." He seemed to flinch slightly when mentioning Danny.

"No, he wasn't, but Rhys and Paul found two of Cole's brothers. One of the cousins is a good candidate for the transplant. I think it cost Cole a fortune, but the cousin agreed to give his marrow. They've started the chemo, and if all goes well, she'll have the transplant in about a month. Dr. Weitz is optimistic, at least as optimistic as that man is capable of being."

"Are the kids okay?"

Hesitating, she started to say how much they missed him, but decided not to risk sounding negative. "They're good."

Annie waited until after they ordered, then approached the subject of the meeting. "Have you told anyone that we're separated?" she asked, trying to keep any emotion out of her voice.

Shaking his head as he dipped a piece of bread in the oil and herbs the waitress had left, Dan replied, "We're not separated, Annie."

She suppressed a smile. *Don't get your hopes up, Annie. He's still cold as a frozen fish.* "Have you told your parents anything?"

"No."

Without preface, she blurted out, "Danny is your son." *There it is.*

He looked at her, but didn't respond. Annie tensed. *Why isn't he reacting? Isn't this good news? I might as well have said I bought a loaf of fresh bread.*

"We did the DNA test. He's yours, Dan."

"How did you manage that without me?"

"Cole." Reaching into her purse, she pulled out a folded piece of paper. "Here.... Read this."

Glancing over the document, Dan looked up and said, "So Cole agreed to the test." His voice bore the trace of a sneer. "When did you tell him?"

"The day after I told you—or more accurately, the day after you overheard me talking to Molly. Danny is your son, Dan." *React, damn it.*

He looked pensive for a moment and then appeared to relax. "It is good news, Annie, real good news—but under the circumstances, you'll forgive me if it takes a little time to process. I've spent the last weeks trying to adjust to the idea that Danny wasn't my son."

Oh Dan, I'm so sorry I've hurt you so. You've been suffering as much as I have. "But, he is your son, and he misses you, Dan." *Stay cool, Annie. Don't let your nerves take control.* "He asks me every day where you are. Faith does too. Some afternoons, she goes to the front window and stands there, looking out. When I ask her what she's doing, she says she waiting for Daddy."

Her words were reaching him. She could tell from his expression, but before he could respond, the waitress appeared with their food, providing him with an excuse to dodge. He immediately turned his attention to his steak sandwich.

Annie took a sip of hot tea, but only toyed with her Cobb salad. She didn't even bother to put dressing on it. Watching Dan devour his sandwich and French fries, she wondered what he was thinking.

"Aren't you going to eat?" he asked, breaking the silence.

"I had a big breakfast," she lied, then corrected herself. "Actually, that's inaccurate, but I'm not very hungry." *Should I tell him that the rape was a misunderstanding? No, that would be pushing it.*

However, she couldn't contain herself. Leaning forward, in a low voice she said, "Cole may not have exactly raped me."

Matching her low tone, he said, "Now, that's interesting. How could he have not exactly raped you?"

Annie told him the entire story, and when she finished, he asked, "And you believe him?"

"I think I do. I know it sounds crazy. The whole thing is so bizarre, but why would he lie at this point?"

"I could probably think of a reason or two."

"It does make sense. Alex was so scatterbrained, she could have forgotten to call me and never had any reason to mention it later."

"I thought you told him to stop."

"I did. But he said Alex liked sex games, so he thought because of the way I had dressed for him that I was playing a game. Don't you remember that tiny bikini I had just to wear in the back yard when working on my tan? No one ever saw me in it but you."

"And apparently, Cole. Annie, it's all been a little more than I can handle. I've got to get back to the office, now. You can stay and finish your salad. I'll take care of the check. Is there anything you need before

I leave?" There was no trace of a smile on his face. He was a man she didn't know.

"No."

"Call me if you need anything. There should be plenty of money in the account to take care of you and the kids."

"When are you going to see them?"

"Soon. I'll let you know."

And with that he left. Annie remained at the table, rearranging the vegetables in her salad and fighting tears.

CHAPTER FORTY-EIGHT

On the Saturday, after the having lunch with Dan, Annie was folding a load of laundry when the doorbell rang. Danny was visiting with a friend from his Sunday school class, and Faith was down for a nap. Fearing Faith would wake if the caller rang again, Annie hurried to the door. A delivery man stood on the front porch with a flower arrangement in his hand. Surprised, she thanked him and took the flowers in the house, her heart racing. Putting them down on the coffee table, she tore open the card, praying that they were from Dan. *Who else would send me flowers? It's not my birthday.*

Her hands trembled as she unfolded the florist's card. The inscription simply read, "I'm sorry."

He's apologizing. He still loves me. Happiness spread over her like icing on a warm cake. *Our marriage isn't over.*

For a moment, Annie reveled in the idea that Dan had sent the innocuous arrangement of lilacs and white daisies as a token of regret for his actions. But then doubt crept in. The card's not handwritten. It was impersonally typed by some florist employee.

Turning it over, she saw that the arrangement came from a florist in Atlanta. *Did Dan have a secretary send the gift?* What if she was misunderstanding the intent? What if he was saying that he was sorry that he could not forgive her—could not come back to the family?

Afraid to think about it more, she took the arrangement to the dining room table and put it down, tucking the card under the green pottery container. She then went back to the unfinished folding, trying to distance herself from further speculation. But it wasn't easy to get off her mind. As she took each item from the basket, her mind repeated, *"I'm sorry."* What is he sorry for? Why couldn't he say more?

Then it hit her. *Oh no! What if the flowers aren't from Dan?* She stopped folding and stood still, staring at the wall of the laundry room. But would that be bad? It was certainly better if someone else had sent them than to believe Dan was giving notice that he had made up his mind not to return. But, if not Dan, then who sent the arrangement?

It was a curious choice of flowers. There were no roses, the symbol of love. There was only the somber shade of lavender, the green of the foliage, and the white of the daisies. Therefore, no suggestion of cheerfulness was suggested. Was that intentional?

Then it struck her—Cole. *He couldn't have sent them. He wouldn't. He never sent Alex flowers.* She was jealous that Dan sent them to me.

But who else could it have been? Annie knew she could not call either man to inquire or verify. Her only choice was to call the florist. Leaving the laundry, she retrieved the card and noted the name of the flower vendor. Dialing 411, she asked the service for the number and let it dial automatically. Her heart was pounding again. With three possible explanations, she was not sure what she wanted to hear, but knew she wanted the mystery solved. But it was not to be. After speaking with three people, at what sounded to be a large business, all she was able to learn was that the order had been placed in the shop and paid for with cash. The clerk taking the order had no specific recollection of the sale.

Back to where she started, she sat down at the table and looked at the flowers, and then dialed Molly.

"Surely, luv, they be from Dan," Molly said, after Annie explained the reason for her call.

"I'm beginning to lean more the other way. It's far more in character for Cole to be sneaky and not sign his name. I think Dan would have. Either one could have gone to the shop in Atlanta. Cole is there a lot when he takes Sunny to the doctor. But would he have apologized? Could he really be sorry?"

"How would you feel, if he were sorry?"

"Not really any different. What he did, he did. He could have listened to me. He knew me well enough to know that I wasn't a game player. It's too little, and way too late."

Hanging up, Annie looked at the flowers again. *If they are an apology from Dan, I want to savor them. If they are a "kiss-off," I can't look at them. But, it they're from Cole, I want to trash them. What do I do?*

As she heard Faith calling, she got up, took the container to the kitchen, removed the flowers, and threw them in the garbage. That settles it. But, she took the card and slid it under the papers in one of the drawers of the kitchen desk.

Nearly three weeks passed with no communication from Dan. Annie continued to make up excuses for his absence, but knew the day was near when she would have to admit they were separated. Molly remained her only source of support.

On the third Friday night after the lunch date, the doorbell rang just as the late TV news came on. Startled, Annie felt a wave of panic. *Who could be at the door so late?* Her hands grew clammy, and she called Heidi. The old dog got up from where she was laying and followed Annie to the door. Trying to look through the peephole didn't help because it was fogged. *Why didn't I clean that thing?* Her knees were going weak. From what little she could see, it appeared to be a man. Her heart raced as she looked to Heidi for a sign. *Surely, you would bark if this is a stranger. Maybe it's Ray...or Cole.* Pausing longer, she wasn't sure she wanted to open the door for either one, especially Cole.

Swallowing hard, she shouted, "Who is it?"

"Dan Cameron."

Her heart beat faster. Was it really him? It sounded like Dan, but what if it was an imposter? She tried harder to see through the peep hole, but it was useless.

Annie took a deep breath and opened the door, keeping the safety chain in place. Dan put his official ID through the opening. Instantly recognizing the familiar card and badge, she fumbled to unfasten the chain—her hands trembling. Once the door opened, he stood there, looking to Annie like the most handsome man on the planet in his traditional black suit, white shirt and striped tie.

"What are you doing here?" she said, her voice shaking, tears welling up in her eyes.

"I live here—that is if my wife hasn't replaced me."

"Never." She moved aside to let him walk in. She wanted to throw herself in his arms, but wasn't sure yet what his appearance truly meant.

"We need to finish a conversation we started a few weeks ago."

"I thought it was finished."

"Not by a long shot," he said, taking her hand and leading her to the living room couch. Before sitting, he turned to face her.

"The kids asleep?"

"Of course."

"Good."

"They're going to be upset that they missed you."

"They'll see me in the morning. That is, if you let me stay."

With that, she threw herself against him and wrapped her arms around his neck. "Do you mean it? Are you really going to stay?"

"For a short while."

Her heart sank, and she pulled back.

"Something along the lines of fifty or sixty years," he continued, with a mischievous smile. He then pulled her back and kissed her hungrily, igniting passion in both of them. Pulling away, he said, "Okay, hold on to that thought for about fifteen minutes because we need to talk just a little before I take you upstairs."

They sat down on the sofa. Annie was almost afraid to hear what he would say.

"Annie, I'm not going to lie to you. This may not be easy, and I'm likely going to lose my job when I beat the hell out of Cole Dalton, but if you're willing, I'm willing to give this marriage my best shot. I love you. I'm not going to pretend I'm not wounded, but I've come to understand you were in an untenable position. I wish you had trusted me enough to tell me from the beginning. But then, I'll never know how I would have reacted. If Danny had been Cole's child and if I knew before I grew to love him, I would hope I could have been the father he deserved, but we'll never know. But even understanding the hell of a mess you were in, it still cut deep that you could believe he wasn't my son and keep such a secret from me. Thank God, you were wrong, and I don't have to untangle my position in Danny's life."

Annie's eyes had grown large; her heart was pounding. "What made you willing to come back?"

"I never wanted to leave, but I couldn't be with you while I worked through it. I wanted to hate you, but I couldn't stop loving you. Then your friend Molly called and reamed me out."

"Molly called you?" Annie asked, incredulously.

"Damn right she called me. Told me that she would kick my blue-blood, Scottish arse if I didn't get my act together and look at what her precious girl had been through. She described how you suffered from the time of the attack, your breakdown at the abortion clinic, how many times you cried about deceiving me. I'm telling you—that is one tough old broad. We would do well to have her on our team at the Bureau. But in the end, angel, she cut through my damned false pride and made me see my priorities. I think I would have gotten there on my own, but she put me on fast-forward."

"What are your priorities?" Annie asked, tears gushing down her smiling face.

"You—the only woman I've ever loved—and our children. This is no fairy tale, so I'm not promising happily ever after. I have to delete a lot of mental images and diligently work to regain my trust; and you're going to swear on everything you hold sacred, including that little white Bible on your night table, that you'll never lie to me again about any-thing."

"Done—anything else?"

"Yeah. Don't expect me to go line-dancing with that son-of-a-bitch your sister married."

***

Ten months later, Sunny Dalton stood at the Baptismal Font of St. Peter's Episcopal Church, holding her four-week-old godchild—blue-eyed Molly Alexandra Cameron.

ABOUT THE AUTHOR

Judith Erwin practiced family law for over twenty years before retiring to devote fulltime to writing novels. Prior to obtaining her law degree at the University of Florida, she was a freelance writer and photographer and worked on the staff of a literary magazine. *Shadow of Silence* was her debut novel, first published in 2014. She currently lives and writes in North Florida.

www.ingramcontent.com/pod-product-compliance
Lightning Source LLC
Chambersburg PA
CBHW030628110726
47901CB00002B/367